The Black Horse Diaries

A Year in the Life of a Small Town Ontario Pub

A novel by Bill Perrie, Ken Jorgenson, Alissa Heidman

To: Erin - Miss you! We must have a wine night with the mothers next time you are home!!

Copyright © Bill Perrie, Ken Jorgenson, Alissa Heidman

The rights of Bill Perrie, Ken Jorgenson & Alissa Heidman to be identified as the authors of this work has been asserted by them in accordance with the Copyright Act of Canada.

This book is a work of fiction. Names, characters, places, organizations and incidents are either products of the authors' imagination or used fictitiously. Ant resemblance to actual events, places, organizations or persons, living or dead, is entirely coincidental.

All rights reserved. No part of this publication may be reproduced, stored in a retrieval system, or transmitted in any form, or by any means (electronic, mechanical, photocopying, recording or otherwise) without prior written permission of the authors.

ISBN: 9781693385490
Imprint: Independently Published

The Black Horse Diaries

A Year in the Life of a Small Town Ontario Pub

Foreword

When the regulars and staff of the pub become more like an extended family, you know you have found your true "local". People from all walks of life sitting at a bar chatting away about their day, the upcoming weekend, and of course, their favourite sports teams and how agonizingly bad they are. Planning golf games together and making fun wagers on the outcome, laughing at the same jokes heard over and over again, but holding your tongue and being polite when they are being related to a pub "newbie". Your local is a home away from home, a place to share happiness and sadness, never wanting to miss a day in case you miss out on some new epic tale, or then again, maybe just feeling secure with more of the same old, same old. That welcome feeling you get when the bartender nods and places your beer on the bar and you haven't even said a word yet, or the comfort of a friendly pat on the back from the regulars as they pass by to sit at their own bar "thrones". Yes, you love your local pub.

We would like to welcome you to our very special local, where you will meet a great bunch of regulars. Many will make you laugh, some will maybe make you angry, a couple might even make you cry, and a few will have some deep, dark secrets that are bound to be revealed. You are about to enter the Black Horse Pub; so please, pull up a stool, order a drink, and let John tell you a joke or two as you sit back and pass some leisurely time with us all.

Cheers!

Bill, Ken & Alissa

The Black Horse Pub Interior

Meet the Black Horse Staff

Rosie
Owner & Landlady of the Black Horse Pub, Rosie is an attractive, hard-working woman in her late forties. She is dedicated to her staff and customers, especially her "regulars".

Mel
One of the Black Horse's full-time servers, and a favourite of the customers, Mel is a friendly & cheerful woman in her early thirties who is always outgoing and generous. While the regulars all love her, they can't stand her obnoxious boyfriend.

Dylan
Dylan is Rosie's millennial nephew who tends bar at the Black Horse and operates his own "private" taxi service in his spare time. Though he loves his Aunt dearly, it hasn't stopped him pilfering & stealing from the pub on occasion.

Nancy
Another of the Black Horse's staff, Nancy is an older, experienced waitress, though often grouchy, irritable and slow with her service. She likes to stick around after work for a few drinks and to flirt with the customers.

Evelyn
Evelyn is one of Rosie's closest friends and has been the pub's chef from day one. The pair will often spend the night in Toronto performing "research" on other pubs, bars, and restaurants.

Brian "the Piano Man"
Brian "the Piano Man" provides regular entertainment events for the pub, belting out Rock & Roll classics

and hosting karaoke nights.

Meet the Black Horse Regulars

Garnet "the Grump"
Garnet is a retired farmer who is always complaining about the evils of immigrants, urban sprawl & development, and technology. He talks non-stop about how good things used to be "back in the day".

Claude
A handsome, successful engineer recently arrived from Quebec, Claude has an eye for the ladies and the good things in life. Often rubs Rosie and the other regulars the wrong way with his arrogance.

Sammy
Sammy is a mysterious, intimidating man of indeterminate age & ethnicity who is the acknowledged leader of the group of hard-core regulars affectionately known as the "Dog Pound".

Gary
Amiable, intelligent and very well-read, Gary is a flooring contractor with a problematic home life. He seeks solace in the Black Horse to escape his troubles for a few hours several times per week, often found with his nose stuck in a book.

Ben
A quiet, heartbroken young widower, Ben pops into the pub occasionally to visit his friend Mel.

John
John is a boisterous, blue collar member of the "Dog Pound", fond of telling jokes and dominating conversations. A likable guy with no "off switch", he also has a fetish for women's feet.

Tony
Tony is a stylish young real estate agent with an attitude, often condescending, and always bragging about his success. Drives a Porsche and wears an Armani suit, but is hiding a big secret.

Rhonda
Recently abandoned by her extremely wealthy husband, Rhonda still maintains her designer wardrobe and snobbish airs, using her good looks to her advantage whenever possible in the search for her next husband.

Mary
Mary is a dentist from Nigeria who enjoys a glass or two of red wine in the pub a couple of times per week. A natural "watcher", very little goes by without her notice. Mary is content to stay on the periphery by herself, or with Gary, and observe all the happenings that occur around her.

Tommy & Jack
Two retired, genial and argumentative friends, these characters sit in the pub's snug and banter back and forth with their argument of the day over their 2:00 pints. Tommy is a Scottish immigrant, yet to lose his accent despite his many years in Canada, while Jack is 6th generation Canadian.

The Funeral: Mary's Story

If there was one thing that Mary was most proud of, besides keeping herself in good shape, it was her fastidiousness. A place for everything, and everything in its place, that was her motto. Having to share a small room with her three sisters while growing up in the outskirts of Lagos, Nigeria, taught her this reality at a very young age. Receiving punishment from her mother for having a messy room only reinforced it. Being the youngest, her sisters would often blame Mary for any indiscretion they knew would set their mother off, clothes not neatly folded and put away, toys or books left out, even an empty water glass left on the lone nightstand. She could still remember the horrible smacking sound and the sting of the wooden spoon her mother had used to spank her bottom. She would stubbornly fight back the tears during these punishments, her sisters giggling and urging her mother on. Only after, when she was alone with her face buried in her little pillow, would she allow herself to cry and silently scream that it wasn't fair, that she'd done nothing wrong, it wasn't her fault.

When she was older and started at the Academy school, she quickly gained a reputation as a most serious young girl, neat, tidy and dedicated to her studies. She was proud of her awards for penmanship, being allowed to use cursive in her assignments before any of her other classmates could, and for getting straight A's in her course work. While the other students were out playing, or dancing, Mary would be off in a corner studying or reading a book borrowed from the school's tiny library. Her sisters were popular, always leading the crowd, but she knew she was smarter than all three of them and she had already, at the age of twelve, begun planning for her future. Mary would become a dentist, the best dentist in all of Lagos. And nothing, no one, would stop her from achieving her dream.

Mary laughed at the memory as she tidied up her small basement apartment. *It's funny how dreams work out sometimes, where life can take you.*

Here she was, 10,000 km from her childhood home, in the small town of Ashington, Ontario, getting ready to head out to the local pub for a well-earned glass of wine.

She had indeed gone on to become a dentist in Lagos, graduating near the top of her class, but life had still been difficult. After working in a clinic for almost eight years, she was no closer to running her own practice. The wages were just too low for her to make the leap and set up her own shingle. So, not getting any younger, at the age of twenty-eight, Mary made the decision to emigrate and move to Canada, where she could start again with a much better opportunity to realize her goals.

Unfortunately, as many newcomers found out, the transition to working in Canada was not always as smooth as the immigration consultants make it out to be. Her Nigerian dental credentials were not recognized by the Ontario Dental Association, so she could only find work as a technician until passing her Canadian exams and becoming fully qualified. Just a slight bump on the road, but she was fortunate to have found work in the clinic in Ashington, just an hour or so north of Toronto. Her boss, Dr. Sharif, was very supportive and understanding, being both female, and an immigrant herself. Dr. Sharif was eager to help her prepare for her examinations, even hinting at an opportunity for Mary to work her way towards a minority ownership position within the Ashington office, one of two locations that she currently owned. To Mary, this would be her dream come true. She enjoyed living in a small town, and although there were not too many other dark faces around, she generally felt very safe and welcomed by most of the townspeople. She had even managed to make a couple of friends in the short time she had lived here, a real achievement for a "loner" like her. And the occasional trip into the city satisfied her need for adventure, the hustle and bustle that only a large city could provide.

All in all, Mary was satisfied with her lot in life. She still had a plan, she had a roof over her head, and a promising career ahead of her. In a few months she would sit her exams and become, for the second time in her life, a qualified Dentist. If only her twelve-year-old self could have imagined this future, she laughed. What a crazy dream that would have been.

Grabbing her current read from the night table, John le Carré's *"A Most Wanted Man"*, Mary headed out the door and began the ten-minute walk to The Black Horse, Ashington's authentic British pub. She had become a semi-regular there over the past few months, popping in once or twice per week for a glass or two of red wine. It satisfied her need for social interactions, even if she didn't seek to interact very much herself. She just enjoyed the sights and sounds around her when she visited, watching, listening to the regulars laughing, chatting and gossiping, as she paged through a book. For her, it was enough. Enough to feel a part of the crowd and that she belonged. All her life had been spent on the periphery, away from the popular people and the "in-crowd", and now she was finally getting to the point where she could relax and be herself in public. She had even managed to find someone to chat with regularly at the pub, a young flooring contractor named Gary. He frequented The Black Horse most days and shared her love of reading, amongst other common interests. Like her, he was introverted, only he didn't seem to realize it. He became irritable and self-conscious when surrounded by loud, boisterous people, so she would try to keep a stool available for him beside her where they could talk quietly and take in the noise from afar, or as far as the little pub would allow. The L-shaped bar was at the back of the room when you entered the pub, with seating for sixteen people. Gary even came up with a cute name for their regular seats at the corner of the bar, "Library Corner". It seemed that each of the regular patrons had their own assigned seat at the bar, just like school children in a classroom, and they would glare daggers at any unfortunate soul who dared take their seat. The sit-down section contained seating for about fifty people, including a couple of booths and bench seating along the sides.

Mary hoped that Gary would be there today, she hadn't been in for a couple of weeks and missed seeing and talking to him. He had recommended the le Carré book, and she wanted to let him know how much she was enjoying it. They had exchanged phone numbers, but Mary still felt a little uncomfortable texting him, as he had a girlfriend and she didn't want to cause any problems. Maybe she was just being a bit old-fashioned, but he was a very nice man, and "better safe than sorry" was usually the best approach to take in these situations.

Mary had always been a cautious person, except when she let her alter-ego personality come out. She smiled and shook her head as she walked. If any of the regulars found out about "Cherry", it would blow their minds. At dental school in Lagos, Mary had taken up "brezking" dancing with one of her colleagues, a way to relax and let loose when the pressures of studying became too great. Trying to invent a new expressive style of dancing, the two had come up with an upper-body version of twerking, while wearing ornately fashioned bras or revealing tops. It was incredibly fun, and they felt powerful for probably the first time in their lives. She was able to let her inner wild-woman out and it felt fantastically freeing, both self-fulfilling and a bit of an "up yours" to the norms expected of them. They would go to each other's rooms, blast some music and dance for hours until the sun came up. Mary had lost contact with her friend after graduation, but she'd never forgotten how good it felt to let "Cherry" come out when the stresses of life became too much to handle. So now, when she felt the pressures of life and work getting too serious, she would release a new brezking dance video on her YouTube channel and Instagram, dancing provocatively in one of her sexy outfits. She had developed quite a big following, mainly African, and she enjoyed both the anonymity and the excitement her alter-ego allowed her to foment. It was a huge secret though, her secret, and she would die if anyone in Ashington found out about it. Fortunately, the chance of that happening was extremely remote. She was careful to use a fake name and persona, and always wore colourful wigs and lots of makeup to disguise her face. Realistically, she highly doubted that any of the people she knew would be interested in searching for such subject matter to begin with. It wouldn't even be on their radar.

As she turned the final corner towards The Black Horse, Mary noticed an unusually high number of cars parked in the pub's lot. In fact, the lot was completely full, and it was only 3:00 in the afternoon. She debated turning around and heading home, as she didn't think she could handle such a crowded scene, but since she was almost there it would be worth the effort to see what in the world was going on.

Mary pulled open the door and entered the pub to a cacophony of sounds and voices. She had never seen it so busy. Everyone was dressed nicely in dark suits or dresses, and every pair of eyes was now looking directly at her. She spied one of the regular servers, Nancy, struggling to move across the floor with a full tray of food. Poor woman, she looked more like a chicken with its head cut off, running around in a panic, than anything else. Mary felt sorry for her. Nancy was a little older than the rest of the staff, and she tended to struggle with a half-full pub on the best of days. Mary didn't know what to do, it was a nightmare. Her first instinct was to just turn around immediately and leave, but she felt frozen in place and couldn't make herself move. Panic was setting in until she locked eyes with Rosie, the pub's owner. Rosie smiled warmly and waved Mary over, pointing to her regular spot at the bar which amazingly was currently unoccupied. It was the sympathy in Rosie's eyes that finally broke the spell, and Mary somehow regained her poise and slowly made her way over to her seat.

A wake, that's what it must be. A gathering like this could only be one thing. But whose funeral had it been? She wondered who had passed. Obviously, it must be a regular to have drawn this type of crowd. Her first guess would be Garnet, she even felt a pang of remorse for hoping it was him, but she spied the crusty old farmer scowling at her from across the room as she sat at the bar. No such luck. He was one of the few people who made her feel unwelcome. His views on the evils of immigrants invading Canada were clear and often loudly expressed. He didn't like her, and the feeling was quite mutual. Garnet was a small-minded, bitter old man, ignorant of the big, wide world around him. She had encountered many versions of him back in Nigeria too, it seemed no city or country was immune to such people. As if by magic, despite the hustle and bustle all around the place, Rosie placed a large glass of wine, Mary's special glass, in front of her at the bar.

"Here you go dearie, this one's on the house," Rosie said before rushing off to serve another customer.

It had been awhile since she'd been to the pub and she had obviously missed hearing about a death in the family, so to speak. Mary casually scanned the packed room to see who was missing. She felt too embarrassed to ask who had died. It would make her look foolish. Worse, it would make her appear even more of an outsider.

The regulars at the Dog Pound area of the bar were all present and accounted for; Sammy, John, Claude and even poor Gary, who looked like he'd rather be somewhere else. A quick glance at the little snug confirmed that the two old retirees, Tom and Jack, were still alive, still hanging out together and bickering at one another. One of them would have been her next guess for a sudden demise. That smarmy young real estate agent, Tony, was holding court off in the corner, talking to Ben but chatting up Mel the waitress whenever she passed by with a tray of hors d'oeuvres. Even that rich bitch Rhonda was here, dressed head to toe in designer labels. There were a lot of strangers in the Black Horse as well, but Mary's heart sank as she realized the one person who was always there, every day, between 3:00 and 6:00 like clockwork, was not there. "Uncle" Dave. Dear old Dave, the gentle heartbeat of the pub. That sweet, sweet man who had been the first person to introduce himself to her and make her feel welcome on her very first visit to the pub. He was missing.

When she had first realized that her desire to go out for a glass of wine and to socialize was greater than her nervousness about going to a bar where she probably knew absolutely no one, Mary had gathered up all her courage and made her way to the local watering hole. Dave had smiled at her as she entered the Black Horse for the first time, sensing her nervousness and hesitation.

"Why, hello there, young lady, welcome to the Black Horse." Approaching her with his hand outstretched, she held out her own in return.

"My name is Dave, it's a pleasure to meet you."

"I'm Mary. I'm new to the area and I was just

hoping to have a nice glass of red wine and relax for a little while."

"You've come to the right place, Mary, and now you know someone here as well. A stranger is just a friend you haven't met yet, you know."

She couldn't help but take an immediate liking to this kind man.

"Thank you, Dave, it's good to meet you too."

"Ah, here comes the one person you must be introduced to above all."

Mary saw a lovely blonde woman, in her early middle years, come out from behind a door at the bar.

"Mary, please let me introduce you to the wonderful landlady of this establishment, Rosie. Rosie, this is Mary, our newest regular, who is in search of a relaxing glass of red wine."

The two ladies exchanged greetings and a handshake, Rosie happily led her to a seat, her "seat" at the bar, and poured her a glass of wine. The two of them kept her company, friendships were quickly made, and they introduced her to some of the other Black Horse regulars who had wandered in and out that day.

"Oh no," she uttered to herself. "He seemed so full of life."

Uncle Dave had been a daily regular at The Black Horse for many years, since even before Rosie's rat of a husband had taken off with a waitress, leaving her to sort things out on her own. Good riddance to bad garbage. But Dave was always there, laughing, smiling and being the life of the party. He was still relatively young too, maybe 60 or so, far too young to die. He was a dear man too, a true gentleman. Poor Dave, he didn't even have any family to mourn his passing, other than the bar regulars of course, who all seemed genuinely affected. Mary would eavesdrop when Dave talked about his family. It was a sad story to be honest, but very compelling. His wife had up and left him many years ago, taking their young son with her back to England. Mary thought it probably had something to do with his drinking but was never certain. Dave had never been able to reconnect with them and had ultimately become completely estranged. He'd never recovered from losing his family. There was a heavy sadness about it that would come out at times.

He would still receive periodic updates from his ex-sister-in-law though, and then he would regale the regulars with great pride about his son Michael, the now grownup RAF fighter pilot. It hurt Dave that 'Mikey' had never reached out to him over all these years, but maybe that was all for the best.

Mary's concentration was shattered by Sammy loudly slamming his hand on the bar, shouting for more shots of tequila for him and John. He was an intimidating man, big and strong, with a few noticeable scars on his face. He looked dangerous too. Not in a crazy way, he just looked like a man you wouldn't want to mess with. His eyes had the look of someone who had seen things that most people would never want to see. Truth be told, he scared her, but everyone else seemed to love him. He was the acknowledged leader of the regulars, and other than being loud sometimes he hadn't really done anything to warrant that fear. It was just a gut feeling that Mary had. She wouldn't want to be there if he ever lost control, that's for sure.

John, on the other hand was harmless. Annoying yes, obnoxious certainly, but generally he was harmless. He was a close talker too, and he loved to talk, mostly nonsense, bouncing from one person to the next like a pinball. He could be rude at times, especially when going on and on about women's feet and his obvious foot fetish, but she knew he didn't mean to be. Mary had heard him begging Mel to see her toes on more than one occasion. So gross! He was colourful, that's for sure. She knew he was just lonely, plain-looking, forty-something man who worked in a factory and had no social life other than at the pub. He could be funny and charming at times but tended to get increasingly louder, and increasingly more obnoxious with each beer. At least one thing Sammy had going in his favour was the ability to never appear drunk. Mary had seen him put back shot after shot, with pints on the side, and still maintain the exact same demeanor he had when he began, that strange, inscrutable, mysterious aura that he just seemed to project effortlessly.

Right now, John was haranguing Claude, the handsome French Canadian, with another story about Dave. Claude was a bit of an odd one too. He was a very good-looking man, about John's age, but he seemed so much younger due to his charisma. He was apparently a very successful engineer who had designed some type of machine for processing and packaging dry soup mixes, and he didn't mind flaunting his success in other people's faces. Mary didn't much care for him. People like Claude would usually fall back to earth eventually. The women, especially the younger ones in the pub, always seemed to fall for his charms though. He would slither through the room like a serpent, eying his target from afar before making his approach with a flourish of French-accented English. Mary knew that it was all an act, and that he was just laying it on thick. He'd even tried it on with her before. Only once though, and he seemed shocked, almost angry, at Mary's quick dismissal of his attempted seduction. But Claude, give him credit, racked up a lot of successes and it drove some of the younger guys crazy. They couldn't compete with his money and sophistication and would inevitably end up as the shoulder to cry on after Claude quickly tired of his latest conquest.

"Do you remember when that craft beer rep came in with those samples of pumpkin spice beer?" John asked.

Encouraged, John was now shouting at the group. "Holy shit, that was hilarious!"

Mary turned and watched as John began to act out the scene for everyone within hearing range, which meant, at his current decibel level, everyone.

"The rep gives Uncle Dave a bottle of that pumpkin crap," he mimicked swallowing a big swig of beer, puffing out his cheeks in imitation. "Dave gets the most hideous look on his face and then proceeds to spit the entire mouthful onto the poor bastard!"

John was laughing hysterically now, loving the attention he was getting from the room.

"Now that's what I call customer feedback!" he said choking on his words. "Oh man, poor Dave was so embarrassed. He really must have hated that shit."

John's story seemed to break the spell and set the tone for more stories about Dave. One after another, the regulars and guests recounted stories about him. Rosie's was especially moving, bringing many to tears.

"My husband left me, I know you all know all about this, taking all our money but leaving our many debts behind. I was struggling so badly. I really didn't know what to do. The pub wasn't making any money and my old car wasn't running, so I couldn't even go out and get supplies. We'd been cut off by most of our suppliers and I was so close to just giving up and closing this place for good."

Tears rolled down her face as she went on, "But Dave was there for me. He told me not to worry and gave me his car to use to go to the beer store and to the grocery store for supplies. He even fronted me a good amount of money to make sure the pub would stay open and our accounts were in the black. He made sure that the lights would stay on."

Other than the odd sniffle, there was not a sound in the room as Rosie continued with her memories.

"He told me that he believed in me, that I would get through the heartache, the betrayal and the struggles, and come out the other side stronger than ever. He truly believed in me! He made sure that I was OK when I needed someone to be there for me the most, and I will always cherish and love him for that."

Rosie smiled and pointed to the heavens, and everyone raised their glasses in unison with hers as she spoke some more, "So here's to that dear, sweet man, Uncle Dave, who we were all blessed to know and love. We will miss you so much. I will miss you. May you rest in peace."

Mary was touched by the outpouring of affection she witnessed. She too was crying for the loss of Dave, and for the sadness in the room. Everyone remained silent for what seemed like minutes before John broke the spell with a shout.

"The only reason that old bastard helped you out was because he didn't want to have to find another place to drink!"

And with that, the roar of laughter led people to once again relate their stories about Uncle Dave, one after the other, memory after memory. How he ran the NFL and NHL pools each season without fail, how he organized the annual football bus trip down to Buffalo to watch the Bills play, telling jokes and singing songs the whole way there and back, making sure that everyone was having a great time.

The sombre mood had changed wonderfully to one of celebration. The drinks were flowing, trays of food were devoured, and Dave was eulogized, over and over again, with the love and devotion he had earned from his friends.

Mary was on her second glass of red, observing all the commotion and activity around her. While she had seen many new faces in the pub this day, there was one stranger who stood out from all the others. He was quiet, standing to the side almost the entire time, blond-haired, late thirties and with a distinct military bearing. She had overheard him when ordering a drink, definitely an English accent too. This surely must be Michael, Dave's estranged son. She wondered how he had even found out about his father's passing. It was so sad that the two had never reconnected, never found the peace that Dave must have wanted very much. Their estrangement was the one thing that had haunted him. It looked like Michael was getting ready to leave, when Rosie wandered over.

"Hello, you must be Michael," Rosie said quietly. "Your dad always called you young Mikey."

Michael smiled and shook her hand, replying equally quietly, "Thank you for your kind words and for hosting this wake. I thought it was the least I could do to drop by."

"Your father loved you very much Michael. He was always talking about you, about your achievements and activities. Your aunt Pamela would give him regular updates about your life, just so you know. You were always on his mind, he never once stopped caring. He just figured it would be best to love you from a distance."

"I'm glad that he managed to find a sense of family here with you, with all of these people." He looked across the room, adding, "I was only three when we left, I have no real memories of him, but I'm glad I came. He seems to have been a good man, at least for all of you he was. Maybe that's enough."

With that, Mary watched Michael quietly make his way past the boisterous throng of people and leave The Black Horse, unnoticed by everyone but herself and Rosie, who just went up a few notches in her estimation.

She put her hand on Rosie's and whispered, "That was very nice of you to say, it must be so difficult to deal with the loss of a father for the second time. I hope he can make peace with the situation."

Rosie gave her hand a squeeze and replied, "He will. It will take time, but he will sort out all the emotions and guilt. He's a good young man."

And then she was off again, first into the kitchen to get more food, then helping pour drinks at the

bar.
Reflected in the bar's mirror, Mary saw the front door open. A baby stroller entered, followed by a visibly angry young woman. The chaotic din of many overlapping conversations was soon shattered by a piercing scream.

"Gary! Where the fuck are you?"

Everybody not named Gary immediately shuddered and looked down in relief, but poor Gary looked ashen and speechless. The woman quickly spotted him in the crowd.

"Get over here right now! We're leaving! You were supposed to be home half an hour ago!"

Looking like a naughty child, Gary made his way towards the door as Sammy and John mimicked her shout of "Gary", making the sound of a whip being cracked and giggling amongst themselves.

"Time to go home Gary!" John added in his best 'harpy' imitation.

"Steph, I was just leaving," Gary finally managed to say, pleading for understanding.

"Bullshit!" You were going to hang out here with your loser friends all night, weren't you? Weren't you!" she demanded.

All Gary could do was shake his head in embarrassment and make his way towards the door.

"You know it's my night to go out, now let's go home right this fucking minute!"

Head down, Gary took the handles of the stroller and led the way out of the pub, not daring to look back at the laughing crowd of mourners.

Mary noticed one of the regulars not laughing though. Claude. The look on his face was not one of glee, not even one of embarrassment for a friend. To her, Claude was sporting a look of recognition. He knew that girl that was for sure. She was probably one of his conquests.

Poor Gary, she hoped he would be alright. He'd probably tell her all about it the next time they shared a quiet moment at Library Corner.

Mary figured it was about time for her to go home as well. This had turned out to be a most unusual visit to The Black Horse indeed. She'd seen, heard and experienced too much sadness to enjoy her visit. She swallowed the last of her wine in one quick gulp, grabbed her book, and headed out the door.

Rosie's Story

Rosie tumbled off the cliff, and as she fell towards the rocks 80 feet below, she turned and saw the figure of a man looking down at her. As always, she woke up before she hit the ground and failed to recognize who this mysterious person was, the person who must have shoved her.

This dream was one that Rosie experienced frequently. She had no idea what it meant, but she would make sure that there weren't going to be any cliffs in her future anytime soon.

The alarm sounded. On Wednesdays, Rosie got up an hour earlier than usual. Wednesday was beer delivery day and her pub was the first stop on the delivery driver's route. Better not miss it, or all you would get is a note saying, "sorry we missed you."

Rosie was the landlady of the Black Horse, a cozy traditional style pub in the heart of Ashington, a small town about one hour north of Toronto, where she had lived for over 20 years. Rosie and her husband Aaron had moved there when they had purchased the little bar from someone desperate to get out the business. It had been a sports bar back then and Aaron and Rosie had turned it into an English style pub. The food was good, the beer cold, and Rosie was a wonderful host. In no time at all they had become quite the busy little place.

Rosie loved the Black Horse, it was her little "Queendom". Aaron, on the other hand, drank more than he worked when he was there. He would often get belligerent with the customers, and many a time Rosie would be forced to step in. It didn't matter in the end, as after only a few years Aaron ran off with a young waitress named Sally. She had never heard from

him since, and to be quite truthful, she did not really care. She was better off without him.
After he had taken off, many of the regulars that Aaron had offended, and who had vowed to never drink in the Black Horse again, began to trickle back and frequent the place again, mainly because they all loved Rosie.

Rosie was forever smiling and always had the time to chat to everyone, even though she might have a pile of stuff to do. Rosie was in her late forties but looked ten years younger, strawberry blonde hair, pale blue eyes, and a wonderful smile that had many people wondering why she remained single. The truth was that Rosie never had the time to think about finding someone special, the Black Horse was a full-time job and more. There was someone at the bar, however, that made her feel a little giddy, but she knew that he didn't share her feelings for her. So, when it came to romance, that was that.

Rosie got to the bar at 9:30 am. It was time to clean up the place and get ready for opening. Wednesday was never an overly busy day, but in this business, you just never knew what the wind would blow in. Evelyn, her chef, would be in at 10:30 and Mel the waitress would be in at 11:00. Rosie and Mel could handle the Black Horse together, no matter how busy it got.

She looked around at her little slice of heaven. The sit-down L-shaped bar with its 16 seats was at the back of the room as you entered. Between the entrance and the sit-down bar was a 48-seat dining section containing a couple of booths and bench seating along the left hand and right hand walls. At the front of the bar, by the large window, there was a semi-private little "snug", with cozy seating for two. This was a very popular spot for couples, as the four-foot high partition with the open entrance gave you a hint of privacy while you could still see the whole of the bar from the elevated step up to its

small table and two seater padded red bench. The snug was where the pensioners, Tommy and Jack, sat seven days a week, at 2:30 on the dot. She smiled and wondered what they would be arguing about today.
The Black Horse had many regulars, god forbid if you sat in one of their seats. By 3:30 in the afternoon the 16 seats at the bar were usually taken up by regulars, and if a stranger happened to be sitting in one of "their" seats, they would not know it, but a pair of eyes would be burning a hole in their back.
Rosie liked most of her regulars, they were a jovial bunch, a bit loud most of the time but hey, they supported her and were indeed a loyal gang. A couple of them she maybe would like to see move on though. One was a bit brash and a "know-it-all", and the other just couldn't handle his alcohol anymore.
Then there was Sammy. It was very strange, as he would talk to everyone at the bar but never said more than a few words to her. Oh, he was polite enough when ordering his beer, but that was it. He would then look away and converse with the guys but would never engage her in direct conversation, which was a pity as he made Rosie weak at the knees every time she looked at him. Anyway, now was not the time to think about him, as the beer truck was pulling into the parking lot.

Rosie always had to double check the order, these guys just wanted to get in and out as quickly as possible and were not always on the mark when it came to getting her order right.
After Rosie checked the delivery, she offered the guys a pop and some water, then got back to work getting the bar ready for the day. Taking the chairs down from the tables, Rosie looked out the window and saw Garnet driving by. He would be in later today to talk about how the country was "going to hell in a hand basket."

Garnet "the Grump", as he was known by the regulars, was in his early seventies and had lived in the area all his life on a large property that was once a thriving dairy farm. Nowadays it was rather run down, no more cattle, just one old horse that seemed to be as old and grouchy as Garnet. Garnet was all doom and gloom and didn't like the fact that civilization was creeping closer to his beloved little town. His favourite saying was "back in the day". She could just hear him now, "Back in the day, you worked hard to earn a living not like these new Canadians who live on hand outs from bleeding heart liberals."

Rosie did feel a little sorry for him though. He was a lonely old man. She could tell that his daily visits to the Black Horse were what he lived for now. She wondered if he was on his way to the dump and it got her thinking about an episode a couple of months back when he had brought a lot of attention to the pub, and the Black Horse had even been forced to close its doors for the night.

It had been a busy Friday evening, and the crowd was already starting to thin out when all hell had broken loose. Garnet tinkered around with old radios and juke boxes as well as collecting old junk. Now and again though he would have a big clean-up and drive his old Dodge truck to the local dump with a load of cast-offs. This time, as he was leaving the facility, an alarm had sounded. The attendant on duty told him that the radioactive alarm had been activated. Together, they looked over the truck and discovered nothing amiss, so the worker took down Garnet's name and number and explained that the authorities might be in touch.

Garnet thought nothing of it and blamed it all on faulty equipment and the incompetence of local government workers. He headed straight to the pub, arriving a little later than usual, but he knew someone would be there to listen to his story. As he was at the bar, telling Rosie and anyone else who would listen about being stopped at the dump his phone rang. Garnet's face turned white as a sheet as he listened to the voice who had called him. Garnet put the phone down and told Rosie that the "authorities" were on their way immediately, and he had to stay put and not go near his truck. Sure enough, the whole street lit up when a convoy of over twenty vehicles surrounded the pub. There were cops, firefighters, paramedics, and a few white SUV's marked "Nuclear Response Team". This shit was real, guys in Hazmat suits came into the pub and ordered everyone out. No one could believe that in the little town of Ashington, at the small local pub, World War 3 had apparently just broken out. At least that was what it felt like.

The emergency responders made everyone move their cars from the large eastern parking lot where Garnet's truck was parked. The Chinese take away next door was also forced to close, which certainly annoyed and inconvenienced them on their busiest night of the week. Garnet's truck sat alone in the parking lot, and Garnet himself was marched outside and given a chair in the middle of the large lot where he sat looking forlorn and completely lost. At least they gave him a blanket while a robotic arm was used to search his truck. Rosie's cell phone was going nuts with family, friends and regulars texting and calling to find out what the hell was happening at the pub. Had someone died? Had there been a fight? What was going on? Enquiring minds wanted to know. Poor Garnet sat alone in the lot surrounded by guys in white suits who had even set up a portable shower in case it turned out that he was contaminated.

Garnet was a heavy smoker, but his cigarettes were in the pub, which was now closed. He breathed a great sigh of relief when a friendly fireman passed him a couple of smokes. Garnet ended up having to sit there until 2:30 in the morning. The emergency response team had discovered a small capsule-shaped item lodged in the crack between the trucks bed and tailgate. Someone in authority told Garnet that it contained enough radiation to last another fourteen hundred years. The same expert had stated that the capsule was actually a surgical implant from the 1950's that was used to eradicate cancer tumours through mild radiation. This now made sense to Garnet, as a month or so ago he had picked up an old medicine cabinet on one of his scavenger hunts at the dump. He had left it on it's side in the back of his truck for awhile, before deciding it wasn't worth keeping, tossing it into his trash pile at the farm. Eventually the experts told him that he was free to go, and all was clear. He could even drive his truck home. Garnet's thoughts wandered to who he could sue for this over the top reaction, but then considered it best just to let it go.

Rosie remembered Garnet coming in the bar the next day and all the gang putting napkins over their mouths. They all laughed hard at that one, except of course Garnet. The jokes about that incident lasted for weeks and even now, someone would occasionally have a dig at him. She had felt sorry for him though. It could only have happened to old Garnet she laughed.

Rosie went into the kitchen to chat with Evelyn about the daily specials that she would have to write on the large chalk board. Evelyn had been with her from day one, an excellent cook who came up with outstanding specials. Evelyn was a couple of years younger than Rosie, and now and again when they both had a night off, they would take an Uber down to Toronto and go bar hopping. "Research" they jokingly called it.

Her nephew Dylan who bartended most nights, drove a private taxi, a small business to help make ends meet. Lately, she had become worried about him. He seemed to be drinking on the job behind the bar. A couple of customers had informed her that after she left for the night, he would pour himself a few

Jameson whiskeys. One morning she had checked the Jameson's bottle and left a small mark at the top of the liquid. Dylan had worked that night, and when she examined the bottle in the morning at least eight ounces had been poured out, yet sales had shown only three shots rung in. Rosie had decided to let it go for now, as she was very fond of her nephew. She would deal with it another day.

She was happy to be working with Mel today. Mel was a ray of sunshine and the customers all loved her. She was a very good looking woman in her early thirties, so obviously, when she first started working there, she was asked out on a date several times a day. By now though, everyone knew that she would always politely decline the advances. She had a boyfriend, Richard Wainright, the local golf course pro who considered himself so much better than everyone else. So much so in fact that he would not even deign to step foot in the Black Horse, preferring instead to frequent the very exclusive golf club bar where he worked.

Rosie never understood what Mel saw in him, as Mel was a very down to earth and a fun-loving person. Oh well, to each her own she thought, the heart wants what the heart wants.

On many days Rosie would work with Nancy who was a female version of Garnet. "Could you imagine the pair of them together," she laughed to herself. Nancy would complain about the heat, the cold, even the price of eggs. You name it, she would groan about it. It wasn't all bad though, she had her good days, especially if her kids and grandchildren had visited the night before. Nancy lived alone in a small apartment just around the corner from the pub, which was just as well, as many times after her shift she would stay behind and sink a few back. Rosie didn't blame her though as she knew what it was like to live alone, and sometimes staying later to have company wasn't a bad thing. Today though she was glad that it was Mel's shift as she was not in the mood to hear about bread going up half a cent.

She unlocked the front door, as it was now 11:00 and any minute her first customer of the day would be driving his Porsche round back to park before walking back around to the front doors. He did this almost every day. She never really understood why he parked round back, maybe he didn't want clients to see him frequenting the pub so early in the day. That's if he even had any clients, as he would park his butt on the same stool until late in the afternoon. Tony Romano was a realtor and according to him a very successful one. The weird thing was, Rosie had never seen a "For Sale" sign with his name on it anywhere in the neighbourhood. Maybe he did all his sales in the city.

Oh wait, there was one sign nearby with his name and number on it, it was the old bungalow that his mother lived in. She was selling up and going to live with her daughter in Collingwood. Tony told everyone he owned a condo in Markham and yet his car always seemed to be parked in his mom's driveway. When asked, he would say that his Mom needed him that night to fix something or other. Strange fellow, he was a good looking man, Rosie would give him that, and he always wore a really sharp suit that looked very expensive, although it appeared that he wore the same suit every day. The door opened but it was not Tony, it was Gary. Rosie liked Gary, he was one of her favourite customers.

"A bit early for you Gary, isn't it?"

"Not in for a drink Rosie," he replied with a big smile. "I came in to fix that loose floorboard by the washrooms. You said that someone would break their neck tripping over it one day."

"I guess I should have twigged to that now that I see you carrying your toolbox," Rosie laughed.

As Gary walked towards the washrooms, Tony entered the pub.

"Morning Rosie, pint of Moosehead please."

As if he had to ask, he had the same thing every day thought Rosie.

"Cold pint of Moosehead coming up, Tony my man."

As Rosie went behind the bar to start pouring, the door swung open and in rushed Nancy.

"Sorry I'm late Rosie, I slept in. Well it wasn't really my fault, it was that bloody alarm clock, cost me a fucking fortune too."

It just dawned on Rosie that Mel and Nancy had switched shifts, as Mel had a dental appointment. Let's just hope her grandkids had visited her last night, thought Rosie. Otherwise, it was going to be one of them days.

Meanwhile, back in the snug...

Meanwhile, back in the snug, Tommy was staring at Jack as if he had suddenly sprouted a second head. For many years, between two and five o'clock each day, Tommy and Jack had been meeting up in The Black Horse Pub, as regular occupants of the pub's small corner "snug". Tommy was seventy years old, originally from Glasgow, and despite having lived in Canada since his mid-twenties, still maintained a strong Glaswegian brogue. His best friend, Jack, was fifth or sixth generation Canadian, living two doors down in the nearby subdivision. They enjoyed their daily walk to the pub, where once settled in, and over serious conversations about the most important dealings of the day, Tommy would have two or three pints of Guinness and a single malt to Jack's three pints of Canadian.

"Jack, in all the years that we've been coming here, I think that is the stupidest thing I've ever heard you say. And that's really saying a lot!"

"I don't understand," replied Jack, feigning disbelief. "CFL football really is more exciting than the NFL."

"You must have hit your head on something very, very hard to believe that nonsense. The NFL is the biggest league around. The Argos can't even fill BMO field. The Super Bowl is watched by a billion people, they even make special TV ads for it. The Grey Cup, who cares? There's no comparison."

"I didn't say it was more popular, just that the CFL is a better, more exciting game. You really should clean your ears out one of these days."

Tommy was shaking his head emphatically, "The NFL has the best athletes, the biggest, fastest, strongest players in the world. The best coaches too. What does the CFL have? NFL rejects and Canadian college players. It's not even a point worth debating. Any NFL team, even the bloody Bills, would absolutely destroy a Canadian team! Maybe it's time to go see your doctor, you're obviously losing your mind."

Jack only smiled at this latest jibe before continuing, counting out his points with stubby fingers, one by one. "There's a reason they call the NFL the No Fun League. Because it's boring! Smaller field and smaller end-zones means less room for open play. Fair catches? Another excuse not to run a punt back. And don't get me started on the way coaches run down the clock at the end of the half or end of the game. It takes ten freaking minutes for the quarterback to take a knee three times. It's boring!"

Tommy was going to interject, but Jack, sensing he was on a roll cut him off quickly. "In the CFL there are only three downs, right? That means more punts and more punt returns, with no sissy fair catches either! And all that extra room that the players have to run, the much wider field, means more scoring! Nobody runs the clock down either. There can be two or three scores in the last minute of the game!"

Sensing victory at hand, Jack leaned back casually before hitting Tommy with his coup-de-grace. "The 'rouge' Tommy, the single point. That's the exciting part."

"You mean rewarding a team for missing an easy field goal?" Tommy replied sarcastically.

"Yes. In a tie game or one-point game, that single could mean all the difference. Players scrambling to run or even kick the ball out of the endzone, only to have the attacking team kick it right back in. Now that's fun to watch. That's excitement. And that's why the CFL is a more exciting game you doddering old fool."

Tommy made to offer a rebuttal but decided to acknowledge his loss gracefully by ordering his single malt, and a final pint for Jack. After Rosie had placed their drinks in front of them, Tommy arched his eyebrows and nodded at her retreating form. "Would you?"

"Oh yeah, Tommy," Jack laughed. "I most certainly would!"

Garnet "the Grump's" Story

Garnet pulled into the Black Horse parking lot, it was 1:30 in the afternoon, the time he arrived almost every day. As usual he hoped no one would be sitting in his seat at the bar, the seat he had occupied every day since he first walked in 10 years ago. Once in a while a stranger would be sitting in his chair and he would stand patiently until the guy finished his beer and lunch and left. Sometimes he knew that the other regulars would invite someone to sit there just to piss him off. Bunch of clowns thought Garnet but without them his days would be more miserable than they already were. At least they had stopped with the "Radioactive man" jokes, referring to the time when he had been surrounded by a Nuclear response team and made to sit in the parking lot on his own for 5 hours or so. He knew they called him the Grump, shit, they even said it to his face once in a while, but he did not care. He liked being a Grump. The world really had gone to hell in a hand basket these last few years.

Garnet usually got there before the rest of the gang, namely John, Sammy, Gary and that annoying French bastard Claude. They all sat in the same seats at the end of the bar, Rosie had jokingly called that section the "Dog Pound" and the guys loved that. Gary though, would often grab a magazine and go sit by himself or join the mysterious African woman who came in a few times a week. They would both bury their noses in books while quietly chatting away. What the hell was wrong with Gary? Garnet walked in and surveyed his domain. Tony the grease ball was sitting in his usual chair looking like a million bucks and boasting about his million dollar deals to Rosie, who was loading the glass washer behind the bar. Looked like Nancy was working, the guys always joked about how much of a moaner she was, but Garnet kind of liked her. Why, if he was a couple of years younger he might have even asked her out on a date, but that would mean spending money and getting dressed up. No way Jose.

Garnet sat on his chair and Rosie put his bottle of Export down in front of him, gave him a wink and went back to the glass washer. Garnet reflected on his life, he was now 72 years of age and lived alone on a 200 acre spread, mostly brush but at one time it was one of the biggest and best dairy farms in the area. He did not miss the early hours when as a boy his mom would yell upstairs, "Garnet, get your sorry ass out of bed, cows don't milk themselves." He would get up then trek on down to the milking shed and put in a good three solid hours before school. He would then go to school smelling like cow shit, but back in the day so did every other kid. It was almost all farmers around here back then, not like now where people lived in little boxes in them new subdivisions that were going up every day and making Ashington look like a town rather than the quaint little Hamlet that it used to be. Lots of different faces too. The Liberals were letting anybody and everybody in the country. Refugees my ass, they just came for the "free money" and benefits.

As he listened to Tony chatting to Rosie about his latest condo sale in Toronto, Garnet wondered if the grease ball was so busy how come he was in the pub every day? As far as Garnet knew, Tony was first in when the doors opened and often stayed even after Garnet left at 5:00 on the dot. Maybe has an assistant, lucky bastard. The door opened and Sammy walked in.

"Hey Garnet, how's it hanging?"

Garnet liked Sammy, he was a genuine bloke, a hard worker who would do anything to help anyone. Sammy was the local mechanic who worked seven days a week at his shop across the street from the pub. He started early then took his daily Black Horse lunch break, then would go back to work before coming back in the evening. He was a big guy and Garnet could not think of anyone in the pub who would or could tackle Sammy.

"Hi Rosie, usual please, and get Garnet one on me." Sammy was generous too and would often buy the Dog Pound a round or two. Not a bad guy at all, especially for an immigrant!

"Cheers, Sammy."

Sammy sat down two spaces away from Garnet, Gary always sat in the seat between them. The code of ethics was strong in the Dog Pound.

As Garnet was yakking to Sammy about why the price of gas was being raised for no reason, the female "grump" Nancy was complaining to Rosie about her air conditioner not working and how she couldn't sleep because the apartment was too hot.

Rosie uttered, "Christ it's still only June, wait until July and August, what's it going to be like then."

John and Gary came in, greeted Garnet and Sammy and took their seats at the bar. Rosie had seen them park and get out of John's car in the parking lot, so their beers were on the bar waiting for them. Rosie was a "good 'un", no doubt about it.

The Dog Pound was nearly complete except for Claude who got in an hour or so later. Garnet knew that Rosie liked the guys who were there now. Claude was another matter, as everyday he would hit on her, then pretend he was only joking, but she knew he wasn't. John was the funny one, or at least thought he was. But apart from telling bad jokes, he was a smart cookie who would not harm a fly. Then there was Gary, the happy go lucky guy who always had a smile on his face and was ready to jump behind the bar if a keg needed changing.

Garnet the Grump knew he was sometimes hard work after he had sunk a beer or two, although Rosie knew behind all his complaining there was a lonely old soul inside. Garnet got up and made his way outside for a smoke, Gary usually joined him, but he was listening to one of John's long-ass jokes and could not get away. Garnet had heard the joke a dozen times, something about a dyslexic agnostic, and he still didn't get it. Standing at the side of the pub, cigarette in hand, he looked across the street and shook his head at the construction going on in what used to be old Jack Tremont's fields. Jack had died a couple of years ago and his kids sold his land to a developer. Jack would have turned in his grave, greedy little bastards.

All the houses would be filled by Chinese or East Indians, why did they not stay the hell away from rural life? Go live in Toronto with the rest of the refugees. The country was going to hell in a hand basket.

He thought about his daughter who lived on Prince Edward Island. She had married a farmer and they loved it down there. Maybe he would visit them this summer. It had been quite a few years since he'd seen her. He hated being on his own, his wife Mary had passed away 10 years ago, gone too soon. She was a fine woman who would not have appreciated his daily pub visits. Oh well, what else was there to do. Nancy popped out to grab a quick smoke with him while her section was still quiet. Gary looked out the window and decided to listen to one more of John's jokes rather than come outside and listen to them trying to "out grump" one another.

Nancy darted back in as a table of four had just entered through the front doors. Garnet watched Claude pull in the parking lot, he was a bit early today. Garnet thanked God that Claude did not sit next to him, "me, me, me, me," that was Claude, it was all about him. If you climbed Mount Everest, he would have done it twice with a broken leg and suffering from Parkinson's. Good thing was he didn't usually stay long as he would go home and change then come back out later. Garnet had heard he was often thrown out late at night for arguing with everyone and anyone. The guy was annoying and always hitting on Rosie and Mel along with any other woman who came in the pub. He would make a beeline for them and make his accent stronger thinking that it would turn them on. The original "Lounge Lizard", was this frog.

Once, he had said something to Sammy about Rosie's ass, big mistake. Sammy grabbed Claude's arm and squeezed really hard, Claude's face went white as a sheet and he never talked about Rosie in front of Sammy again. Funny, Sammy did not mind if Claude hit on other women, only Rosie. It was not like he fawned over Rosie or anything, as he never really paid her much attention. The Dog Pound was a strange little group.

"Hey Garnet, are the boys all in?" Claude asked as he walked by.

Garnet stubbed his cigarette butt out. "The gang's all here," he replied.

Just as Garnet was about to re-enter, he noticed a large Chevy Suburban pull up and five men, who looked East Indian, got out and started walking around the lot looking over at an empty field next to the construction site. They were holding drawings and taking pictures and Garnet thought, "Oh Fuck, they are looking at the Johnstone place, the world sure is going to hell in a hand basket."

Garnet shook his head and turned his thoughts to actually visiting his daughter. He thought about it every year but always found some sort of excuse not to go. The real excuse was the fact he could not leave the Black Horse. What would the place be like without him? He was not even sure how old his grand kids were, but he knew that there were two of them, a boy and a girl. Maybe they would have odd jobs for him to do, fix some fencing or tinker around with some old machinery. He would like that very much.

Just then the door opened behind him and four of the five gentlemen who had been taking photos and looking at maps, presumably of the old Johnstone place, came in. They seemed excited and went and sat at a table. Nancy approached them and walked away angrily as all they ordered was water. Garnet mentioned that they should be kicked out for not ordering any food or real drinks. John leaned over and told Garnet that their religion probably forbade alcohol.

When Garnet began to turn away, John added, "Did I tell you the one about Kraft opening a factory in the Middle East called Cheesus of Nazareth?"

Garnet groaned and went back to daydreaming about P.E.I.

Just then the fifth guy walked in and was shaking his head as he walked to the table.

"No good guys, it has already been purchased by another developer. Two nine-story condos, and a small plaza."

The other four groaned in unison, stood up and walked out just as Nancy approached with their waters. Without a thank you or even a wave of their hands, they were out the side door and babbling loudly to each other.

Garnet was glad they had not gotten the land but saddened by the fact that it had already been sold. Shit, even more newbies coming in. The world was going to hell in a hand basket. Ashington would never be the same. Garnet picked up his bottle of Export, at least here was one thing that had not changed. When he was younger a case of it would sit in the kitchen just by the back door. It was ice cold in the winter and piss warm in the summer, but either way he had not minded. John was telling his joke to Sammy and Gary, while Claude was now further down the bar talking to two ladies who had probably come in for a quiet bite and a catch up. Claude had no social graces, let the women eat for Christ sake. Then

Garnet’s jaw dropped as one of the women, the prettier one, handed Claude her business card. Claude said thank you, turned and winked at Garnet before going back to his seat. If that Frenchie could be so successful with the ladies, the world definitely was going to hell in a hand basket!

Claude's Story

Claude looked across his bed to the girl getting dressed, Brianna, or was it Brenda? He couldn't be sure of the name, but she seemed the good type, not the kind to make a fuss about leaving, or even worse, wanting to talk about when they could go out again. He hated when they made a fuss or wanted to stay for breakfast too. She wasn't bad looking either, a little chunky in the thighs and ass, but she had a pretty face and didn't have to wear too much makeup. He'd been shocked by some of the horror shows he'd seen in the morning. He blamed the "beer googles" for making him ashamed of whom he had just fucked. Well, almost ashamed. What was that old saying again, "any port in a storm". Brianna, or Brenda, was fun though, and he had really enjoyed his night. He actually wouldn't mind spending another night or two with her in his bed. She definitely knew what she was doing, that's for sure.

It was far too early to have Dylan's private cab come back and drive her away from his life though.

"I'll call you a taxi," he muttered as he reached for his phone, "where are you headed?"

For a split second, he almost even considered offering to pay for it too. Ha, that would be a first!

"Newmarket. Bayview and Mulock area." She smiled at him as she zipped up her jeans. "I don't suppose you have $20 for the ride, do you?"

Fuck, why did they always expect him to pay for the cab? He'd already shelled out for the ride last night, why should he be the only one to pay? He'd even picked up her drinks at the Black Horse. What more did she expect?

Making a big show of looking at his Rolex on the nightstand, he replied, "No I don't. And I'm actually running a bit late, so if you can hurry it up I'd really appreciate it. The cab will be here in five minutes."

He could tell by the angry look on her face that a second, let alone third, encounter was definitely off the table now. Oh well, fuck it, there would always be someone else willing and able to take her place.

"Just let yourself out."

Glancing back to his watch as she left the room, Claude knew that he had plenty of time to get ready for his tee time. Sunday morning golf was always the best way to clear the cobwebs from his head. And he was playing with Richard Wainwright today, which made it even better. Richard was always good for a few laughs. He got up and made his way to his ensuite bathroom for a shit, shave and a shower, leaving Brenda (or Brianna) on her own to wait downstairs. Hearing the front door slam a few minutes later put an even bigger smile on his face. It was going to be a great day.

People could say what they want about the Black Horse, but he liked it well enough. For Claude it was easy pickings. There were usually a few single women in there on Friday and Saturday nights, and compared to the regular riff-raff found there, he stood out. He had money, he had looks, and he found speaking a bit of French was more than enough to charm his way into their pants. And if the odd married woman happened to fall into his bed, what could he do? If they didn't want to be there, they wouldn't go home with him in the first place. They deserved a little pleasure too, didn't they? As an added bonus, the drinks were much cheaper at the Horse than at his old haunts in Toronto.

Living in the Ashington Estates also meant that the Black Horse was just a short hop home after a few too many drinks. Having Dylan give him a special rate for his regular business made it all the easier to manage.

Claude did not drink and drive anymore, not since the "incident" two years ago. It had been a real wake-up call for him though. He was lucky not to have been found out and he knew it. He hadn't even been really drunk when it happened, but it wouldn't have mattered anyway. It would have ruined everything for him. Thankfully, it was all ancient history now. He had managed to get past the guilt too, mainly because he didn't believe it was truly his fault. He hadn't had any time to react, there was nothing he could have done anyway. No one would ever discover the truth, and he hardly ever thought about it anymore. Everyone makes mistakes, but his was an accident, he hadn't set out to do anything wrong.

Claude still worked downtown most days, but now he saved his drinking for the Black Horse or occasionally stayed in a hotel near his office if he went out for a few in the city. He'd played it safe from then on.

Claude was fortunate too in other ways. His career had taken off since transferring to Toronto from the Montreal office. His engineering firm had landed some large accounts, and the machine that he had designed for sorting and packaging dry soup mixes was soon sold to several companies in the Greater Toronto Area, making him a lot of money in the process. He kept himself busy with designing modifications and overseeing the service and maintenance of the machines he had sold and reaped the rewards with large annual bonuses. He also enjoyed taking advantage of the relatively cheaper cost and luxury of living in Ashington. Retiring by the age of fifty was no longer just a dream, it would become a reality in just a few more years. Yes, life was good now and Claude was happy with his situation.

From his house in "the Estates", it was only a five minute drive to the clubhouse of the Royal Ashington Golf & Country Club. After he signed himself in, Claude changed into his golf clothes and hit the driving range for a quick bucket of balls. While certainly not in Richard's class, Claude was still a very good golfer. Though not a big hitter, he was accurate and rarely found himself in deep trouble on any course. The Royal Ashington was a challenging eighteen but suited his game, with narrow fairways and plenty of mature trees and water to keep it honest and interesting. His familiarity of the course was another of his strengths, which made him a good partner for Richard, the Club's professional. Playing regularly with Wainwright and learning from his experience had improved Claude's game immeasurably. As they both were popular with the ladies, they also got along well for other reasons. It always made their outings more pleasurable, he never tired of sharing their recent exploits as they walked the course.

With his handicap, their rounds were usually very tight, Claude having come close to winning on many occasions, but never quite managing to beat Wainwright. At first it felt like he was being hustled a bit, but he soon learned that Richard was hyper-competitive and thrived on humiliating his opposition at every opportunity. He'd never intentionally throw a match to anyone. The fact that they continued to play regularly, and he was able to actually push the pro, only added to his confidence an improved his game.

"Claude! You're looking good this morning. Maybe today will finally be your day."

Richard walked up and shook his hand warmly, looking him in the eyes. "On second thought, you look like shit," he said laughing. "What was her name?"

"Brianna. Maybe Brenda. Does it really matter?" Claude too was laughing as he gathered up his clubs.

"What about you? Did the delightful Mel grace your presence last night, or did you seek your pleasures elsewhere?"

"Don't ask. She came over but was too tired to do

anything but sleep. Had I known I wouldn't have asked her over after she finished work."

"That's a shame my friend. She really is a most wonderful piece of ass. I hope it doesn't affect your game today."

Claude had attempted to sleep with Mel before knowing that she was going out with Richard, but she had turned him down. He still hit on her occasionally but generally respected his friend's relationship as best he could.

"She's been more like a big pain in the ass lately to be honest. If she asks to move in with me permanently one more time, I swear to God I'll smack her. She should know what a good thing we have. I like it the way it is, why can't she be cool with it too?"

"Come on, let's get moving. Today's the day you're finally going to be buying the drinks!"

By the twelfth hole Claude's hopes had come crashing back down to Earth. He wasn't playing very well today. Two three-putts on five and eleven had allowed Wainwright to pull too far ahead. Only a disaster of epic proportions for Richard could save him now. Seeing the beer cart approaching, he turned to his friend.

"There's the beer girl now, care for a couple of cold ones?"

Slapping him on the back, Wainwright replied, "Since you're buying, it would be rude to refuse."

As the cart pulled alongside the pair, Richard smiled and elbowed Claude in the ribs.

"That's her, that's the one I was telling you about last week."

Claude turned to see a beautiful and athletic young woman, tall, blonde and barely out of her teens, staring at his friend.

"Hi Richard," she purred, "What can I get for you?"

"More of the same Denise, and soon, I hope. But for

now, we'll just have two Coors Lights please sweetheart."

By the way she began to blush, Claude knew that his friend Richard was not lying about his encounters with the "new girl". He had been quite graphic and reveled in relating all the details of their wild nights together. Claude felt a hint of jealousy creeping in, the lucky son of a bitch! Girls like that did not set foot in the Black Horse Pub very often, and from what he heard it appeared that Wainwright had her whenever and wherever he wanted. What a lucky prick!

After pouring their beers into cups, Denise and Richard wandered off to speak privately for a few minutes. Claude could only imagine what was being said but his friend had his hands all over her while whispering in her ear.

"See you later," she called to Richard a few minutes later as she drove away, not even once glancing at Claude. That really stung!

"Holy shit, man, she is unbelievable!"

"You don't know the half of it, buddy. She's going to be here all summer long. I just have to make sure that Mel doesn't find out about her before she goes back to University. It's good that Mel hates it here at the Club."

Claude knew that what Mel hated most was the pretentiousness that was always on display at The Royal Ashington, and he agreed with her. He loved the facilities and the golf course, but aside from Richard he didn't have many friends from the Club. The bar in the clubhouse was swanky, yet artificially so. He would sometimes have a quick drink there after his round, but never attended any of the Club dinners or other social events. It was a deeply snobbish place, rife with new money, and despite his recent success, he was not a snob. In fact, he loved inviting John from the pub as his guest for the occasional round of golf, just to see the members shocked reactions to his boorish antics. Fuck them, they deserved every ounce of distress he caused. Wainwright, on the other hand, loved the atmosphere of the place. To each his own he guessed.

"You just better be careful. You've obviously got a good thing going here," he said, taking a sip from his beer.

"You know Claude, I never understood what you see in that dump of a pub of yours. It's just a bunch of low-rent hicks and loser drunks. I feel dirty every time I go there."

"It's not without a certain amount of grit, I agree with you there. But you know what, it's comfortable and friendly. There's something to be said for that. No fucks given."

Claude knew deep down that he wouldn't stand out from the other members at the Club nearly as much as he did at the Black Horse. Here, he was just one of many successful forty-something year old men, nothing special. At the Horse he was a big fish in a little pond. A pond that was often full of younger women who could be swayed by his relative success, and where he was usually welcomed. They weren't offended by his French-Canadian origins either, like they were at the Royal Ashington. At the Black Horse, he was just one of the guys. One of the "Dog Pound". There was real camaraderie there, real friendships, and he could never see himself in the same situation with the "elites" of the Royal Ashington. No, Richard could have his club and his status, but he would stick to his roots with the regular people of the town.

"Whatever you say, pal. It sucks there, trust me. Alright, enough bullshitting, let's get back to me kicking your ass!"

Claude pulled out his driver and teed up his ball. He took a few extra practice swings but couldn't quite get comfortable. He was too distracted, and his drive veered off to the right, slicing into the woods, a very rare occurrence for him. He could not get the image of Denise's perfect ass out of his head.

"Shitfuck!" he said to the sound of Wainwrights laughter. Shaking his head, he added, "How the fuck did you ever get into her pants?" He couldn't help but laugh himself. That lucky bastard!

A few weeks later, Claude popped into The Dugout Lounge, a bar two blocks away from his office, to meet a client for an early dinner. He had frequented the place over the years but hadn't set foot there for quite some time. They always served good food and were never too noisy or too busy. He'd heard it was a good place for gamblers, but he liked it for its quiet, dark ambiance and for enjoying a decent steak while watching the odd hockey game. Claude recognized Mike, the bartender, but ordered a Perrier instead of a beer and a shot of bourbon, which was his "usual" order. He was a bit early, so just sat quietly at the bar going through his emails and reviewing some documents on his phone.

There was only one other person at the bar, a large, middle-aged man in an expensive suit, quietly chatting away with Mike. Claude wasn't eavesdropping, but when he caught the name Tony Romano his ears perked up.

"Any luck finding him?" Mike asked.

"No clue. He's not been seen or heard of for months. Not working out of his real estate office anymore either."

Claude wondered if he was referring to the same Tony Romano who he knew from the Black Horse. The real estate reference was quite the coincidence, and Tony did live in the city when not taking care of his mother.

The man finished his last sip of scotch and got up to leave. Mike cleared away the empty glass.

"Good luck, I hope you find him soon."

Claude watched the man leave the bar and motioned the bartender over.

"I'm sorry for overhearing, but why are you looking for Tony Romano? I think I might know him."

Mike's expression showed amazement for a few seconds before he relaxed with a smile.

"Oh, he won some money on a game here a while ago and we haven't been able to pay him out. It's a good chunk of change, and it's just been gathering dust here. He used to drop by regularly, but nobody's seen him for months. Why do you ask?"

"It's probably just a coincidence, but there's a guy named Tony Romano who hangs out in the pub near where I live. He's a real estate guy too."

"Oh yeah? It's a common enough name, I guess. What does he look like?"

"Good looking dude, late-twenties, always in an Armani suit and talking about major deals. Want me to pass on the message?"

Mike stared at him, conflict apparent in his eyes, but simply shook his head.

"No, it's a different guy for sure. Your description doesn't fit at all." After a couple of minutes, he added, softer, "We don't see you much around here anymore Claude, where do you live now?"

"I'm up in Ashington, about 90 minutes north. Quiet town, but nice enough I guess."

"Sounds quaint."

"Here's my colleague now," said Claude as he waved towards the opening bar door. "We'll move over to a table. Can we grab a couple of menus please, Mike?"

"Just sit anywhere, I'll send the waiter over in a few minutes." As Claude guided his dinner companion over to a booth, Mike turned around and made a quick phone call.

"Yeah, it's me. He's been spotted. A small town up north a ways. Ashington. It's definitely him, boss. It's fucking Romano."

A month later, Claude was sitting in the Black Horse on a busy Friday evening. He took a long sip from his pint as he considered how to respond to the text he had just received.

We need to talk

He recognized the number. That fucking bitch Stephanie again. Just about the last person on earth he wanted to talk to. He took a look across the room. The Black Horse was rocking, still full of after work regulars, with some of the early dinner crowd already arrived and taking up many of the tables.

He decided to bluff.

I'm busy. Still at work

The response came almost immediately. It made his blood run cold.

I know you're in there . Come out now or I'm coming in

Shit. Claude glanced over at Gary. He was sitting at the corner of the bar, away from the Dog Pound, talking to that dentist woman, Mary. Another fucking bitch.

Claude hated public scenes more than almost anything. He avoided them like the plague. And he didn't like communicating this way by text. Screen shots of text conversations could be taken and used against him. He would have to go out and talk to her. Gary's fucking girlfriend, or was she his wife now?

The biggest mistake he had ever made here at the Horse was shagging Stephanie for a month or so two years ago. What had he been thinking? He knew she was Gary's girlfriend, but he wasn't in his right mind at the time. She'd kept coming on to him, and she did look very hot back then, not like now. Gary was an idiot. If he had only taken care of her like he should have, there never would have been a problem. But now it was too late, and he was caught in the middle of a major situation. Fuck.

I'm coming out

Stephanie was parked around the side of the building. He got in on the passenger side and closed the door. She was staring daggers at him.

"Gary's inside, did you know that? Pretty fucking risky don't you think?"

"Of course I fucking know that! I'm not here to talk to him. I'm here because you won't answer my fucking calls."

"We've talked about this already. I'm not the father of your kid. Gary is. I was wearing a condom every time. You're full of shit, I can't be the father, so quit bothering me with this fantasy of bringing him and you into my life!"

"Bullshit! Condoms can break, it happens all the time. You're the fucking father and you're going to fucking pay. Big time."

The certainty in her voice was beginning to concern Claude. Maybe she was just crazy, but she seemed pretty sure of herself.

"How can you know this for sure? You were probably fucking Gary and half of Ashington at the time."

He was expecting an explosion but was startled by her sudden calmness and the wicked smile that appeared on her face.

"I had Gary's DNA sampled, from some of his hair. He is not Ryan's father and I can prove it."

"That doesn't make him my kid. He can't be."

"The timing fits perfectly asshole. You are so screwed. I'm finally going to be able to leave Gary and you're going to pay for everything I want."

Stephanie leaned in towards Claude, emphasizing each point with a finger.

"A nice place to live, food, a new car, monthly support. You're going to fucking pay!"

Claude felt trapped and was struggling to maintain his calm. He needed to find a way out, and fast. Before this whole fucking thing blew up in his face and ruined everything.

"I can't be the father, Stephanie." He figured the best way to respond to her calmness with some of his own sureness. "You're way off, you dumb bitch. It must have been one of the other losers you fucked. I had a vasectomy five years ago, just before I moved to Toronto. I have hospital records to prove it. You're blackmailing me, you fucking bitch. That's a crime, and if you fucking continue to harass me, I will ruin you, and ruin whatever it is you have with Gary."

He enjoyed seeing the way his barbs struck home, seeing her shock and rage.

"You will never get a fucking penny from me."

"You're a liar!" She was starting to cry now, "A fucking liar!"

It was a lie, but it was the only thing he could think of at the moment to dig himself out, and it was working. He needed to double down and end this shit-show now.

"It's going to cost you thousands to try and prove it Steph, thousands, and we both know you don't have it. It's going to absolutely fucking ruin you. I can afford the best lawyers around and drag this out for years. You'll be calling one who advertises on the side of a fucking bus. You will never win. You'll lose everything, including Gary. We'll drag your name through the mud so deep you'll never see the sun again. You're going to end up being shown to be just a dumb slut who doesn't know who her baby's father is, Steph. You're nothing. So, fuck off back to Gary and shut your fucking mouth. I never want to hear a single word about this from you again. Ever. Do you understand?"

"You're such an asshole. It had to be you. There was no one else."

She could barely get the words out between sobs. Her collapse was proof that he had won, had saved himself from another personal disaster. A part of him felt bad, he never wanted it to come to this, but she just wouldn't back off. Fucking gold digger. Gary was alright, still a bit of a loser, but he was better than nothing, and he was taking care of her. And the child too. Stephanie should have just left things alone and been happy with what she had. But she got greedy. He actually felt bad for Gary too. Steph would make his life miserable from now on. She was not the kind of woman to let things lie. She'd never get over the lost opportunity and take all her frustrations out on the poor guy. Fuck it, it was no longer his problem.

"I'm serious, you fucking bitch. If I hear even one word of this from you or anyone else again, I will come after you with everything my lawyers can think of. I never want to see you ever again either, do you understand?"

Still crying, Stephanie nodded but said nothing, blinded by her tears and rage.

Out of the corner of his eye Claude sensed a shadow moving away from the car. Shit, was someone there? How long had they been standing there? He had been careful to look around before entering the car and hadn't noticed anybody around then. They'd only been talking for five or ten minutes, but he hadn't really been keeping an eye out for anyone coming out of the pub. Maybe he'd somehow missed someone. He hopped out of the car and looked around, and saw a figure, on foot, turning the corner onto the side street. He couldn't tell who it was, but he thought it was likely a woman. It was probably nothing to worry about, but just to make sure he leaned back into the car one last time.

"Get the fuck out of here Steph, before someone sees you. And go clean yourself up before Gary gets home. You look like shit."

With that, he closed the door and walked back to the front of the Black Horse. Taking a deep breath to collect himself, he opened the door, walked calmly back into the cozy confines of the pub and headed for his regular seat. Everything seemed normal, the Dog Pound still noisy and full of conversation.

He glanced towards the corner of the bar to see Gary sipping a beer and reading a magazine. Poor guy, sitting all alone. Alone? Shit, where was Mary? He thought he had recognized that figure off in the distance. It must have been her. What could she have possibly seen or heard as she passed by? Or had she been lingering beside the car the whole time. Nosy bitch. He'd have to keep an eye on her now too. Fuck, it was always something with these women.

"What can I get you Claude?" asked Dylan, just coming on to the bar.

He looked up, still lost in thought.

"Beer and a bourbon, thanks. Better make it a fucking double!

Meanwhile, back in the snug...

Meanwhile, back in the snug, Jack was taking a long, slow sip from his pint of Canadian and staring at Tommy, his daily companion in the Black Horse's "snug".

"You're not British, Tommy, you're Scottish," he said after carefully placing his pint glass back on the table. "You've told me a million times that you're Scottish. You have a Scottish accent for Christ's sake, not a British one!"

Tommy stared back with equal parts ferocity and pity. "What do you mean by a British accent? What the hell is a British accent supposed to sound like, you daft prick?"

"You know, that pompous way of talking that Brits are famous for. Like in Monty Python!"

"You mean like John Cleese?"

"Yes Tommy, a British accent."

"That's not a British accent you idiot! Well it is, but it's a toffee-nosed accent, spoken by an educated person from the south of England."

"So, I'm right."

"No Jack, you are miles and miles away from being right. You are as wrong as wrong can be. And then some!"

"But most people think that's a British accent."

"Then most people are morons. I am Scottish and I'm also British. A Welshman is also British despite his Welsh accent, which, by the way, is also a British accent. That's the problem over here, people think that only the English are British. It's bloody annoying actually!"

"Well, maybe it's because the English are the ones that have a Queen."

Tommy choked on his Guinness before spluttering, "For fuck's sake Jack, she isn't only the Queen of

England. She is the Queen of the Scots, and the Welsh, and the north of Ireland too. She is the fucking Queen of Britain. Great Britain. The United fucking Kingdom!"

"But she has a British accent Tommy!"

"Because she was raised in England, she has an English accent. Christ, you're a dumb twat!"

Tommy was struggling to come to grips with his friend's lack of comprehension.

"Look Jack, it's like here in Canada, there are different provinces, but they are all part of Canada, even though Quebecers and Newfies speak with a different accent. Do you understand now?"

"But we're not different countries Tommy! Scotland plays against England in soccer, don't they? How could they be British if they compete against England in the World Cup or something? Shouldn't they be on the same side? Who would the Queen cheer for then? Answer me that Tommy."

"I don't know Jack, with her ancestry, probably the fucking Germans! Or she'd be neutral, or…"

"No need to get upset pal, she probably doesn't even like soccer."

Suddenly, a smile crossed Tommy's anguished face as he leaned forward to make his winning point. "The Olympics! The Olympic games, you dumb bastard. We all compete as one team at the Olympics, the British team. Team Great Britain. English, Scottish, Welsh and Northern Irish. All together on one great, beautiful, unified fucking team!"

"Like North and South Korea!"

Tommy laughed as he had to concede once again. He was a victim of not only Jack's lack of knowledge and sheer hard-headedness, but also his determination to show off that ignorance in a most spectacular way.

"Yes Jack, just like North and South Korea." He motioned to their empty glasses. "One more pint before we go?"

"Absolutely. My shout this time," Jack replied.

As he turned towards the bar to signal for another round, he saw Rhonda alone at a table, nursing a large glass of wine and looking caustically chic as usual.

"Hey," he said as he motioned towards her with a nod, "Would you?"

After a few moments of quiet contemplation Tommy answered soberly, "Yes, I would. I most definitely would. She'd probably tear it right off of me when she was finished, but I'm sure it'd be worth it!"

Sammy's Story

"Dylan! Four more shots!" shouted Sammy towards the bar, "And no fruit."

Sammy hated to drink tequila any other way than straight up and in a simple shot glass. Lemons were for pussies. Salt spoiled the taste. Why did people want to ruin such a good thing?

As was his habit at this time of night, Sammy was constantly shifting his weight from one foot to another with pent up energy, almost pacing in place, as he stared at his three companions.

John was getting pretty fucked up. He wasn't usually here this late and it was beginning to show. John could be annoying at the best of times, but Sammy still liked him, admired his honesty. And John would always buy a round for the group, even if he really couldn't afford it. He was good that way. He was the kind of guy who would say whatever was on his mind and not give a single shit. Just like he was doing right now with Tony, riling him up, intentionally or not, with his running commentary on the deteriorating quality of Porsche automobiles. Sammy was a mechanic by trade, well up on most foreign makes too, but even he wasn't sure if John was full of shit or not. That was the problem with John, he sounded like he knew what he was talking about, and seemed to have his facts straight, but there was always the possibility that he was just talking out of his ass because he loved to hear his own voice. A voice which was becoming louder and louder with each drink, to the point that the entire bar was getting annoyed with his obnoxious behaviour. At least he wasn't talking about how much he wanted to suck on Rosie's toes anymore. Sammy would always shut him up quickly when he veered onto that subject. He didn't mind that John had a foot fetish, he just didn't like him talking about Rosie that way.

Sammy figured he'd get in on the action with a little dig at Tony as well.

"I don't see your car parked out front Tony. If it's not running well, you can always bring it in to my shop for some work."

Tony's eyes were expressive, and right now they were moving all over the room in a very guilty manner.

"I like to park out back now, so no one dings the doors or scratches the paint. You can't trust anyone these days. Especially in this podunk, little town."

Tony loved his Porsche almost as much as he loved himself, which was a lot. And Sammy had to admit that he drove a nice car, unlike the beaters he drove himself. Tony was supposedly a bigtime real estate agent and loved to be seen driving around town in a flash car when making his "million-dollar" deals. Flash car, flash suit, flash haircut. Fast talker too. That was Tony in a nutshell. Never paid for rounds of shots when it was his turn though, and that's what was pissing Sammy off tonight. Maybe that was how he stayed rich, letting all the little guys pay. Or maybe he was just full of shit. Sammy had good instincts, and right now they were telling him that not only was Tony hiding something, he was also lying about all his successes.

"Well, let me know when you need more work done. I'll give you a good deal."

Dylan placed their drinks in front of Sammy, and he handed them out, making sure to spill a little on Tony's sleeve. He didn't really know the fourth guy, someone John had invited along from work. He was the polar opposite of John, tall, quiet and sullen looking. But he'd already paid for a round, and needed some work done on his car, so Sammy guessed he was alright.

Peter was his name. Sammy was very good with names and faces. Sometimes it took a while longer to recall a name, depending on how many drinks he had sunk, but he never forgot a face.

"Here you go, man. Drink up!"

All four tipped back their heads and swallowed the tequila in unison, as was Sammy's way. Only John and Sammy seemed to enjoy their shots. Peter looked like he was going to throw up and Tony's face betrayed his discomfort.

"Fucking pussies," thought Sammy.

He wished that Rosie was working late tonight. He liked the way she moved around the bar, making sure that everyone was being taken care of. People thought she was tough and stern, but from the very first time they met, Sammy saw through her act. She was a very kind woman, a good woman and a very good-looking woman at that too. Maybe it wasn't completely an act, but he had seen too many small gestures of kindness and generosity from Rosie to think otherwise.

Sammy noticed everything, something he had picked up back home before coming to Canada. It was a necessary skill if you wanted to survive in his former career. He'd been in Canada for 15 years now and still couldn't believe how different it was, how peaceful life could be. He just wished that he could find someone to share his life with. Someone like Rosie. Who was he was kidding, Rosie was the only person he wanted to be with, not that there was a chance of that ever happening. He was too rough around the edges, too different, too ugly.

"She would never go for a guy like me," he thought to himself when looking in the mirror, glancing from his reflection to his rough, calloused hands. *She's too pretty, too settled.* And he knew how he came across to other people - he was an ogre. A mean one at that!

He had studied hard to improve his English and become a mechanic, and now sort of operated his own shop. He didn't actually own the business, but it was his. He ran it and called the shots. And, he took his share when there was a profit. For Sammy this was a dream come true. Not everybody got a second chance at life. Sammy understood this more than most people ever would.

Something was off with Tony tonight though. He was acting very nervous, more nervous than usual. He was constantly scanning around the pub, looking out the window, searching for something, or someone.

"What's up Tony? Looking for better company?"

Tony spun towards him with a start.

"Better than you losers? That shouldn't be too hard to find."

Tony smiled as Sammy laughed. Yes, he was definitely nervous about something, but appeared to relax as he pulled their little group in close.

"Listen up, this is what we're going to do. Everyone got a loonie or a toonie on them?"

Sammy and Peter nodded. John fumbled around in his pockets and eventually pulled out two bus tokens and a nickel. Sammy shook his head and handed him a toonie, then all three faced Tony again.

"Now for the hard part. Everyone got a twenty?"

"For fuck's sake, Tony!" Sammy shouted, "Just get to the fucking point."

After a convoluted explanation of the bet, and the further lending of twenty dollars from Sammy to John, four twenty-dollar bills were piled on the bar, and each man held a coin between their fingers.

"Remember, gentlemen, heads wins, tails loses," Tony said a little too loudly. "Unless we all get the same side. Then we have to start again. We keep going until someone wins the pot."

At his call, the four coins were spun on the bar top and four pairs of eyes watched as the coins fell one by one. John's fell first, a head. Sammy and Peter both came up tails. Tony's coin fell last, he was obviously a practised "spinner". It finally landed with a head facing up.

"Shit!" Sammy almost spat the word out. He hated losing, but especially hated losing to Tony. He was tempted to check if Tony was using a trick coin. He wouldn't put it past him.

Tony smiled his snake-like smile.

"It's just you and me now, Johnny boy."

Sammy took a deep swig from his beer and looked on as the two remaining coins were once more spun upon the bar top. John again landed a head and pumped his fist animatedly in the air.

"Yeah, baby!"

Tony squinted his eyes as his coin flopped over. Tails.

"Fucking hell," was all Tony said. He appeared devastated.

Sammy couldn't understand the utter dejection he saw on Tony's face. It was only twenty bucks. Maybe he was just a sore loser. A really sore loser. Rich guys never like losing money he guessed, even when it was their idea to gamble in the first place. But this felt different, more like he couldn't afford to lose.

John was laughing and waving at Dylan behind the bar.

"Garçon! Four more tequilas, please. My shout!"

Peter interrupted and said he didn't want one, he had to go. No one else seemed to mind, even John, who had invited him along.

"See you at work tomorrow John. Sammy, can I get your number so I can get my brakes fixed."

Sammy nodded and pulled out his wallet. From between some cash and a stack of faded receipts, he pulled out a tattered business card.

"Do you have a pen?"

Sammy scrawled his name and phone number on the back of the card after crossing out the name and number on the front, his "business partner's".

"You can reach me here. Ask for me direct."

"Any idea how much it will cost?"

Sammy looked at him, quickly sizing him up. A decent guy, honest and probably hard-working too. "Two fifty. Cash."

Sammy only ever dealt in cash. Always.

"Or just bring it by the shop tomorrow afternoon."

He grabbed back the card, scratched out the address and wrote in a new one, before handing it back to Peter.

"If I'm not there, have them call me. I'll take care of it myself."

Peter looked confused but nodded and smiled anyway before turning and walking out the door.

John and Tony knocked back their shots and went outside to smoke a cigarette. Sammy stared at his drink for a moment before doing the same. He didn't feel the need to smoke much these days, he just wanted to get a little fresh air. He was happy to see that John had pushed the twenty he had borrowed back towards his shot glass. John really wasn't a bad guy. He had kept the fucking toonie though!

The night air was cool on his face and Sammy instinctively looked up at the stars. He had camped out often in the mountains near his home when he was a child, had always loved to look at the night sky. They reminded him of better times. Peaceful times, before the shit hit the fan.

His thoughts were interrupted once again by John's loud voice.

"You going on the Bills bus trip this year, Sammy? You missed a great one last season."

Sammy was not a fan of American football in general, but he really loved the Buffalo Bills. No matter how bad they were, they were still his team, and he watched their games whenever he could, especially in the Black Horse. The roar of the crowd, the fans in the pub, and the action of the game all made him feel a part of something, like he actually belonged. He didn't usually like big groups, but Bills games were the exception. Every year, Uncle

Dave had organized a bus trip for the "Black Horse Bills" to go down to Buffalo, tailgate for a few hours, and watch the game from the actual stadium.

Sammy had wondered if it would even happen this year after Dave's passing, but apparently someone had taken over the role of organizer, probably John. He had never gone on the trip himself. Dave had always encouraged him to go, to board the bus and enjoy the day with all the rest of the crew. And Sammy had really wanted to go, but he had his reasons not to. He didn't want to cross the border into the US, show his passport, have his movements tracked. He just couldn't explain all of that to Dave, bless his heart, and he hated lying to the old man, coming up with some lame excuse, year after year. Dave knew something was up though. Sammy really missed him, missed his genuine soul, his kindness. He looked up to Dave, and he knew that Dave respected him too. One season, a few years ago, Dave had taken him aside, held his arm and looked him in the eye, man to man. Like a father prepared to speak to his son. That meant a lot to Sammy, he remembered Dave's words clearly.

"It's okay son, you don't have to tell me. Just let me know if there's anything I can do to help. Anything at all."

Sammy knew that Dave meant every word and he loved him for that. For understanding that sometimes secrets just have to remain secret, no matter what. Those few words meant so much more than Dave would ever know. Uncle Dave understood, and what they had shared in that moment was worth more than any silly football game could ever be. Yes, he missed Dave. It seemed that men like him were found fewer and further between these days.

Sammy would just end up watching the game on the pub's big screen, looking for some familiar faces in the crowd. Later, he'd stick around just to listen to the wild tales of the drunken group upon their return, stories of their idiotic one-upmanship more numerous than the memories of the actual game itself.

"No. Maybe next time, John. I have to work."

"How about you, Tony?"

Tony looked as if he had just taken a whiff of rotting garbage.

"Are you kidding? Stuck in a bus for hours with the likes of you guys? Forget it. When I go to their games I watch from a private box with the civilized people. 'Jim Kelly Club' bro, free drinks, free food, the whole shebang. I never hang with the toothless hicks in loser central."

John laughed at Tony as he stubbed out his cigarette and blew out the remaining smoke.

"You don't know what you're missing, pal, the real fans watch from the cheap seats. That's where all the action's at!"

"Whatever. I'm out of here. I've got a big meeting in the morning."

Tony turned and walked around the corner to the back lot, but not before, Sammy noticed, checking first to see if there was anyone back there. Something was definitely up. He knew that look well. Tony was scared. Very scared.

"Those fucking Bills, when are they going to get a real fucking quarterback?"

John laughed again before replying, "It doesn't really matter if they can't get an offensive line to protect him first. You really should come on the trip you know. You love the Bills, Sammy! You'll have a blast. Guaranteed!"

"Next year, John. Next year. What do you say, one more pint?"

"Why not, my bus doesn't come by for 30 minutes."

Sammy attempted, for what was to him a smile, and opened the door for John.

"Why not!"

He slapped John on the back and followed him into the warmth of the pub after glancing one last time at the night sky and the stars.

Once comfortably back in their seats Sammy signalled for two more beers.

"On me, Dylan."

After their first sips, he turned to his seatmate who, for once, was being unusually quiet.

"Hey John, any idea why Tony's been acting so weird lately? Has he said anything to you? Or to the other guys?"

"Tony? I haven't noticed anything. He was a douche last week, he was still a douche tonight. He'll be a douche tomorrow. He's a douche."

"I don't know. There was definitely something off about him tonight. He's been behaving differently for a while now. I think he's in some kind of trouble."

"What do you mean?"

"Do me a favour, okay. Just let me know if you notice anyone looking for him, you know, or asking around about him or something. Anything out of the ordinary."

He had John's full attention now.

"No problem, Sammy. I'm sure he's just worried about one of his deals though, nothing serious."

"Let me know if you hear anything from any of the other guys too. Let me know right away."

Sammy was only half listening now. Something else had attracted his attention. Dylan had just poured another shot of whiskey. Jameson's, not the cheap stuff. It was the third one he'd seen him pour in the last hour, but nobody in the pub was drinking whiskey. He had to give Dylan credit, he was definitely being very discreet about it. He hadn't noticed him drinking on the job, but he obviously was. And there was no way he was paying for these shots out of pocket, no way in hell. He was stealing. Stealing from Rosie, his own Aunt! What a sneaky little shit.

Sammy turned back to face John again but watched Dylan from the corner of his eye as John nattered on about the shitty music Dylan was playing.

"Shitty millennial angst on a stick, he wouldn't know real music if his life depended on it."

Where did John come up with stuff like that? He seemed to have a never-ending reservoir of colourful comments.

After a few moments, Dylan turned around and then quick as lightening, he tipped the Jameson's back and palmed the empty shot glass. If he hadn't been watching out for it, he never would have noticed anything amiss. He wondered just how often, and for how long, this had been going on. John and Claude often got a ride home from Dylan after the pub closed, Dylan ran his own "private taxi" service. Sammy doubted this service was legal. There was no way he'd have the proper insurance for something like that. He was likely just making a few more bucks on the side, but if something bad were to happen he didn't want Rosie to get hit in the crossfire.

"Hey John, you get Dylan to drive you home a lot, don't you?"

"Yeah, man. All the time! Way cheaper than a cab or Uber, more convenient than taking a bus. He's great!"

"Do you ever smell alcohol on him when he's driving?"

"Haha, all the freaking time! I mean it's not like he's wasted, or anything, but he usually has a couple shots after closing, while he's tidying up and stuff."

"Hmmm," Sammy wasn't impressed and was having a hard time not showing it.

"Anyway Sammy, thanks for the beer. The beers, actually. I'll get you back next week. I gotta head out now before I miss my bus."

John got Dylan's attention, not a hard thing to do for him. "What do I owe you?"

Dylan punched out a receipt and plopped it on the bar in front of him.

"Do you need the machine?"
John's eyes opened wide when he saw the amount on the bill. He hesitated for a moment before pushing it back towards Dylan.
"You know what pal, just put this on my tab. I'll take care of it on Friday when I get paid."
"You better. I'm not supposed to do this you know."
"Don't worry, you know I'm good for it."
With a flourish, John gathered up his backpack, said goodnight to Sammy, spun around and walked quickly out of the Black Horse to catch his bus.
Sammy shook his head and laughed. John was a hard one to figure out sometimes, but he never worried about him stiffing the pub for his drinks. He'd always take care of his tabs. Eventually.
"Hey Dylan, you got a minute?"
"What do you need Sammy?"
"I need you to come over here so I can talk to you."
Requests from Sammy generally tended to be accepted, almost like an order, but Dylan was showing some resistance. He was uncomfortable. Sammy just sat calmly and stared at Dylan until he eventually walked over.
"What's up Sammy? Are you ok?"
"No, I'm not ok Dylan."
He continued to stare at the bartender before continuing.
"I saw you drinking some shots tonight. Does Rosie know you drink on the job?"
"What the fuck are you talking about, I wasn't drinking!"
Sammy slapped his hand down hard on the bar but kept his voice even and calm. Dylan almost jumped at the sound.
"Don't lie to me Dylan. I saw you drink some Jameson's and I know you didn't pay for it. I know you had at least three or four shots. You're stealing from the pub. You're stealing from your own aunt. How

long has this been going on?"

A range of emotions crossed Dylan's face, fear first, which eventually turned to confusion, and then to anger.

"It's none of your fucking business what I do Sammy, who the fuck do you think you are? Bartenders always take a drink after their shift, it's no big deal!"

Images of long-ago interrogations flashed quickly through Sammy's mind, ugly images from his past. Dylan didn't know how lucky he was that he was beyond all that now, that he had moved on. But he was starting to get angry, and it was about time Dylan started to get the picture.

"You listen to me Dylan, and you listen good."

There was an edge to his voice now, even though he was nowhere near yelling. A very hard edge, and Dylan was starting to show some fear again, despite his false bravado buoyed by alcohol.

"Don't bullshit me about an after-work drink, asshole. I'm talking about drinking while you're supposed to be working. I'm talking about stealing shots from the bar instead of fucking paying for them like a man. Stealing from the woman who gave you a place to live and a fucking job. Do you understand that? Rosie has put everything into this place, who the fuck are you, to take it from her?"

Dylan started to protest again.

"Come on man, it's hardly anything. Everybody does it. It's not like I'm stealing money or anything. Nobody's getting hurt."

At the mention of money, Sammy wondered if that was indeed true. Maybe he was skimming from the till as well.

"It's worse Dylan, it's way fucking worse. Each shot you steal is money. It's money for the pub, money for Rosie! It's not yours. I don't know how long you've been doing this, but it better stop. Do you fucking hear me?"

"Or what? You'll go running to my aunt like a little bitch? You think she'll take your side over mine? Fat chance. I'm family, you're just a loser customer. She thinks you're an asshole anyway!"

Sammy doubted that was true. He believed that Rosie would be very, very upset, and embarrassed for Dylan too. She may not like Sammy the way he liked her, but she trusted him, she even confided in him upon occasion. She was a good, honest woman and wouldn't put up with Dylan's behaviour for long if she ever found out. Dylan's liquid courage was very telling as well. How drunk was he?

"You know what Dylan? What do you think would happen if you got in an accident driving one of your 'customers' home after a night of drinking in here? You're probably drunk off your face and too stupid to even care, but what do you think would happen?"

Before Dylan could even say a word, Sammy stood up and leaned forward.

"I'll tell you what would happen. Your aunt would be fucking liable, not you. You'd go to jail or something, but the Black Horse would be responsible for allowing you to drink on the job, to drink and drive your private little bullshit 'taxi'. You have no proper insurance, I know it, you have nothing. But Rosie, she'd lose everything, her business, her home, everything! Don't even start to deny it or I'll smack that stupid look right off your face!"

Dylan was finally starting to panic. Sammy looked as if he were about to reach over the bar and strangle him, and Dylan was looking for a way to escape.

"Okay Sammy, Okay. I get it. Don't lose your shit, I'll stop. Fuck, it isn't that important."

Sammy knew he was lying. He'd seen this same reaction before from men much tougher and with much, much more to lose than Dylan. Men who usually ended up dead, face down in the middle of nowhere with a bullet lodged in the back of their head. In a different time and place, a different world, thank god.

He liked Dylan, and for the most part he was a pretty good kid. Rosie had confided to him about his situation, and he did have some sympathy for him. But Sammy wanted to keep an eye out for Rosie, and he wouldn't let this little punk blow it for her. Dylan needed a good scare.

"We'll see, Dylan, we'll see. Just know that I'm onto you now. And I'm irritated. I'm irritated by all of this. But listen carefully," he was pointing at Dylan's chest now, with his powerful, gnarled finger, coming close but not quite making contact. "Don't make me get upset. If you know what's good for you, you don't want to get me upset. Do you understand?"

Dylan swallowed hard and just nodded in reply.

Sammy reached into his pocket and pulled out a wad of cash. He didn't need to see a receipt to know how much money he owed. He always calculated the total in his head with every order he placed. Peeling off a couple of fifties, he threw them on the bar. More than enough, and with a great tip too. He had to give Dylan credit, he was a pretty good bartender and his service was excellent.

"Take care, Dylan. I'll see you tomorrow."

With that, Sammy made his way out of the pub. He really hoped that Dylan would take it to heart. He meant it. He really didn't want to get upset.

Mel's Story

Sitting on the end bar stool Mel sipped away at her coffee, she had just swept and mopped the floor and taken the chairs down from the bar and dining tables. Fifteen minutes to opening time! Mel liked to have a sit down and a coffee before the first customers arrived.

She suddenly recalled that this was the same spot she had sat when she'd first entered the Black Horse four years earlier. She did not know anyone and had just found a small apartment in town. Mel had been working for The Golden Leaf insurance company at their head office in Newmarket. She had applied there fresh out of University as a customer service rep, and over the years she had risen to the post of 3rd floor office manager. The 3rd floor had the job of handling all the claim requests and it was a challenge. The reps handled the initial calls, but they all eventually ended up with Mel, as the clients usually demanded to speak to the manager. Mel hated telling people that their claim was denied because they had not read the small print, or their husband had lied on the application 30 years ago about how much he drank. People broke down and sobbed on the phone and this broke Mel's heart. She was also told by many that they would come down there and cut her fucking throat, or such similar threats.

The stress had gotten too much, so much so that she dreaded going into work, she could not eat, was losing weight as well as sleep. One day Mel had gone in to work, and after a dozen calls where she'd had to tell people, "**CLAIM DENIED**", she finally snapped. On her last call she told the client that the company had made a mistake and the claim would go through. Mel fudged the forms to suit the case, threw it in the approved file, and walked out the door, never to return.

Rosie had been behind the bar that day. Mel was one of the few customers in, and Rosie had asked how her day was. Mel had no idea why, but she had suddenly burst out crying and told Rosie everything. Rosie had sat beside her and put an arm around her shoulder in comfort. The two had since become great friends.

Mel informed her that she had found a small apartment nearby and would look for a new job that definitely wouldn't have anything to do with insurance.

Rosie responded thoughtfully to her, "Why not come and work here until you find something?"

She needed someone reliable and finding capable staff in a small town was not always easy. Mel politely said no thank you, but two days later she had started her first shift. Life was strange sometimes.

Mel was quite surprised when she realized that she truly loved the job, no worries to take home, she made good money, and was quite flattered by the attention she received. She had been asked out half a dozen times within her first hour and a half of work! Mel always replied with a polite "no thanks," but appreciated being asked out nonetheless.

She got on great with the regulars and had even put the Dog Pound in its place when a bombardment of wolf whistles had greeted her every time she walked by. Now the Pound knew exactly where they stood with her and they'd eventually become quite protective of "their Mel".

She smiled fondly as she thought of her favourite customer, Uncle Dave, who had sadly passed away a few months ago. Dave was the life and soul of the pub, he ran all the golf, hockey and NFL pools, he'd even arranged the now infamous annual Buffalo Bills road trip. Everyone loved Uncle Dave. She never knew who had first called him "Uncle", but he was like everyone's favourite uncle, so the name had stuck.

Uncle Dave loved Mel, he always had a great big hug for her and would bring her in little gifts periodically. Dave had a dog called Kelly, named after Jim Kelly the Buffalo Hall of Fame quarterback. Kelly was a sweet dog and she would get tied up to the patio fence in summer where Mel would bring her doggie treats and fresh water. Now and again Mel would bring Kelly into the pub for a quick visit to the kitchen, where Evelyn the cook would give her a piece of meat.

When Dave died Mel took in Kelly and loved her just like Dave had loved her. This had caused problems with Richard. He hated dogs and would not allow her to bring the dog over to his place, as he claimed to be allergic to dogs and cats.

"Bullshit," she thought.

As for Richard, he was certainly a horse of a different colour. She had known Richard at Markham District High School, he was part of the Geek Squad and hung out with the dweebs and "trekkies". She had never really talked to him at school, he was a quiet kid, kinda shy and skinny. Imagine her surprise when three years ago she had bumped into him at the local Foodland. He was tall, well built, and ruggedly handsome. "Richard, Richard Wainright, is that you?" she had asked.

"Well, well. If it isn't Melanie, how have you been and what are you doing up here in this neck of the woods?"

"I live here now and work at the Black Horse," she had replied.

"No way, that's great! I'm the golf pro at the local country club, the 'Royal Ashington'. I just started a while ago, need any lessons?"

"Hmm, no thanks, golf is not really my thing, but that's awesome for you. I never thought of you as the sporty type," she had laughed.

One thing led to another, and after exchanging phone numbers, and having a few dinners together, they had started dating. It was very passionate and exciting in the beginning, but she always thought that Richard just might not be all that she thought he was. He hated the pub and its regulars, "blue collar crap" he had called them. He never visited her at the pub and bragged about how wonderful the country club was and how lucky they were to have him as a pro. Once, when attending a country club function, Richard had asked her not to tell anyone that she worked at a pub. This slight had only motivated her to tell anyone and everyone who would listen that she worked at the Black Horse! Richard had become more evasive lately, not showing up for dates and then using the golf club as an excuse for not calling her, important client this and important client that, he would say. When they were together, he always looked at his watch as if he was late for something more important than her.

The guys at the pub detested Richard, except for Claude, who occasionally golfed with him. Even Uncle Dave, who liked everybody, would say to her, "What do you see in that asshat?"

Maybe it was finally time to have it out with Mr. Perfect. Where was this relationship heading anyway? She wondered if Ben would be in today, Ben had been to school with Mel also, they had hung out a bit there along with the love of Ben's life, and one of Mel's best friends, Lydia. Lydia and her daughter were killed by a hit and run driver about two years ago in Toronto. Ben had moved up to Ashington soon afterwards, as he could no longer bear to stay in the city. He always looked so sad and Mel tried her best to cheer him up. No one at the Black Horse knew about the tragedy as Ben had asked Mel not to say anything about it. He kept to himself at the quiet end of the bar, although he would nod a polite hello to the regulars as they came in.

"Poor Ben," she thought, so much sadness and grief to carry around all day and everyday. Maybe she would ask him if he wanted to go with her and Kelly for an early walk in the forest. The great outdoors sometimes had a soothing effect, it certainly did for her.

Well, one minute to opening. She guessed that Tony Romano would be the first customer in, he almost always was, then the gang would show up one by one, quiet at first then louder as the day went on. She also wondered what Tom and Jack would argue about today. It was always something at the Horse, but Mel loved the place. It was her second home, her second family.

Meanwhile, back in the snug...

o the fuck is this arsehole in the penny
rs," Jack said to Tommy with a wrinkled
ead.
y in the hell would you even ask me that, Jack.
I would know."
an walked over with hands on his hips. "Easy
, fellas. Dwight is a beer rep, he's here from
ickled Banana Brewing Company. I asked him to
in and let you folks taste some of their craft
It's seriously good, you'll like it.
rst of all, what kind of fucking name is Dwight,
econd of all, who's ever heard of a pickled
ng banana?" Jack burst into laughter fighting to
his breath.
one, Jack, that's the point. They're an indie
ng company. Their beer is super exclusive, I
it would be really cool to get their stuff in
' Dylan said, rather annoyed. "These geezers
absolutely nothing about culture these days," he
it to himself.
right Dylan, you've talked us into it," Tommy
with a grin. "Well, not really. But let's try
of this shit so that we can get back to our
"
ght walked over with his pair of thick black-
l glasses and slicked side-parted hair. "How's
ing fellas! I'm here today to have you guys try
our most popular brews." He laid down a row of
plastic cups.
rst, I've got for you the Sunny 70, our American
e Ale. It's sweet and malty with light fruity
. Second, we've got our Scottish Ale. We've
this one the Scottish Racoon. It's been
ured with herbs and spices and has a slight
ness to it. Last, but not least, we've got our

Oatmeal Stout called Nana's Kitchen, enjoy, boys!"

Tommmy and Jack look at Dwight in silence for an uncomfortably long time. Their mouths held wide open while each of their bushy brows furrowed in the middle of their wrinkled foreheads. Dylan stood by knowing exactly what was going to come next.

"What in the fuck did you just say? I didn't understand a lick of what just came out of your mouth," Jack said.

Tommy smacked Jack on the shoulder before the two burst out into a roar of laughter, "Oh, come on Jack, give the god damn guy a break," he said between gasps of air and giggles. "He's just doing his job!"

"Well honestly, Tom. What in the hell type of beer has fruit in it? And since when are there raccoons in Scotland? This is a bunch of bologna!"

Dwight stood awkwardly in front of the snug.

"Don't worry about this grumpy old bastard, Drake, we'll try your beer," said Tommy.

"It's Dwight."

"Sorry 'bout that, Doug."

Reluctantly, Tommy took a swig of Nana's Kitchen, while Jack knocked back a sip of the Scottish Raccoon. Dylan and Dwight stood by anxiously waiting for their reaction. Before Dwight could even get out a "So…?" Tommy spewed his Oatmeal Stout out his nose and all over the table top.

"Jesus Christ! I've never had anything more disgusting in my entire life," he said while coughing, and wiping his face. "Nana's Kitchen my ass, I don't know whose Nana made this shit, but she should be shot!"

Jack, with a sour look on his face after tasting the Scottish Raccoon, mocked his pal.

"He's just going his job, Jack. Give him a chance. Whattya say now, buddy?

Rhonda's Story

Another glorious morning. I mean, what other kind of morning could it possibly be when you're waking up in your mother's basement? Ok, it's probably time to tone down the sarcasm. Although, it does seem to be the only thing keeping me even the least bit positive lately. Well, that and my daily talk show lineup. I've got to say, some of those whack jobs on Dr. Phil can really make you appreciate what you have in life. And, I guess what you don't. Like a good-for-nothing husband. It's been almost four months since he took off with Little Miss Perfect. Ha, joke's on her. I can't wait until she finds out what kind of loser she chose for herself. Or *stole* from me I should say. Boy, I'd give anything to be a fly on the wall for that conversation.

"Sweetheart, I've got something to tell you. I'm a professional cash embezzler, this isn't our vacation home, it's our safe house from the Feds!"

Pfffft, I can just see it now, he begs for her to stay, she grabs the keys to her ugly white Bentley and heads out the door. She barely gets down the driveway when she realizes she's got nowhere to go and nobody who cares.

I'm sure he's doing the same thing to her as he did to me. Isolating her from her family, "hating" all of her friends so that she won't see them anymore. Yep, those young, stupid girls can be pretty damn pliable. I should know. I used to be one. I can already see the Botox wearing off. Each day I get a little older and a lot uglier. The least that asshole could have done was leave me a couple thousand to keep up my injection appointments. How the hell does he expect me to find anyone else looking like this? Oh, right. He doesn't give a shit. Never has.

I guess that's the only plus side to being in a

loveless marriage for 22 years – not giving a shit. No heartbreak, no love lost. Now my bank account on the other hand, that's a different story. In one sense, I think him leaving is one of the best things that's ever happened to me. On the other hand, I don't even know who I am anymore.

I used to spend Tuesday mornings with Susan at Pilates. Now I'm sitting here watching some bald guy with a brutal moustache tell people how dysfunctional their lives are, although I know mine's not much better. My unlimited bank account has now dwindled down to a point where I'm afraid to look at my bank receipts. I haven't felt that way since I was in my 20s, before Sir Scam-A-Lot swept me off my feet and rode me off into the sunset of mansions, designer clothes and a life of luxury.

Things were much simpler when we first met. He had the money, I had the look of a trophy wife, that's all there was too it. All I needed to do was keep up with my wifely duties and perfect figure and he supplied me with a life I never would have had. That was the deal.

You know what wasn't part of the deal? Finding out 20 years into the marriage that your husband is nothing but a fucking scam artist, that's what. The scam artist thing I might have been able to deal with if I had managed to ignore it. What I couldn't deal with was the cops catching on. I would NOT do well in prison and that's probably right where I was headed if Donald hadn't done a runner. Who knows what kind of accounts he put under my name? I wouldn't put it past him to try and drag me down with him, or even instead of him! Drag me down? Sure he would have! But, you know where he wouldn't drag me? To some fucking mansion on a tropical island. Nope. Clearly there was only room for him and his little slut there.

She can have him all she wants, that's fine with me. Not my loss. What's not fine with me is the fact the rug was ripped out right from under my feet. This little bitch is off sipping mojitos on some island and I'm watching Dr. fucking Phil in my mother's basement. That former life is still mine and I refuse to think otherwise. Being in the mindset that I'm now an unemployed 45-year-old woman living with my resentful mother (which I am) will only lead me further down that mediocre path. Ugh, the thought makes me sick.

I may not be an "official" member of the Wallace estates any longer, but I've got just enough to keep up my image. My Louis Vuitton luggage is still filled with more designer goods than I know what to do with. My 45th birthday gift is safe in my mom's driveway. Although, a Concept S-Class Coupe does look a little out of place in this subdivision of bungalows.

"Rhonnie! I've got some stuff for omelets up here. Do you want me to whip some up?"

"Alright, Mom. Sure."

Being here with her feels like I'm in another life. *Rhonnie?* Boy, does that name bring me back…and not in a good way. I'm Rhonda now, Mrs. Rhonda Wallace. Now *that* has a nice ring to it, which is exactly what I was thinking when I married Donald. *Rhonnie?* Not so much. She might as well have given birth to me in a trailer park. Ugh, I shouldn't be so harsh. At the end of the day, I guess I'm lucky she came to my rescue. She may hate who I became when I entered the lavish Wallace lifestyle, but I know she does love me. "A bond between a mother and child never dies", is that how the saying goes? I mean, I really wouldn't know much about that seeing as Donald never wanted kids. I guess I really didn't either, although it would have been nice to hold something, or someone over his head at this point.

Later that day

Two pointless hours of Oprah reruns with two crappy glasses of merlot, this day couldn't be ticking by any slower. Its 3:00 in the afternoon, I should be good to head down to the Horse. All of the Stepford Wives should be back home with their kids by now. I just can't stand to see them anymore. I can't tell if I've outgrown them or they've outgrown me. They used to be my closest friends, and by closest, I mean the people who I spent the most time with.

It was Pilates with Susan on Tuesdays, tennis with Bethany on Thursday, and then Saturday brunch with the whole lot of them. I used to have so much to talk about. I used to be so much better than them and I loved that. At home I was next to worthless. With those women I was the queen bee. But as we all know, things change. Now the only people I'm better than are the Black Horse regulars. Well, at least I seem better than them.

Jesus Christ, I'm only five steps into the pub before realizing someone's in my seat. I can't stand that. I mean, I've only been coming in here regularly for the last few years! Who doesn't know that's my seat?

Sometimes I feel like it's time to find a new watering hole. If I'm going to find a man to get me out of this mediocre life, I'm sure as hell not going to find him here. We've got everything from dirty old farmers to attractive widowers, but certainly not any men that are going to give me what I need.

"Hey there, John! You're parking beside me today, are you?" Oh great, I get to sit with the creepy guy who stares at my feet all the time.

"How's it going, Rhonda? Yep, the end of the bar's a little crowded today. I figured you might be in soon, so I came down to see ya," he said with a nervous laugh.

"Aw, aren't you sweet. Say, I'd love to join you, but it seems my seats been taken!" I'm barely halfway into giving John a hug before the oddball in my seat takes the hint. "Ahhh, well that's better! All is right with the world again now isn't it, Johnny."

"Hi there, can I get you something to drink?" I turn my head to the left and see a perfectly manicured little bartender, Mel, the "Belle of the Bar". She's very pretty and I don't like it.

"Sweetheart, if you need to ask me what I want to drink they clearly haven't trained you properly. Why don't you go and have Rosie pour me my usual." I can feel her roll her eyes at me as she turns away. See, I knew she was a little bitch.

"Hey there, Rhonda, large or small glass today?"

"Is that a serious question, Rosie? What is up with this place today?"

She finally put my 10oz red on the bar. I know she's not a fan of me. Why should she be? I'm the well put together woman who pays her bills. I have a life. She has a shitty little bar.

"Anyway, John, how's life?"

"Oh, as good as it can be. Workin' lots. You know, that sort of thing."

"Ah, I feel your pain. I honestly never have time for myself. I just spread myself so thin some days."

"You still running that business?"

"Well, yep there's that. Then there's a charity gala I'm planning. I'm also in the midst of looking for some condos to buy downtown. You know, some income property." Wow, I'm really good at this lying thing.

"You know who you should talk to about that? Tony." Out of nowhere, a roar of laughter rips down the bar like a tidal wave.

What's so funny? That didn't sound like a joke to me. Am I losing my sense of humour too?

I'd heard of Tony Romano before. I've definitely seen him here a bunch too. Come to think of it, he's not a bad looking guy. Always well dressed, that's for sure.

"Nothing, nothing, Rhonda," said Sammy from two

seats over. "Tony's one hell of a realtor. He's got a very exclusive clientele. As a matter of fact, they're so fucking exclusive he never even talks about any of his sales. It's almost like he doesn't make any at all!"

Another roar of laughter fills the bar.

"Huh, you don't say." I'm clearly not getting everyone's sarcasm.

Strange. Donald and I dabbled in our fair share of Ashington area real estate over the last ten years or so. I never remember hearing anything about Tony being in the luxury home market. He must deal more in the downtown area.

"Yep, if you're looking for condos, he's your guy," Sammy continued, as the end of the bar barely held back a snicker.

What the hell are they laughing at? Well, then again maybe if I'd been drinking since 11:00 am I might be a little giddy too.

"I have no idea what you bunch are on today, but I want some!" I say with a laugh.

"Mel, wanna grab Rhonda another drink on me?" says Sammy.

"Yep, sure," Mel responds with a smirk.

"Well thanks, Sam. That's very kind of you."

That's got to be a first. I've had men buy me drinks here now and again, but never Sammy the Neanderthal.

I know that the men here have heard that I'm single. As quiet as I tried to keep the split between Donald and I, this is a small town and word travels fast.

While they might know I'm single, I don't think they know that I'm broke. Guys buying me drinks these days have me suspicious. I mean, Sammy? I've talked to him a quite a few times, but I never thought he'd ever be buying me a drink.

I'm still trying to decipher what him and the other men in this bar are getting at pumping me up full of wine. If they think they have even the slightest chance with me, it's comical.

They know I am, or was, more than capable of buying my own drinks. No one would have ever offered to buy me a drink before the split, I would have been offended. Now, I can't help but accept. I've been getting the feeling some of these bottom feeders in here might be feeling bad for me, how embarrassing. You know, coming here isn't too bad in terms of getting me out of my mom's little bungalow. But some days I can't help but feel totally pathetic for hanging out with this crowd of folk. This town just has too much of a mixture for me. I've always thought that. In Ashington Estates you've got the classy folk. The ones who make at least six figures and who know what the world holds beyond this little town. Meanwhile, you get a few klicks down the highway and you're in the land of farmers and hillbillies. The Black Horse is the only pub in town and so the entire mixture of Ashington flocks here. It's a place to socialize, it's a place to eat and it's a place to drink. So, I guess I can't really complain too much. Let's see, who do we have here today.

Well, first we've got Garnet. I've never seen a more disgusting hillbilly in my life. The only thing grosser than his toothless grin is his ridiculous politics. He couldn't sum up the stereotype of a racist white farmer any better.

Then we've got Claude. From the outside he looks alright, but there's something seriously off about him.

Gary's a nice guy. It's too bad he's a labourer. Poor guy won't have two dimes to rub together for the rest of his life. On top of that I've heard his girlfriend is a real bitch.

Thankfully it's almost five o'clock. The day drunks should be leaving any minute now to make room for the more sophisticated dinner crowd. The bar's already starting to empty.

Oh, and here comes the door swinging open again. What kind of character is the cat dragging in now? Huh, talk about speak of the devil. It's Mr. Big Shot himself, Tony Romano. It's funny, whenever I see him in here he never seems to catch anyone's attention. I guess that was even true in regards to me, up until today.

I remember when Donald and I would take trips down to the city every now and then. We'd walk straight into some of the best restaurants down there and would be treated like royalty. Everyone knew who we were. Everyone respected us.

Then you've got places like Ashington. A well-dressed, well-respected man walks into the bar and no one bats an eye. He walked over to the nearest empty barstool he finds and started fiddling around on his phone. Still, no one even acknowledged him except Mel.

"Moosehead pint, Tony?" she offers.

"I'm gonna go with something a bit stronger today actually. Maybe a red, it's been one of those days," he replied with raised eyebrows.

"Sure, what kind would you like we've got a shiraz, a cabernet sauvignon, a merlot…"

"Go with the merlot!" I blurted out without even thinking first. "That's what I always have. It's good stuff."

"Why thank you for the recommendation, Madame," he said with a laugh. "It's Rhonda, right?" he said, reaching out to shake my hand.

"You got it. What's your name again? I feel like I recognize you."

Ha! Told you I'm good at this lying thing. Of course he knew who I was, but I couldn't possibly let him know that I knew who he was.

"I'm Tony, it's nice to meet you."

"Well hello, Tony. It's nice to meet you too. I promise you you're going to love that merlot. Do you usually drink red?"

"I'm more of a beer drinker to tell you the truth, but I've had quite the day. Lots of showings. I'm a real estate agent."

"Are you now? What areas do you serve?"

"Oh… just here there and everywhere," he says with a nervous laugh.

"It's funny. I don't think I've ever seen any of your signs up in this area. I've got a place in Ashington Estates. Or, I mean I did, but I'm currently looking for something a little more spacious."

"Ahhh, the estates! Nah, I did a few sales in there around ten or so years ago but my career sort of took off after that and I started focusing closer to the city."

"Well I can't blame you for that. I mean, Ashington's nice and all but I could definitely picture myself living elsewhere. My husband made us stay here for his business. Sorry, my ex-husband."

"I'm so sorry to hear that, you and Donald split?"

"You know Donald?"

"Not too well, but he and I had definitely met a few times. I think we played in the same golf tournament once."

"I see. Well, yes, we decided to part ways. He wasn't supportive of me trying to venture off into my own business endeavors. It really caused a strain."

"Well, it happens I guess."

"What about you? Do you have a wife and kids at home?"

"Ha! That's a good one. Nope, that life has never been in the cards for me. I'm very job oriented and that's been a problem in my past relationships."

"Really? What kind of woman doesn't appreciate a hardworking man?"

"A lot, apparently!" he said with a snicker.

"Well, I'm certainly not one of them."

These wines are going down a little too smooth. I started to feel myself lose my inhibitions.

Would Tony and I make a good match? I'm starting to think so. I was never really anticipating putting myself back on the market but sometimes things are just meant to be, aren't they? I mean, he's rich, I'm broke. Sounds like a match made in heaven to me.

"You here for dinner Tony, or are you just having a quick drink? I heard Evelyn has some pretty great specials planned for tonight."

"I wasn't really planning on it, but I am a little hungry. How about you?"

"Well when I heard Evelyn has lobster on the menu tonight, I figured I might stay."

I hoped he took the hint, because I couldn't afford that lobster tonight.

"Lobster! Well, how could I turn that down."

"Well, uh it looks like Tommy and Jack are out of the snug there. Did you maybe want to take a seat in there with me and we can get away from this old riff raff?" I said with a laugh.

"Huh, that doesn't sound half bad," he says with a surprised look on his face.

Well what do you know. There's a lot more to Mr. Tony Romano than a lot of people give him credit for. Thinking back, I have heard the bar crowd snicker at him in the past. They say he "brags" too much.
Of course, they would consider a man talking about his successful career "bragging". I can imagine there aren't many interesting conversations that come out of talk about farming or flooring.

He's certainly got his life set for him. Now the question is, could he set up a life for me?
By the sounds of it he could. Now it's only a matter of making him fall for me. It shouldn't be too hard, I attracted one rich guy, I should be able to do it again.

I felt that our little impromptu dinner date went well. Trying to keep up with my little fibs proved to be a bit difficult, but he didn't seem to catch on.

I can't have him knowing the situation I'm in right now. Two rich people falling for each other makes sense. One poor person trying to attract a rich person seems suspicious. And so, in Tony's eyes I'm still the richest bitch in town. I enjoy going on weekend drives in my Mercedes and am sure to take a few exotic vacations per year to let me decompress from all of my business endeavors. Now that I know his Black Horse schedule, I'll be heading to the pub a little later from now on.

Perfume, check. Chanel pumps, check. My favourite summer dress, check. I'm ready to go. I've been practicing my pick-up act all night, it better work. I think he seemed fairly interested. I didn't come off too strong, but just enough for him to know that I'm single and ready to mingle.

It's just passed 4:30 pm now, I better get going. I've got to be there before him. I can't just walk in after he's already there and pull up a chair beside him. That would seem too desperate. I'll go in, sit in my usual spot and see if my mere presence can reel him in.

I'm two glasses in and still no sign of Tony. Figures, the one day I doll myself up for something special in this god damn pub and this is how it turns out.

Did he go somewhere else? Did he know I would be here and is trying to avoid me?

That's when I see him. Wow, I really wish I hadn't have dressed up, because he sure as hell didn't. Now I just look like a fool.

He looks disheveled. His hair is out of place, his shirt's untucked and he looks like he just ran a marathon. Beads of sweat are collected on his forehead. He gives a quick nervous nod to everyone at their seats and then beelines it for the bar.

"Hey, Tony…are you alright there?" Mel says with a

confused look on her face.
"I'm fine, thanks, just a shitty day. Give me a shot of Jameson if you would."
"You haven't been having much luck with shitty days lately now have you?" Mel replied.
"You could definitely say that," he says as his eyes light up with to the sight of his shot.
I never pegged him for a liquor drinker, but I guess some days you need something with that extra bite. I should try and turn him onto brandy, much classier than Irish whiskey.
He catches me staring at him. I'm embarrassed and I don't know what to say. He's clearly had a bad day, maybe today isn't the best time to chat him up.
I can see him walking in my direction from my peripheral vision. Ugh, I just want to crawl into a hole. This is so awkward.
"Good evening, Rhonda," he says.
"Tony! Oh hello there, you're…I mean how was your…um, how are you?" Jesus, that was hard enough to spit out.
"I've definitely been better. I'm skipping the beer and the wine today and going straight for the whiskey if you know what I mean."
"Ahh I sure do."
He seems distracted. Every time the pub door opens, he's rubbernecking to check who it is. What's up with him today? Maybe this whole plan of mine isn't the best idea. I mean, I don't even know this guy. He could be a total psycho and I wouldn't even know it.
"Yeah. I was basically running around like a mad man all afternoon. I had about four different showings all in the matter of a few hours. On top of that, each showing was in a different building around the city. So, I definitely need to blow off some steam tonight."
"And? How did your showings go?"
"Oh, they went great! If there was any silver lining to the whole ordeal it's that I think I've

probably got a few huge deals coming my way. Hard work pays off I guess, right?"

"Well, that's excellent then Tony. Pull up a chair and have yourself another drink, you deserve it."

Okay, see? That's jumping to conclusions at its finest. He's not a psycho, he's simply a hard-working man who has crazy days now and again. Totally understandable.

"Well, I was thinking, if you're hungry maybe you wanted to hop into the snug again for a bite to eat. I don't think I've had more than a coffee since breakfast, I'm starved."

"I'd like that!"

"Hey, Mel. Would you mind brining a bottle of that merlot Rhonda likes over to our table here?" he says loud enough for the entire bar to hear.

We set up shop in our little snug and I can see the eyes of the bar crowd staring at us.

What's the big deal fellas, never seen two good-looking successful people out on a dinner date before?

Then again, they probably haven't. Not in this pub anyway. "Ha ha, we seem to be drawing some attention," I say to Tony as I see the bar's whispers.

"Huh. Well, you know, Rhonda, the only thing they're used to around here is themselves guzzling beer and talking nonsense. No wonder the two of us draw attention."

"Isn't that funny, that's exactly what I was thinking."

John's Story

I knew that I was going to get Garnet all riled up again, but to be honest I really didn't care. Truth be told, I liked it when he got all flushed in the face and spitting mad. I saw it as my civic duty to get him out of his crusty old shell once in a while and let loose. It made him look "alive" instead of like a raggedy old scarecrow.

"Listen, I don't disagree with you Garnet. Of course, Gordie Howe was one of the best, and maybe one of the toughest players ever. He just wasn't the greatest. Not by a longshot!"

And with this simple statement all hell broke loose in the Dog Pound. There is nothing I love more than a spirited debate amongst friends, especially at the pub, and especially when it comes to old-time hockey. Or music. I find that I always have to ask the bartender to change the music. None of them would know good music if their lives depended on it. Classic rock rules, that's not even up for debate! Music is a close second, but nothing breeds chaos more easily at the Black Horse than talking hockey with a bunch of half-witted, half-drunk assholes. Myself included! And I love chaos. Wasn't it Anais Nin who said, "In chaos there is fertility"?

Garnet's eyes were bulging, and he was almost frothing like a rabid dog, barking out, "Back in the day you played for the shirt, not for the millions of dollars that they pay these namby-pambies today! And back then they played like real men! No helmets, no shoulder pads, no woosies allowed! And let me tell you, Gordie Howe was the best of all time! The very best, he was a legend in his own time."

"He could hardly fucking skate, you old bastard," Claude chirped, "I've seen the old video clips. He wouldn't last a minute in today's game."

Gary was laughing but managed to goad Garnet even further, "No wonder he scored so many fucking goals, the goalies didn't have hardly any padding either. There was so much net to shoot at! Fuck, I could have scored 50 goals back then."

Garnet was raging now. "You guys don't know what you're talking about. Gordie Howe played in the league when it was the toughest league in the world. There were only six teams for Christ's sake! Only the best players too, no dipsy-doodling cherry-pickers like there are today. And he played for over twenty-five seasons! That woos Gretzky needed a bunch of goons to protect him so he could score. Gordie was his own god damn goon! He backed up his play with his fists and elbows, nobody wanted to piss him off. You guys are too young to understand what it was like back in the day." Garnet made a half-assed effort to smile and looked directly at Claude before adding, "Even the frenchies were okay back then. Dirty players, mostly stick work and cheap shots, but at least they'd work hard, not like today."

"Garnet, chill the fuck out. We're not saying Gordie Howe wasn't a good player," Gary added, "just that the game has evolved beyond him. The speed, the technology today, the athletes, they are so much fitter and stronger today. It's a completely different game, and without a doubt, Wayne Gretzky is the greatest player of all fucking time. How can anyone in their right mind argue with what he's done, argue with his stats. He has more assists than any other player has total points! He scored over 200 points in a single season several times. Nobody will ever touch his records, he is the greatest. Ever! Period! If I had a fucking microphone, I'd drop it right now!"

Before Garnet could reply, Claude leaned in and put an arm around both of them. "Listen to me now, you dumb fucks, you're both wrong." He looked from one to the other before adding, "As usual."

His strong French accent was suddenly gone, even though he was obviously very tipsy. I knew he always played it up a bit for the ladies, the exotic 'French lover'.

"You can't compare apples to oranges, you have to look at things structurally. I'm an engineer, I know these things, and the greatest player of all time is the one who changed the game the most, who changed the way it's played!"

He was looking at us directly one at a time now, an intense, intimate moment of eye contact for each of us. I could understand now why the ladies loved him. This was the "business" Claude, the director, the Claude we guys rarely saw in the Black Horse.

"Nobody changed the game more than Bobby Orr did. Nobody could touch his skill. If he hadn't wrecked his knees, there's no telling how many records he would have set. A defenceman who led the league in scoring two times! A fucking defenceman! Nobody could touch him, and he was tough too Garnet, you know it. Very tough."

"He didn't play long enough to be the greatest," Gary stated, but at this point, I felt the need to interrupt him.

"Claude's made a good point Gary, I can't believe I'm saying this, but he's absolutely right. Orr was the best player, in the best era too, when hockey was fast and freewheeling. No neutral zone traps, no giant goalie pads. Just good, old-fashioned, fire-wagon pond hockey. You're too young to remember, and you're a fucking idiot too, but Orr was untouchable. He was Howe and Gretzky combined. He could do anything he wanted with the puck, and he was a leader too. A quiet, tough, natural leader."

I looked at Claude, who was nodding in agreement. Even Garnet was listening, shaking his head, but at least not wanting to bite my head off anymore. It was time to end this discussion.

"Bobby Orr was the greatest hockey player who ever

played," I repeated. "Now let's all drink to the greatest ever!"

We all raised our glasses and downed our beers, even Garnet the Grump, although Gary was rolling his eyes and muttered "whatever" under his breath.

At this point, the ever-delicious Mel walked over, seeing our empty pint glasses, and took our order for re-fills. I loved it when she worked nights.

"Mel, I will pay you twenty dollars to see your toes."

"For fuck's sake you freak, will you stop with the foot fetish crap. It's disgusting!"

Gary, although laughing, was always so willing to play the hero. But Mel doesn't mind. I know, because once she actually did show me her feet, probably just to shut me up, but my oh my, she does have beautiful toes! Claude was drunkenly trying to put his arm around her for comfort, but she was having none of that. She was not one to fall for his charms and judging by the look on her face she was more disgusted with him at the moment than she was with me! "Let chaos reign!" I thought.

Mel just laughed her wonderful laugh and told me to behave myself. I'll tell you one thing I know for sure, she is the best waitress any pub could ever have. She is the Bobby Orr of waitresses, and there is no debate about it. She just has a natural way of making you feel like you matter, that you are at home. She and Rosie make a formidable team, the dynamic duo. That's why the four of us are still here arguing about stupid shit on a Wednesday evening, because she makes it a fun, welcoming place to be. Especially for me, and I love her for that.

The only thing wrong with Mel is her choice of men, specifically one man, her golf pro boyfriend. That Wainright punk is such a monumental prick. None of us can figure out what she sees in him. I mean, god bless her, he is a good-looking guy, and is pretty successful I suppose, but he is a complete and utter twat if you ask me. He thinks his shit don't stink, and the rare occasion when he lowers himself to enter the Black Horse, he makes sure that we all know how high and mighty he is. He won't say more than two words to any of us, nose in the air as if he was sniffing something rotten. Well, fuck him if he prefers to drink at the country club where he works. You know, it's best that he doesn't spoil our little home away from home with his pretentious airs. He treats Mel like shit and that's what gets us all upset. Who does he think he is telling her what to do all the time, mocking the Horse and all of us. Claude and I have golfed together at the club a few times, it's not that shit-hot, I've played better courses, but the "members" make you feel like you're walking on holy ground. Claude is very successful himself, he is a member at the club after all, but he never behaves like a douchebag about it. He's a douche for lots of other reasons, but not about that. We don't want Wainright in our pub either, but we would never treat him like the asshole he is, because it would upset Mel. I think Mel understands this, because she is always extra nice to us after one of "Sir Richard's" visits.

Gary was here later than usual and looking nervous about it. "Guys, it's been real fun but I gotta get going or Stephanie will have my balls for lunch."

I couldn't resist, he kept setting himself up for me. "She's had them for breakfast, lunch and dinner for quite a while Gary. Who's kidding who!"

He chugged almost his entire pint in one go, glaring at me the whole time, then shook his head and laughed, dropped a fifty on the bar for Mel, and out the door he went. It's weird, but at the mention of his girlfriend I could feel Claude tense up beside me. No one liked Stephanie, she was good looking, but man was she ever a ball-breaker. Claude would always shut up and turn away at the mention of her name. I always wondered about this, maybe he knew her somehow

from before Gary met her. Knowing Claude, it could even have been after they got together too. When he was in his cups, Claude would go for anything that moved, and he could be quite convincing.
Garnet too looked to be finishing up and getting ready to go home. He was probably the only other regular here that had as lonely a home life as me, living all by himself up at his old farmhouse. At least he had no wife to make him miserable, just his own special brand of misery.

I don't really know where it all went wrong for me, but here I am, 47 years old and wanting to go anywhere but home. It took me three years and thousands of dollars to bring my wife and her daughter over from the Philippines and now they don't even want to have anything to do with me. I met Julie on an online dating site and after hitting it off I decided to go and visit her in Manilla. I always knew that she was looking for a way to come to Canada, but we really seemed to hit it off, even if the language barrier was tough to deal with. A few weeks after I returned, I proposed and started the sponsorship process to bring her over. If I only knew then what I know now, I'm not sure I would have gone ahead and done it. Immigration consultants, lawyers, obtuse government officials, multiple letters to the editor, and three years of paperwork, ever-increasing fees and stress, and she finally was able to come over and get her permanent resident card. We were so happy for a few months, but then the demands started. A bigger apartment for when her fourteen year old daughter, Penny, would arrive, and more money to send home to her extended family. I work as a line foreman in a soup-packaging factory, I'm not a millionaire. I earn an okay hourly wage, but I drive an old beater so that I can afford a decent place to live and have enough money to pay for Julie and her daughter. Thank god Sammy keeps the car running so smoothly for me.
I thought it would get better when Penny arrived, but

her English speaking skills are virtually non-existent and even though I pay for extra lessons, she is failing at the local high school and skipping more days than she attends. She never talks to me and spends all her time in her room on the computer, which I bought, or feeding her pet lizards crickets. Talk about "creepy". I don't even sleep in the same bed as my wife anymore. They share the master bedroom while I crash on a futon in the second bedroom of my crappy mid-rise apartment on the outskirts of Ashington. To top it off, after I paid for driving lessons, Julie somehow got her licence and uses the car each day to go to classes at the community college. I have to take the bus to work now, which takes almost two hours each way. They barely even bother to talk to me anymore and disappear back to the Philippines for about two months each spring. For me, to be perfectly honest, right now, my only refuge is the Black Horse.

At least when I'm here, I feel like I'm at "home". I feel like I belong, and that, in a weird way, I am wanted. I know it sounds sad and pathetic, but it's not. Here I am, and here I want to be. I'm taking care of my family, they'll be okay, and I'm doing what I want. I think, after some time, Julie, Penny and I will become closer as they adjust better to their new home. At least I hope it will get better, but I'm getting really tired of being ignored or treated like a schmuck. It's not like I can just send them back to the Philippines after all, I'm financially responsible for them for ten years, and they don't want to leave except for going back to Manilla on annual vacations.

It was a fairly quiet evening at the Black Horse. Sammy was standing at the other end of the bar talking to Dylan, who didn't seem to be enjoying the conversation, but didn't have anyone else to serve. Sammy could be very commanding when he wanted to, and it looked like this was one of those times. There were only a few other people scattered amongst the tables, so Claude and I decided to wave him over and order another drink just to give Dylan a break. I could see the relief in the poor kid's eyes as we sat back in the dog pound. Sammy was non-plussed as always, wandering over and raising his glass.

"Are you guys finally done arguing about stupid shit?" Dylan asked.

"For now. Beer me, please." Claude also ordered another drink. It looked like we'd be here for awhile. "Any chance you can give us a lift home again tonight?"

"Of course, special rate for my favourite regulars."

"Thanks."

Dylan wasn't a bad kid, I know some of the regulars didn't think so much of him, but he was almost always good for a ride home and did a decent job pouring drinks, even if his personality wasn't all sunshine and lollipops.

Claude seemed to be behaving himself tonight too, which was not always the case. Just last week he'd been asked to leave for being too drunk and obnoxious. From what I heard, he had been sloppily hitting on someone's girlfriend, spilling their drinks when he'd leaned over too far to make a point after not taking 'no' for an answer. He'd almost started a fight with two tables of strangers who tried to step in to help. Claude was a very bright guy, he had personally designed the machines we use at my job, but when he drank too much, he became mean and obnoxious to the point of cruelty at times. After he had insulted pretty much everyone in the pub, Dylan got Sammy to make him leave. Claude had initially even resisted that intervention, but when Sammy grabbed his arm and gave him one of his 'looks', he allowed himself to be marched out the door and into a waiting cab. Like I said, Sammy could be quite commanding when he wanted to! From what I heard, Rosie had given Claude shit the next day, and put him back on "Official" probation. Again. So, he'd be on his best behaviour for awhile, which meant only his regular obnoxious, charming self. I liked Claude, he was interesting and had a wicked sense of humour, but to most people he came off being a jerk. Live and let live I always say.

"Hey Dylan, did you hear about the agnostic dyslexic with insomnia?"

"Fuck no, not again."

"He stayed up all night wondering if there really was a Dog!"

Claude still chuckled at that one, but both Sammy and Dylan were groaning.

"You need some new material. I've heard that a million times," said Sammy.

"Did you hear about the two thieves who stole a calendar? They each got six months!"

I always laughed out loud at this one. Sammy looked like he didn't get it.

"If you promise to shut up, I'll get a round of tequila."

Before I could answer, he had Dylan pour us each a shot. No lemon. Sammy never ordered lemon with his tequila.

"Here's to John shutting up!"

We clinked shot glasses and quickly downed our drinks. Sammy slapped me on the back to let me know that he was only kidding. Everyone was shit-scared of Sammy, but he was probably the nicest guy here. He just hid it well. Very well.

"Have you given any more thought to going on the Bills trip? You'll have a real blast."

I could never understand why Sammy never went on the annual bus trip down to Buffalo to watch a game. He was a huge Bills fan, and loved watching them play on TV, but he always bailed on the trip. The rumour was that Sammy was not in Canada legally and couldn't cross the border. It also maybe explained why he only dealt in cash, at the garage, and even here at the pub. Who didn't use a debit card these days anyway? Nobody had the balls to ask him directly though. I doubted this rumour was true but suspected that maybe he had a criminal record that could cause a problem going to the U.S. Sammy never opened up and talked about his past like most people do, which in itself was very odd. A big mystery was our Sammy, a big tough, scary mystery. I would love to know the real story one day.

Sammy leaned forward and spoke to Claude, "How's the Lexus running? You're overdue for a lube, oil and filter change."

"Oui, I need it done. I'm about a thousand klicks overdue."

Claude seemed shocked that Sammy knew this fact, despite being his mechanic of choice for years.

"Bring it by on Saturday morning."

It was funny how Sammy's requests always sounded like demands. Claude just nodded Ok.

The front door opened, and we all turned to look at who was entering the Black Horse. Everyone but Sammy that is, who was watching the entry through the reflection of the bar's mirror. His seat provided the best view of the doors from the mirror, I suspect that this was why Sammy chose that seat in the first place. Two huge guys walked in, real tough looking guys. One of them was well over six feet tall and almost as wide, while the other could have been his slightly smaller, slightly younger brother. I'd never seen them here before. As they walked towards the bar, they scanned the room but didn't seem interested in anything in particular.

"Can I get you a drink?" Dylan asked as they stood near the bar. The bigger one nodded at the hallway to the toilets and the other one wandered over to the men's room.

"No," said the giant.

After a minute the other guy came back and shook his head. They both turned around and walked out of the pub. Sammy had watched the entire strange scene play out in the mirror. It was obvious that they were looking for someone, I sure as hell wouldn't want to be that someone though.

Claude breathed out slowly, we'd all been holding our collective breaths.

"Fuck me, did you see those monsters? What the hell were they doing here?"

All eyes were on Sammy now, even Dylan's, as if he'd somehow have the answer.

"Maybe he just needed to piss."

I could tell from his eyes that Sammy didn't believe what he'd just said, but it was enough to generate some nervous laughter and return the atmosphere to near normal.

"I'd have been too scared to charge them if they ordered drinks," said Dylan. "Holy shit they were scary!"

Sammy turned and looked at us. "It's not always the 'scary' ones that you need to be scared of. It's the ones that frighten them that you should worry about."

Holy shit. What was he on about? Who the fuck was Sammy in real life?

"I don't know Sammy, I wouldn't want to ever meet those fuckers again," Dylan replied.

"Let me know if they come back here again. Let me know right away, okay."

He was speaking to all of us. They'd certainly attracted his attention.

"Fuck it. Fuck them. Three more shots! And get yourself something too Dylan. Just go check and make sure you didn't shit your pants first!"

Even Dylan joined us at laughing, slapping the bar top.

"Right away!"

Drinks poured, three tequilas and a Jameson's for the bartender, and all was back to normal. Just another night at the Black Horse, as wonderful chaos reigned.

"What did the pirate say on his 80th birthday?"

"Please don't say it!"

"Aye Matey!"

Groans all around, just the way I like it.

Meanwhile, back in the snug...

Meanwhile, back in the snug, Tommy and Jack were trying to work together in order to solve a couple of big problems. Marital problems, specifically their own marital happiness problems.

"Why did she have to escalate the situation, Tommy? I thought we were finally putting all these troubles behind us."

There had been a growing conflict between their two wives that had eventually drawn the two friends into the arena. Jack's wife, Emma, was a long-time, avid gardener, extremely proud of the colourful flowers, plants and water features she meticulously crafted and regularly redesigned. She often entered them in regional contests, winning the runner-up ribbon several times, but never quite bringing home the "Garden of the Year" trophy.

She insisted that Jack maintain their lawn to the highest possible standard too, in order to accentuate her floral pride and joys. And when Emma "insisted" on something, she would tolerate no resistance or even the slightest hint of hesitation. Unbridled enthusiasm was Jack's only possible course of action.

So, he too spent many hours toiling outdoors, over-seeding, aerating, mowing and trimming their little slice of heaven. He fertilized and watered the grass according to the schedule provided by his beloved wife, pulling any dandelions, or other invasive weeds, that managed to creep in, by hand. Jack soon found that he enjoyed the work almost as much as Emma did, but despite his pride in their collective efforts, he never approached the level of zeal that his wife displayed for her gardens.

Ruth-Ann, Tommy's wife, on the other hand, had a much more "laissez faire" attitude when it came to home gardening. For her, there was no aesthetic quality in a thick, green lawn and gardens overflowing with flowers and exotic plants. The simple, natural state of their property included all the local weeds and wild shrubs that were already growing, without the need for continual care, and which helped feed the bees and other insects. She couldn't understand Emma's fanaticism towards landscaping. And she became very annoyed when her own choices were criticized by her friend. It really wasn't any of Emma's damn business what they did or didn't do with their own property, no matter how "unseemly" Emma found it to be. Their personal disagreement had eventually flared up and spilled over to now involve their respective husbands, disturbing the peace of their long-term friendships.

"She has to apologize, Tommy. Please, you have to make her say sorry for what she did. Emma will forgive her. I know she will. And then we can all get back to how things used to be."

"You're asking a lot, Jack. Ruth-Ann has a real problem with apologizing for anything when she thinks she's in the right. She even told me she doesn't want me hanging out with you anymore. Can you believe that!"

"She blew fucking dandelion seeds from a fistful of your dandelions onto our lawn, Tommy, Emma saw her from the window! How can she possibly be in the right?"

"It was just a joke, really, she didn't think it was such a big deal. But Emma had been bragging so much about how perfect your lawn is and how shitty ours is. She shouldn't have riled Ruth-Ann up like that!"

"She knows how serious Emma is about our lawn and gardens, Tommy. For Christ's sake, we have a Garden of the Year judge coming by in a couple of weeks! Why would she find that funny!"

"I don't know, Jack, and if it's any consolation, I am sorry for the whole thing, but I don't know if I can make her apologize. She feels that Emma is putting her down, putting us down, when she talks about our lawn the way she does. She takes it personally. Maybe you can get Emma to apologize for that first."

"There's a greater chance of me walking into the pub wearing a string bikini, than having Emma apologize to Ruth-Ann right now. I can maybe talk to her about being more sensitive when vocalizing her opinions regarding your property going forward, but there is no way in hell I'm going to be able to get her to apologize first."

"Look pal, we have to do something, we have to come up with a plan or all I'm going to get is grief, all day long, day after day."

"I know Tommy, I'm already feeling it myself. But what the fuck are we supposed to do about it? How do we fix this, and fix it fast, because if we don't, there are going to be bigger problems for us to have to deal with."

Tommy and Jack both looked down dejectedly as they pondered quietly about how to solve their dilemma. Just then, Mel came by with their refills.

"Now what are you two gloomy Gus's looking so down about?" she asked as she placed their pints on the snug's little table. "I haven't seen you guys so sad since the last time Rosie raised the beer prices in here."

"Woman problems, Mel." said Jack.

"Yeah, big time." echoed Tommy.

Mel listened intently as Tommy and Jack explained their woes, and the difficult situation they found themselves in.

"That's it?" she asked. "I thought you were dealing with something serious."

"It is serious!" Jack replied, "What the hell are we supposed to do now?"

Mel glanced from one to the other with pursed lips and an intent stare. "You're going to have to fight for your women, boys. You're going to have to fight for their honour. It's the only way."

"Are you out of your mind?" Tommy said. "I'm not going to fight Jack, and I am fairly certain that Jack doesn't want to fight me either."

Jack simply nodded in agreement.

Mel laughed at them both before continuing, "Just tell them that you fought about it, you defended them, and you don't want to see each other again. You don't even want to go to the pub anymore! Then just hang around the house, be your miserable selves at home all afternoon, and I guarantee they'll be so sick of you boys moping around that within three or four days they'll make up and happily send you back to us here, where you'll be our problem once again!"

Tommy and Jack looked at each other and laughed.

"It just might work, what do you think, Tommy?"

"I think we should give it a try, pal."

Mel ended up being right, well, almost right. Tommy and Jack were back bantering in the snug only two days later.

Dylan's Story

BEEP BEEP BEEP
BEEP BEEP BEEP
BEEP BEEP BEEP

"BEEP BEEP BEEP, Dylan, are you deaf? Time to get up buddy, I've heard you hit snooze on that thing at least three times now," Rosie called through the door.

It was always the same routine with her nephew; he got home late, stayed up even later and then couldn't manage to pull himself out of bed in the morning. In one sense she couldn't blame him, he did stay up late working. But, on the other hand, a little bit of time management wouldn't hurt either.
Who was she kidding, he's a 23-year-old boy. Yes, boy. He seemed to keep getting older as the years went by but not more mature.

"I'm getting up, Auntie!" he replied groggy and annoyed.

"Well you better be because I'm leaving in 15 and I'm not waiting around for you," she said from the kitchen. "You want to do that driving gig, that's fine, but it doesn't mean you can just ignore your other job. You live here, you help me out with the pub, you know the deal."

"Obviously, I know the deal, Auntie," Dylan responded as he emerged from his room in boxer shorts and scruffy bedhead. "I'm just so tired lately, working two jobs is hard."

"I know it is, sweetheart," Rosie said with a tousle of his hair. "I'm very proud of you for working so hard. If I didn't know any better, I'd think you might actually be becoming an adult!"

"Ha ha," he responded with a sarcastic tone.

"Now get to it! Brush your teeth and fix that hair of yours!"

Deep down, Dylan was a good kid, he had just got dealt a shitty hand in life. If it weren't for his Aunt Rosie, there's no telling where he'd be right now.

His young life started out as decent as it could have considering the circumstances. His mother, Diane was Rosie's sister. She'd always been a wild child growing up and had her demons. She was twenty years old when her partying got out of control. What started out as recreational drug use slowly became a habit.

By the time she was 22, she took off with some guy she'd met from the city. She disappeared. She didn't tell anyone where she was going, and never bothered to reach out once for an entire three years.

Rosie never had, and never will, forget the day she answered the door 24 years ago to see her battered sister standing there in front of her. She looked absolutely wrecked and she was about five months pregnant.

It took some hard work, but Diane was willing to completely change her life for the baby she was carrying. The father, on the other hand, hadn't been heard from since, and good riddance.

Diane got sober, she became the mom she needed to be for Dylan and all was well until he was about five.

Diane started leaving Dylan with Rosie overnight with no word of where she'd be going. It started as one night every now and then, but it quickly turned to two nights a week and then three until Rosie was basically Dylan's main caregiver.

She gained full custody of him when he was seven. Diane showed up every now and again, but no one really cared to see her.

Rosie was the only real mother figure Dylan had ever known. It hadn't been easy. Kids were never really in the cards for Rosie and so she always really appreciated having her nephew in her life. However, the struggle between being an "Auntie" and a mother figure was a tough one. She did her best to lay down the law when needed, but she never wanted to be too tough on him. He had it bad enough being abandoned by his drug addicted parents, he didn't need anything else to be hard done by.

She knew she spoiled him a bit and he took advantage of that from time to time, but at the end of the day she knew he was a good kid. He helped her out with the pub and he helped around the house. He just needed a bit of a kick in the pants once in a while.

"Thanks for helping me open, buddy. You're a big help," Rosie said lovingly to her nephew.

"No problem, Auntie. I'll be back later on for my shift," Dylan replied, as he headed out the door.

Running a private taxi business was a super handy side job for him. Between that and bartending at the pub he made pretty decent money. At 23, Dylan knew it was about time he got out on his own, but he was really in no rush. Instead of saving his money, his extra cash usually went toward video games, takeout and drinks with buddies. He had it way too easy and he knew it. His Aunt would never dare ask him for rent money even though he knew he should probably chip in a bit. She had always handed everything to him on a silver platter by choice, so what was the point of giving that all up?

In his mind, Dylan's past didn't bother him too much, if his parents didn't want to be in his life then to hell with them.

He figured he'd head back home after helping his Aunt Rosie open up the pub. Maybe catch up on some sleep and even get in a few hours of gaming before going back for his shift.

He'd just gotten to the front door when he noticed

a sheet of paper sticking out of it. They lived in a pretty remote part of town, so this was strange.

"Since when do salesmen come around here," Dylan said aloud as he unfolded the paper to read what was inside. "Are you fucking kidding me, dude?"

Dylan headed back to the pub around 5 o'clock, pissed off and fuming.

"Get a load of this, Auntie," he said to Rosie as he threw the crumpled up note on the bar.

"Oh god, don't tell me."

"Yep, she's back again. Read it."

Rosie opened the note as she dramatically exhaled and read it out loud.

"To my sissy and my boy,
I hope you 2 are well. I was in town and thought I'd stop by but I guess you are both out.
Maybe I'll stop by the pub tonight.
Love you both, Diane."

"Over my dead body will she be stopping by here," Rosie said with two raised eyebrows. "You sure you're okay to be here tonight, sweetie? I don't want her to show up and upset you."

"The only person who's going to be upset by her showing up here is herself, because I have nothing nice to say. I'm done with her showing up, pretending to actually be interested in my life when all she really wants is money."

"Alright, well I'm going to stick around just in case she does decide to make an appearance," Rosie says.

"Hey, how's it going, man?" Sammy said as Dylan jumped behind the bar for his shift.

"Oh, not bad, been better," he replied.

"Yeah, your Aunt kind of filled me in on what happened."

"Oh, she did, did she?"
"Well, yeah. She's worried about you."
"She's got nothing to worry about. I'm fine. My Mom doesn't faze me anymore."
It annoyed Dylan that his Aunt would spill something so personal to a bar patron. He'd noticed that she and Sammy were spending more time together at the bar. It never used to be like that. Usually when his Aunt was done her shift, she'd be off home to get away from the pub for the evening. Nowadays, she'd spend a few hours hanging out after her shift – usually with Sammy. The two seemed to be getting close and Dylan wasn't really sure what to think of it. He was super protective of his Aunt and he couldn't quite put his finger on what Sammy was all about.
Dylan spent most of his shift with his peripheral vision focused on the door. As the hours passed on there was no sign of his mother. Rosie figured the coast was clear at around 8 o'clock and so she went on home. Sammy stuck around and Dylan was sure it was because Rosie had asked him to.
"See, I told you my Aunt had nothing to worry about. My mom saying she's going to show up here is like the Leafs winning the Stanley Cup – it's not gonna happen," Dylan said to Sammy as he poured himself his third cup of coffee for the night. He made sure to be careful around Sammy now, he hated that he was watching him like a hawk. What Sammy didn't know was that he had hidden a bottle of Jameson's in the kitchen and poured a generous shot into each coffee.
"Want one? It's on me."
"Nah, that's okay Dylan. I've gotta get out of here."
"Okay, if you're sure," Dylan said.
"You keep helping yourself to that liquor though and you're the one who's going to need a ride home, eh?" Sammy said as he looked at the coffee cup

inquisitively. "You remember our earlier conversation, don't you?"

"My Aunt always lets me have a drink after work, it's not a big deal," Dylan protested.

"A drink? I'm sure a drink is fine but by what I've seen in the last couple hours you've had at least four or five shots from wherever you're hiding that bottle," said Sammy.

"Four or five shots!" Dylan said in a fit of laughter. "Are you kidding me, bro? This is maybe my second. And my aunt knows all about it."

He was completely bullshitting him, what Sammy didn't know is it was actually his seventh shot. Clearly, his sneaky shot stealing had to be a little sneakier.

"Wow, you seem to be a little too interested in my life lately, Sammy. What's up with that?" Dylan said as his liquid courage was becoming more evident. Why was Sammy being so nice about this now, not all crazy like last time? Aunt Rosie must have spoken to him and told him to back off!

"Nothing man," Sammy said with his hands raised in the air. "I just know you're going through a lot and I want to make sure you're alright. Like I said earlier, your Aunt's worried about you and she cares."

"That's fine if she cares. But I really don't need you to care, bro. I'm a full grown man, and I can look after myself, so, no disrespect, but if you could mind your own god damn business, I'd greatly appreciate it," Dylan blurted out.

Sammy's expression briefly changed to his death stare. Dylan knew that he was pushing his luck.

"Well then, understood," Sammy said, throwing $40 on the bar. "Have a good rest of your night and get these guys home safe."

As Sammy walked out the door Dylan started to feel a little embarrassed. He shouldn't have snapped at him like that, but he couldn't help it. Since when is it okay for a customer to get involved in his personal life? Why did Rosie feel the need to discuss his business with that jerk.

"You fellas ready to get home yet?" Dylan shouted over to John and Claude.

"Just about, how about you John," Claude said to his buddy.

"Ah yeah, I'm ready to hit the hay. It's past my bedtime," he replied.

"Alright, well get to finishing those beers. I've just got a few things to do first."

After completing his shut-down tasks, Dylan grabbed his keys to go warm up the car while John and Claude guzzled the last of the moose piss they'd been milking. They always spent so much time flapping their gums it was a wonder they ever had time to take sips at all.

The floors were swept, the cash was counted, and the "OPEN" sign of the Black Horse was turned off for another night.

Dylan locked up while Claude and John followed behind him.

"Hop in dudes!" Dylan shouted as he made his way to his blue Honda Civic that sat warm and waiting for the three.

"Yeah, yeah, were comin' boy!" John shouted back.

As the trio squeezed into the Sedan, Claude immediately scrunched up nose in disgust.

"Jesus Christ, John. What were you doing? Sneaking shots of whiskey when I was in the men's room? You reek like a drunk!" he said.

"What in the hell are you talking about, Frenchie? You know I don't drink that shit!" John replied in defiance.

"Well, can't you smell that? Dylan, is it just me or do you smell that?"

"Can't say I do, man. Maybe your sniffer is just about as whacked as you are," Dylan said with a smirk in the rearview mirror.

"You son of a gun," John said with a giggle.

As Dylan pulled out of the pub parking lot, he started to realize how tipsy he actually was. And, what Dylan considered tipsy a lot of others would consider downright drunk. If that prick Claude could smell the liquor on him, he knew he'd need to stop at the local gas station for some gum before heading out on his trips for the night.

"You know Dylan, I don't deal with any of this private taxi credit card shit, eh?" John slurred in the back seat.

"I know, I know, I've told you a hundred times, you can pay me in cash. Just because you two are so special, I like to keep these trips off the old meter. You guys are my most valuable customers, you know?"

"Christ, five bucks a day and we're your most valuable customers?" Claude said with a chuckle. "Is that all it takes these days?"

"Okay, maybe you're not my most valuable, but definitely my favourites," Dylan said as he pulled into John's drop off spot.

"Ahh, Dylan. You're a good kid. Drive safe there, boy, and we'll see you tomorrow," John said as he peeled himself out of the car.

Dylan watched as he always did to make sure he made it safely into his building. Once inside, John gave them a quick wave. They both knew it was only a matter of 12 hours or so before they'd be back at it again tomorrow. Then it was off to the "Estates" to drop off Mr. Suave.

"Be there in just a few minutes Claude."

Dylan knew he probably shouldn't be driving. But, he chalked down the shots of Jameson he'd had at the bar down to a bad day. His mom always got him rattled. Up until this point he hadn't seen her since last Thanksgiving and what a mistake that was. She showed up looking like a complete wreck. The only thing she was concerned about was peddling the family for money.

Dylan went against the advice of his Aunt Rosie and "lent" her $1,000. According to Diane, it was going to go toward first and last month's rent at a local apartment. She'd given him a huge sob story about where her life had ended up. She nearly had him in tears while she expressed how sorry she was for how she hadn't been a proper mother to him. Like an idiot, he believed her. He kissed his hard earned money goodbye with the promise he'd get it back once she landed a job in town, but after she left he had never heard from her again until he got that dumb note on his doorstep.

For a while, Dylan tried to make excuses for her, but Rosie set him straight. She knew all too well what her sister had done. She purposely showed up in her vulnerable son's life to manipulate him and swindle him for cash. She'd been there before too. Rosie had completely lost track of how much money Diane owned her at this point. A hundred bucks here and a hundred bucks there sure did add up over the decades. She gave up on the hopes of seeing any repayment a long time ago and she knew her nephew would have to face that reality as well.

"Don't do it Dylan, you'll never see it again, mark my words," Rosie's voice rang through Dylan's head as he logged onto his taxi app. His own mother had ripped him off for a thousand bucks, even more reason to go out and make money tonight.

After a night of driving around drunks and driving around a little drunk himself for that matter, Dylan rolled in the door around 2:00 am. He'd slightly sobered up and was starting to get a hangover headache.

"Hey, how was your night?" Rosie said in a groggy voice as she poked her head through her bedroom door.

"It was alright, what are you doing up?" Dylan

replied.

"Just checking up on you, couldn't sleep," Rosie said.

"Really? Couldn't sleep, eh? Doesn't sound like you."

Rosie put on a robe and came out into the kitchen. "Well, you'd be surprised what kind of things change once you start ageing." She walked over to the electric kettle and flipped on the switch. "Want some chamomile tea? It'll help you wind down from your night."

"Nah, I'm okay, Auntie. I'm already pretty tired and I've got a bit of a headache so I'm going to go to bed."

"A headache? From what?" Rosie asked inquisitively.

"From… an ache in my head? I don't know," Dylan said with a laugh.

"Hmm, I see. Your eyes are looking a little glossy too, you feeling okay?" Rosie said with two raised eyebrows and her hands on her hips.

"Yes…," Dylan said with a confused look as he headed to his room. "I'm exhausted, I'll see you in the morning."

When the door shut Rosie knew she needed to say something.

"I know what's going on here, Dylan and it's going to stop," she said in a stern tone which she hardly recognized.

The bedroom door whipped open, and Dylan could feel his liquid courage starting to sneak up on him again.

"You know what's going on? Let me guess here. This wouldn't have anything to do with you talking to Sammy now, would it?"

"Sammy? What does Sammy have to do with any of this?" Rosie nervously replied.

"You know exactly what he has to do with it and don't play dumb, Auntie. He told me the two of you have been talking about me which I really don't appreciate. I mean, seriously? Talking about my personal shit with customers? What's wrong with you?" Dylan fumed. "Oh, wait. That's right, Sammy isn't just a customer, is he? I've seen the way you and he have been chatting it up at the bar, what the hell's going on with that?"

"What the Hell's with what, Dylan? What are you talking about?"

"You might think you're hiding it, but you're doing a really shitty job," he said.

"I seriously don't know what you're talking about, Dylan," Rosie said absolutely shocked at her nephew's attitude. "Sammy's a friend of mine and he's a good listener. I'm sorry that I brought your name up to him, but I've been worried about you."

Rosie was genuinely stunned at this issue Dylan had brought up, or what he thought was an issue. She'd always had a bit of a crush on Sammy, but she knew nothing between them would ever work. They were two totally different people who had just happened to connect as friends, good friends. Rosie truly appreciated Sammy's friendship. Over the last four or five years of her owning the pub she felt like she rarely ever had time for friends, so this bond she had with Sammy was refreshing and she needed it. Although she had recently explained about Dylan's troubled history to Sammy, she knew that it was her responsibility to handle this and had asked him to cut the kid some slack.

Dylan continued on his Jameson-fueled rant, "Well, you seem to have told him a lot about me, so how about you tell me exactly what he said about me to you?"

"He didn't have to tell me anything, Dylan. I'd have to be blind and dumb to not realize you've been drinking on the job, and a lot at that."

"If by drinking on the job you mean me having a quick shot after work - which you've knowingly allowed me to do for years, then that's pretty fucked up."

"*A* shot? Totally fine. A quarter of a bottle gone after each of your shifts? Not so fucking fine," Rosie said almost feeling the steam coming from her ears.

"Excuse me? A quarter bottle? That's complete horse shit, Auntie and you know it. I have a drink after work and that's it. That's how it's always been."

"You know that's a lie and everybody else at the Horse knows that's a lie. You're not very sneaky, you make it obvious to everyone. I've had more than one customer come to me telling me they've seen you take multiple shots behind the bar and they can tell how your disposition changes after a few. If that's not bad enough you're also driving the damn customers home after. What's going on with you?"

"Who are these asshole customers talking shit about me?" Dylan replied.

"I'm not going to call anyone out."

"Ha-ha, don't worry you don't have to," Dylan said with a sarcastic laugh. "I'm going to assume that by 'customers' you're referring directly to the Dog Pound and Sammy in particular. He's a fucking liar, Auntie. He weirds me out. He always tries to put on this 'mystery man, bad boy' front and it's bullshit."

"He's not a liar, Dylan."

"Pffft, you've known this guy for what, a few years? You've known me my whole life and you're going to believe him over me? I'm your family!" Dylan shouted.

"I didn't need to hear it from Sammy. I've seen it with my own eyes. Do you really think I'm that stupid? I do the inventory, I buy the booze and I look at the reports at the end of the night. You've been stealing from me. Funnily enough, that's not even the part that bothers me. What bothers me is that you're driving around town drunk afterward with god damn passengers in the back seat. I can smell the booze on you now."

"Bullshit you can!" Dylan said as he looked away

knowing he'd been caught red handed. She was right, he'd been ripping his aunt off for a long time now. He wasn't doing it to be malicious, he was just doing it because it was so easy. Bad day? Drown it out with a shot. Good day? Celebrate it with a shot. The Leaf's score? Time for a shot. A few here and there didn't seem like a big deal at the time. But Dylan wasn't dumb, he knew it added up.

"I've never been hard on you, Dylan. You're 23 years old now for Christ sakes so it's not like I can start now, but I really need you to smarten up."

"Like I said before, I'm exhausted and I'm going to bed," Dylan said as he slid into his room with his head down. "Goodnight."

He shut the door and fell backwards onto the bed with an exhale. His aunt was right, she'd never been this hard on him and it was a difficult pill for him to swallow.

He hated disappointing her, and he knew that's exactly what he was doing. But, at the same time he was an adult and didn't appreciate being treated like a teenager under a microscope.

While he knew his Aunt's nagging was brought on by her motherly instincts toward him, the person who really ticked him off in this whole scenario was Sammy. Like he'd told his aunt before, he didn't trust him. If his demeanor wasn't enough to make Dylan uneasy, the fact he was basically keeping tabs on him at the pub to report back to Rosie definitely was.

"Morning, Auntie."

"Morning, bud. You're up early for a change."

"I know. I just wanted to apologize for last night. I'd had a bad day and the way I acted wasn't right."

"Well thank you for that. I appreciate the apology and I want you to know the only reason I worry so much is because I care. I don't know what I would do if something bad happened to you, Dylan. You're like my son and you know that," Rosie said as she reached out to her nephew for a hug.

"I know, I know," Dylan said with a bashful grin. As much as he wanted to make his aunt happy in that moment, he also didn't want to bullshit her. He played the whole sarcastic spiel in his head.

Don't worry about me, Auntie. Everything from here on out is going to be different. I'm going to be the little angel you've always dreamed of.

He wasn't going to go there because he knew it wasn't true. If there was one thing in this life he didn't want to be, it was a manipulative liar like his mom. Meanwhile, little did he know her unfavourable characteristics had been coming out more and more, without him even realizing it.

"So, do you have anything else do say?" Rosie pressed.

"Like what?"

"Like maybe explaining yourself? The missing liquor? The fact you come home smelling like booze more often than not?"

"Auntie, like I said last night, I haven't been stealing from you and I haven't been drinking and driving. I don't know what else to tell you. I've voiced my opinions on Sammy and to be honest, if I were you, I would keep my distance from him. He's been lying straight to your face."

Rosie was more disappointed in her nephew than she ever had been before. She wasn't going to argue with him, it wouldn't solve anything. She'd learned that time and time again.

"Okay then. Well, I'm off to the pub, I'll see you later on."

As Rosie headed out the door, she only had one thought in her head, boy, do some genes run strong.

Gary's Story

I don't recall exactly when I first ventured though the doors of the Black Horse Pub or the details of the actual events of that night. In fact, all I remember for sure is that I was definitely underage, under the influence and absolutely unprepared for the wild night that lay ahead of me. The hangover though, that I do sort of remember. I'd never felt so sick in my life and swore to the porcelain gods, with all the righteous religious fervour I could muster, that I would never get drunk again. And I didn't. For two whole weeks, when the next pay day rolled around and my crew once again bundled their young, semi-willing student and apprentice floorer into the company van and headed to the pub.

I like to think I've matured a bit since then, being a dad and all now. I still like to pop into the Horse after work for a few pints though, to chat with the staff, see some of the regulars, and let the trials and tribulations of my day wash off like so much flooring dust. I know Rosie doesn't always appreciate the mess tradesmen make with our boots, especially when she's just had the place cleaned, but being a regular certainly does have its privileges.

It is also the place that I met Stephanie, my girlfriend. It was another wild Thursday night, Karaoke night at the Black Horse, a drunken night filled with horrible music, endless shots, and laughter. I liked what I saw right away, she looked so beautiful in her skinny jeans and tank top. Her voice wasn't all that bad either. We somehow fell in love after singing every duet from the movie "Grease".

My son is a little over one year old now, and starting to become a real handful, but Stephanie and I take good care of him. We've been together for almost four years and will probably get married one day too, just not right now. Let's just say I'm not exactly feeling the love at the moment. Don't get me wrong, I love Stephanie, and our little Ryan is everything I could ever want in a kid, but sometimes I get the feeling that Stephanie isn't happy with how things are going with our "direction" in life. I know I probably shouldn't stay for a third or fourth pint so often, or maybe even skip the pub entirely a couple of days a week. But you know what, I take care of the rent, take care of all the bills and work my ass off to put food on the table. What's wrong with a little me time? It just so happens I like to spend some of my free time at the Black Horse. I'm still almost always home by 6:30 or so anyway, I don't understand why she gets upset. Steph goes out with her friends a couple nights a week, to Newmarket or down to Markham, and I've never once complained to her about it. As far as I'm concerned, we all need a little time on our own to be happy, to keep things balanced, and spend some one-on-one time with Ryan.

He is a real pleasure to be around too. From the moment I first held him, Ryan has been the brightest light in my life. He's a happy baby, doesn't cause much of a fuss and has the goofiest smile you'd ever see! When Steph is out and we're alone I will sit him on my lap and read to him, and he loves it. Not little baby books or even children's books either. I read out loud to him whatever I happen to be reading at the time. Mystery novels, history books, biographies, poetry collections, fiction, non-fiction, science magazines, whatever I've currently got on the go. I know he doesn't understand almost any of what I'm saying, but I can tell it soothes him and he follows my finger as I run it across the pages, grabbing it with his tiny hand and giggling every now and then. I think he's going to be a voracious reader when he grows up, just like his dad. Steph hates that I read so much, so our little private "Daddy-Ryan" time is now one of the only times I get to open a book at home.

"You love your books more than you love me," she says.

I just don't get her attitude, that's the silliest thing I've ever heard. There is nothing wrong with reading before bed, or while she's watching TV. She just can't stand it when I'm not listening or paying attention to her 24/7, so I've had to seriously dial it back. I think I do more reading now in the pub than I do at home or at the library. Believe me, it wouldn't hurt her to crack open a book once in a while, Steph's not exactly well-versed or knowledgeable about many things. I've tried to encourage her, share some of my books, but let's just say she's not been receptive.

I have a nagging suspicion that Steph is keeping something from me, some big secret, but every time I ask if something is wrong she denies it and starts complaining about our crappy apartment, or our crappy car, or why we can't go on a nice vacation somewhere hot with a beautiful beach and an ocean view. I know she's simply deflecting, I'm not stupid. Trying to change the subject or distract me by pushing some of my buttons. I really do wish we could have nicer things, and go on nice vacations, but with just the one income coming in and three mouths to feed there isn't enough left over at the end of the month to save up. I do what I can to save though. I get a ride in to work with Cameron every day so that Steph can have the car to run her errands, and do the shopping, and take Ryan to the park, but it seems that it's just never enough for her. So, I ask to get dropped off at the pub after work, enjoy my pints for an hour or three, and walk home from there. What's wrong with that? It's not like I'm out hitting on women or getting drunk. Even if I wanted to, I couldn't afford it.

empty bottles
fallen over
dripping the last of their bitterness
onto the floor
lemon peels and olive pits
dying on the cutting board
beside the filthy knife
another night to end all nights
slips quietly into day
and resurrection

gary harrison

I have my own secrets too, I guess, like most people do. Nothing monumentally disturbing or sensational, but still kept hidden nonetheless. The thing is, anyone with half a brain could figure them out just through observation alone. Let's just say that the regulars at The Black Horse are not the most observant bunch. They're mostly good guys, but they're not overly interested in following intellectual pursuits. For instance, I don't really go to the pub to socialize much. Quite the opposite really, most of the time I prefer to be alone now, but alone in a crowd. I know that may not make much sense, but I like to have activity around me while I sit and read a magazine or book on my own while slowly sipping my pint. I like to write in my notebook too, jot down ideas for stories and poems. I love to write, to create. The problem is, the people around me, the regulars, don't clue in and assume I'm there to talk and banter about meaningless things, over and over again. They don't notice that I've got my nose in the latest *New Yorker*, or that I'm not jotting flooring measurements in my book, but words and phrases. They just assume I'm there to talk. Except Mary, of course. If I had a dollar for every time Mary looked at me and rolled her eyes when someone, usually John, and almost always loudly, slaps me on the back and intrudes on my space with some inane commentary about who was the greatest band in the history of the world or some other nonsense, I'd have enough money to go on a proper vacation. And don't get me wrong, Johns really is a pretty great guy, just in small doses, and before he gets all wound up!

Mary gets me, she understands because in many ways, she is a lot like me. She's a "watcher", she notices things. She is my only close friend at the Horse, and the only person there that I look forward to chatting with, other than Rosie and Mel of course. And I also know that I'm pretty much the only one she ever talks to on a regular basis, not that I'm special or anything. We connect in a different way, and can speak about books and literature and music, and about the meaningful things that are happening in each other's lives, without fear of it being gossiped about. She knows I write poetry and reads whatever I'm brave enough to show her and gives her honest feedback. For me that says it all. She likes me enough to take the time to read my stuff, is honest about it, and trusts that my feelings won't be hurt by her opinion. Stephanie would mock me relentlessly if she ever read a poem from one of my notebooks. I wouldn't hear the end of it! With Mary, we can vent about the other regulars in a quiet, playful manner without being overheard over the usual din. She, like me, is also quiet, and reserved, or so she'd like us all to think. I know that there's another "Mary" out there though. I just haven't had the guts to let her know what I know about her, her dance videos and YouTube channel. Man, what a shock it was when I stumbled across that! She'd left her phone on the bar once, when she went into the washroom, and I saw the subject line of an email that popped up, *"Brezking Cherry video"*. What the heck was that? So, I googled it, and found her secret identity in the process! I never suspected she could move like that, and wow, does she ever look so beautiful in them! Anyway, when she is sitting at her regular spot at the bar, drinking the house red from her special glass, only occasionally glancing up from the book she is inevitably reading, at what we call our "library corner", she is often overlooked. Except by Garnet, that bigoted old nut. He notices her alright, because of the colour of her skin, sneering at her from a distance, mouthing off about "too many immigrants", or how "multiculturalism is a plot to make Canada communist". It's not like Garnet is the second coming of Hitler or a member of the KKK, but he just hasn't made the adjustment to the 21st century. Maybe not even the 20th century either! He's too old, too stubborn and too stupid to bother changing. Which is a pity, because in many other ways Garnet is a good guy. He's tough, he's hard-working, and he cares deeply about the land and Ashington's history. He abhors the rapid development that's been happening all over the region, and I have to admit, I kind of agree with him. We need the development, but it seems rushed at times, without enough conservation of good farmland in the process.

Mary ignores him, or even laughs it off, but I know that it wears on her. She is originally from Nigeria and moved to Canada after earning her Dental degree in Lagos. It must have been such a challenge for someone all alone, but Mary is tougher than she looks, and I've never heard her complain once about it. Unfortunately, here in Canada she could only get work as a dental technician at first, but she has worked so hard to study and have her qualifications recognized here in Ontario. She wants to eventually open up her own practice. I'm so proud of her, she recently passed her exams and is now a full Doctor of Dentistry! Mary has more integrity and hard work in her little finger than Garnet will ever possess, no matter what he says about "farming making real men".

Like milking cows should give him a free pass for spewing nonsense. There are times when I want to throttle him and let him know exactly what I really think about how badly outdated his views are, but Mary will somehow sense it, even before I do, put her hand on my arm and tell me he's not worth getting upset over. It's just too bad that she's not always around. Putting up with Garnet's ignorance is almost worth it when she does that.

For instance, just last week, when I arrived a little earlier than usual at the pub, I noticed Garnet, with his usual scowl, staring at two women sitting by the snug. They were just enjoying their lunch and talking quietly to one another. I recognized one as Fahima, the head librarian at the Ashington Public Library. I see her regularly there, but I have a nagging suspicion that not too many of the Black Horse regulars, other than Mary and me, would recognize her. She looked up and smiled hello, but I could sense that she felt concerned about the way that Garnet was behaving. I didn't recognize her companion though, a younger, university-aged woman, very attractive too. She shared the same long dark hair, high forehead and brown eyes as Fahima, so I figured she might possibly be a relative. They were obviously discussing some books that were spread across the table, gesturing at some open pages. It only took me a few seconds to see what they had done to rile up and offend him. The books were in Arabic! "Quelle horreure!"

I could also see the rage forming on Garnet's face as he looked from them to me and back to the table, pointing and silently mouthing the word "Mooslems". The ignorant hick was too stupid to even pronounce the word correctly. I figured that I'd make my way over to the table in order to prevent him from making a complete and total ignorant ass of himself in front of the ladies. When I passed by, I couldn't help but tell him to "fuck off back to his seat". One of the things I hate most in the world is a bully, and Garnet can be a bit of a bully at times, especially when a few pints have loosened his lips. But he's also a bit of a coward when confronted or alone, so I was pleased to see my words hit their target as intended and make Garnet scurry back to his seat at the bar, face purple with apoplectic rage. Why couldn't he just mind his own damn business and let people be who they were. They hadn't done anything wrong.

Fahima waved me over to the table, clearly relieved, and invited me to join them. I was curious about the books, and her companion, so I agreed and sat down. Fahima quickly introduced me to her niece, Nour, who was visiting from Tunisia. I shook her hand and smiled, more so from deducing that they were related than anything else and inquired about her visit. It turns out that Nour was studying English Literature at the Tunis El Manar University and was visiting her Canadian aunt over the semester break. Her beautiful eyes lit up when I mentioned that I had studied literature at University too, although I didn't mention that I dropped out after my first year in order to work installing flooring. My one regret in life is never having gone back to school.

I didn't recognize any of the books she had placed on the table. It turns out that they were gifts that Nour had brought over for Fahima, the collected works of Aboul-Qacem Echebbi. Fahima proudly explained that he was one of Tunisia's greatest poets, and in fact his words were used in the Tunisian national anthem. I love to learn, and the wonderful time spent with Fahima and Nour that day was packed full of introductions to authors and poets that I'd never heard of before but were furiously scribbled down into my notebook. Nour and I were both admirers of William Blake and Oscar Wilde, so the conversation flowed easily and animatedly and Fahima visibly relaxed as well. I occasionally glanced over at

Garnet muttering to himself at the bar, but truly enjoyed the opportunity to talk about books. These moments were far too rare anywhere these days, especially in the Black Horse.

As the women were preparing to leave, I mentioned to Nour that I hoped she was not too offended by the actions of Garnet and explained that he was not representative of most people or viewpoints around here. At this, Fahima let out a small but bitter laugh, looking around nervously as she did so. She leaned in and whispered conspiratorially, "It's only going to get worse for him soon."

Nour and I looked at each other then back to her with eager expectation before she continued. "There is going to be a mosque built in the region, for the growing Muslim community, and from what I've heard, Ashington is the preferred location."

This was stunning news, but as a librarian, Fahima was always well informed about municipal and regional issues, and I believed her. It made sense too, with Ashington being fairly central to the many other small towns in the region, having available land, and being close to the highway.

"Please don't say anything," she said, and I quickly nodded agreement. "Nothing is confirmed yet, but it would be such a wonderful thing to have happen."

I wasn't entirely convinced that all of the locals would think it so wonderful, or be as supportive as she hoped, but with the growing immigrant population in the region it was bound to happen sooner or later. This would drive Garnet absolutely insane. That itself would be worth the controversy any announcement would create. His head would literally explode!

As I walked the ladies to the door, I said goodbye to Nour and wished her well for the remainder of her holiday. We exchanged our email and Facebook contacts. I really hoped to learn more from her.

About her too, she was such a beautiful, bright woman! I also promised to drop in on Fahima at the library more often to catch up on any updates regarding the mosque.

More importantly, I now had another little secret stashed away. Well, in this case, a big secret. Very big! And the only person I would ever dream about sharing it with was Mary.

powerless to resist
beguiled by exotic beauty
this sultry siren's velvet songs
enchant with words
inducing wondrous visions
enticements
to dance
unto her swirling depths
to drown
in dreams
of infinite delights

gary harrison

Unfortunately, I hadn't seen her all week, which was not that unusual, as she didn't come by the pub as often as I did. So, when I pulled open the door of The Black Horse and saw her sitting by herself at library corner, I knew that it was going to be a great afternoon.

Mel was there with her ever-present smile and was already pouring my pint as I neared the bar. Just what the doctor ordered. Mary, seeing me approach in the bar mirror, casually moved her bag from the stool on her left, where I like to sit, and placed it to the other side, all without turning or raising her head from her book.

Mel slipped the pint in front of me, said hello and smiled even brighter while glancing at Mary. Good old Mel, she is always so bright and cheery and welcoming. The perfect server in my opinion, and I know most everyone else feels the same. The Black Horse would not be such a friendly place without her. She has a natural way of making everyone feel welcome, making us feel special, and feel at home. Rosie is great too, but in a different way. I know she appears gruff to most people, but she too is full of kindness, it's just harder to see at times. Rosie definitely has her hands full here, that's for sure. She is like the stern counterpart to Mel, but together they make an unbeatable team. It must have been so difficult for Rosie to have taken on the full responsibilities of running the pub by herself after her husband Aaron left, but she somehow fought through the emotional and financial trauma and just carries on as if nothing had happened. She's a proud woman, hard working too, and The Black Horse is her pride and joy, no matter how humble it is. I respect her for that, admire her strength. Rosie knows what needs to be done and simply makes sure that it gets done. I wish my boss at work had her kind of fortitude. Then maybe we'd have more work and I could actually start making some real money for a change, instead of bouncing from one small job to another.

The pub wasn't too busy yet, which was good for me. Sammy was at the other end of the bar talking with John, or more specifically, John was talking, a lot, and Sammy was nodding his head between gulps of beer. They're both great guys, although Sammy does scare me a little bit. It's not just his physique that is intimidating either. He seems cool and collected most of the time, but I'd hate to be the unfortunate soul that lights his fuse. I've seen his face turn from a smile to a death glare once or twice and it's not a pleasant sight. He's the one guy I've never been able to quite figure out. He doesn't talk about his past much, and to be honest I haven't even been able to pin down how old he is. He could be anywhere from 35-60 as far as I can tell, and I get the sense that he's experienced a very tough life. I've never been able to place his accent, it could be anything from Middle Eastern to Baltic, and even that is just a guess. I've known him for years and I still don't know. How crazy is that? I asked him once after he bought some shots for the group, and that's when I first saw the "stare". I never asked again. All I know is that he runs a busy garage, uses only cash, and can drink like a fish without ever seeming to get drunk. Nope, nothing mysterious there!

I've taken my car to him for repairs a few times and he's always given me a very good deal and done great work too. I like him, he appreciates my privacy, and is one of the very few who will leave me alone if he sees me reading or writing at the bar. Sammy will even send over a shot occasionally, raising and downing his own from across the bar as I down mine. He's good that way, he respects peoples' boundaries. He could be a serial killer for all I know, but from what I've seen and experienced, you can't help but like him.

What I liked best about him at the moment was that he was occupying all of John's attention. I could speak to Mary quietly without interruption. Hopefully. John was the type of guy who could bounce around from person to person, conversation to conversation, like a whirling dervish at times, leaving a trail of confusion and disbelief in his wake.

I remember one time, when I was trying to talk to Mary, he came up to me repeatedly asking about what were my "five most favourite movies" of all time. It is not easy for John to understand subjectivity, especially when it comes to art and creativity, but in order to get rid of him, I'd have to answer. So, despite my best instincts, I blundered forward.

1) The Right Stuff
2) Jackie Brown

3) Henry V (Kenneth Brannaugh's version of course)
4) The Mission
5) Tinker, Tailor, Soldier, Spy (new one)

I should have known better. John spent the next forty-five minutes explaining why I was "wrong", and he not only pointed out, in great detail, the "right" answers, but also added that I was too uneducated to "know better". I heard Mary laughing and as she made her way out partway through his harangue, she whispered "Good luck, dearie."

Well, it was still fairly early and he looked reasonably sober, so I figured we had some time.

"Hello Mary," I said before taking a sip from my pint, "It's been a while."

Mary smiled and closed the book she was reading, Umberto Eco's *"The Island of the Day Before"*.

"Yes, it has. I've been preparing for my graduation ceremony but had to get out of the house for a break."

I nodded at her nearly empty wine glass. "Do you have time for another?"

She smiled and pushed her glass towards Mel who was already reaching for the bottle.

"You look like the cat that ate the canary."

I couldn't help but laugh, and once she had taken a sip from her re-fill, we leaned in close, shoulders touching, and I told her all about last week's encounter that I dubbed "The Adventure of the Grump, the Librarian and the Tunisian Tourist". As I quietly recounted the story, Mary's eyes got bigger, her smile wider, and her wine level lower.

"There's going to be a lot of resistance from some people around here if this is true," she whispered. "This is not exactly Toronto."

"I know, but I don't think it will be as bad as you might think. The region has changed so much over the past fifteen or twenty years, since I was a kid, it's grown so much. Maybe not in Ashington itself, but all around here it has."

Mary looked at me for a moment before replying. "I can see that, even in the short time I've been here it has changed." She looked around quickly, "But a mosque! This is not just more houses and roads, this is cultural. This is a big change!"

"Well, we're going to find out soon enough I guess."

I ordered a second beer, but Mary put her hand over her glass and indicated that she was fine.

"I've got to get back home soon. I'm expecting a Skype call from my sister."

There was something else I wanted to talk to Mary about, and figured this was as good a time as any. I pointed at a poster on the mirror behind the bar, "The pub has organized another bus trip down to Buffalo to watch the Bills play next month. It's usually a pretty fun time."

I had reserved spots for myself and Stephanie, but she wanted absolutely nothing to do with my "idiot friends from that dump again" and suggested that maybe I shouldn't bother going myself. I hadn't been in the mood for another argument, so I dropped the subject, but the game date was quickly approaching, and I had already paid for both tickets. Also, I really wanted to go! These trips were a blast. I hoped that Mary would appreciate the offer.

"American football?" she asked.

"Yes. I have two tickets and thought that maybe you might like to go. It's mostly people from the pub, some friends and family. We'd leave in the morning and be back by nighttime. What do you think?"

"I've never seen a game before, other than when it's on TV here. It might be interesting. Are you not taking your girlfriend?"

I was glad that Mary hadn't discounted the idea right off the bat, and after a brief discussion, mostly about Stephanie's hatred of football, she agreed to take the extra ticket and be the best Bills

Booster she could possibly be. She recounted a few stories about going to soccer games in Lagos to support her local team, and I let her know that she could expect some of the same, just maybe on a larger scale.

The pub was beginning to fill up, John's voice was getting louder and Mary was sipping the last of her wine.

"Gary, there's something I've been meaning to talk to you about."

She looked a bit sheepish and wasn't making any eye contact now, which was completely out of character for her, as we had always enjoyed a comfortable relationship.

"Sure, whatever you want, I'm here for you."

Just then the door opened and a few more people made their way towards the bar. I followed Mary's glance and saw Claude with a couple of his work acquaintances seating themselves at a nearby table. Claude was one of the few people at The Black Horse that rubbed me the wrong way at times. He was obviously successful, some type of engineering whiz, but he could also be rude and condescending. He was a good-looking guy, but I hated how he would often hit on younger women, even in front of their boyfriends. From what I've seen and heard he has had a lot of success with them too. Claude thought he was better than everyone else and that sometimes pissed me off. There are lots of other successful people around who don't have to rub other people's noses in it.

Mary hadn't yet told me what she had to say, so I touched her arm and asked, "What's wrong?"

"Oh, don't worry, it's nothing. Really, I've forgotten what I was going to say anyway. We'll talk again soon I hope."

She smiled, a real smile, and said goodbye before making her way to the door, carefully avoiding Claude and his friends as she passed.

Something was bothering Mary, I hadn't seen her act

so nervously around me since we first met, but I'm sure whatever it was, she'd tell me when the time was right.

there is great beauty hiding in the
Darkness
joyous stings of paralytic ecstasy
found in the sweet poison of
Sadness
no shame to carry when lost
to the clutches of
Melancholy
that is why I have always
preferred
to write by candlelight
allowing
the altering movement of shadows
entry
to hypnotize
revealing the emptiness of illusion
saturating my mind
whispering
wandering words that flutter
little piercing daggers
borne of feathery flames
that take control of my trembling hand
and compel the long abandoned ink
to splatter page after page
with only the deepest
meaningful
silhouettes of truth

gary harrison

I opened the magazine that I had brought along, ordered another pint from Mel, and focused my attention on the pages in front of me, losing myself in their words.

Meanwhile, back in the snug...

Meanwhile, back in the snug, Tommy and Jack were taking the first sips from their first pints of the afternoon.

"How's the Guinness today, Tommy?"

"Divine, pal, simply divine. Mel sure knows how to pour a pint," Tommy replied, smacking his lips.

"That she does," Jack added, "she runs a smooth ship too. I always make sure to tip her a little extra, she deserves it."

"Extra? What for? Just for doing her job? You're crazy, Jack."

"I know you come from a place where tipping is not the norm, but for Christ's sake Tommy, you've been in Canada long enough to understand how it works."

Tommy raised his hands in mock defeat. "I understand how it works, I just don't agree with it, that's all I'm saying. It's the obligation I object to, Jack, the 'automatic' requirement to pay more that I don't like about the whole 'tipping' concept."

Jack merely shook his head at his companion's explanation. "There are so many things to find unlikable about you, my friend, but being a cheap bastard has got to be near the top of the list."

"Now hold on just a second Jacky boy, you know I tip, maybe not as generously as you, but why should I be forced to provide an additional fiscal 'thank you' to someone for just doing their job?"

"You're not forced to Tommy, it's a reward for providing good service. It's also how servers make their money, their wages are crap."

"You're making my point for me Jack," Tommy replied sternly. "Why do customers have to subsidize an employee's paycheck? They're already earning a wage, aren't they? If it's not enough, then businesses should raise their wages instead of masking the real cost of food and drink by passing the responsibility on to the customer."

"You'd have to pay more for that food and drink, Tommy. Would you be happy with that, you old sod?"

"It'd depend, I suppose. If you're expected to tip 15% for lousy service, and 20-25% for good service, a price increase of less than 20% would be fine with me. But if my waiter knows I have to pay him a tip no matter what, then what's his incentive to provide good service? Why would he care? But if a tip is now only expected for exceptional service because a basic increase in wages is already built into the price, then he has a motivation to do so. Can you get your thick skull around that concept, Jack?"

"You're the hard-headed one here, Tommy. Why do you always have to make it so complicated? Just tip the basic 15% and be done with it!"

"Tell me something, Jack. If I order a $15 hamburger, and you order a $45 steak, why should you pay our server three times more as a tip for doing the exact same amount of work as what they do for me? It just doesn't make sense. And the expected 'minimum' tip keeps rising. I choose to tip here by a set amount per drink, not a percentage of how much that drink costs."

"Bah, you're just a crusty old bastard with no heart!" Jack said leaning back. "And you have no sense of compassion for the staff either."

"My way is fairer, more just, and you know it! Makes no difference how good-looking the server is either, I know for a fact you tip Mel way more than Nancy for doing the exact same job just because she's a knockout. More arbitrary advantages to the already aesthetically advantaged if you ask me. How fair is that?"

"It's my money, my choice," Jack started to respond, but was quickly cut off by his friend.

"Just quit while you're behind, Jack, and make us both happy."

Jack's eyes wandered over to Mary, sitting alone

with a glass of wine at the corner of the bar.

"Hey Tommy," he said, nodding towards the bar, "speaking of knockouts, if you had the chance, would you?" he whispered with a carnal wink.

Tommy's gaze remained set on Mary as he replied, "Oh, aye Jack, definitely aye! But I tell ya, I'd probably only use the tip!"

The Day the Music Died

The Dog Pound was loud today, Brian 'The Piano Man' Larter had the crowd singing along to all the oldies, and the guys were joining in with great enthusiasm. Brian played a couple of times a month at the Black Horse. He would take the busy bar through the history of Rock and Roll. The first hour was always quiet, then the beer and wine loosened up the inhibitions as well as the vocal cords.

Gary, John, Claude and Sammy were as loud as the whole bar put together.

"She loves you Yeah! Yeah! Yeah!" they hollered, Ashington's own Fab Four were in fine form. Garnet the Grump was sat in the middle of them and even his feet were tapping, although he wasn't much for music and singing.

Brian told everyone he was taking a break and would welcome anyone who wanted to come up and sing in the next and final set.

Sammy slapped John on the back, "John, get up and do an Elvis, you'll bring the house down."

"Yes," said Claude, "do 'All Shook Up' like you did the last time."

Gary nodded in agreement, "Come on John, you can do it."

Now they all knew that John could not sing worth a shit, but John did not know this, and when he had a few drinks in him, John not only thought he told the funniest stories in the world, but that he could have actually been the next coming of Elvis.

"I don't know guys, it's been a while since I sang and I'm not sure if I'm drunk enough yet."

On that note Sammy shouted to Mel who was doing the bar shift.

"Four tequilas Mel and get the Grump a bottle of Export please."

"Coming up, Sammy," Mel smiled back.

John left to visit the bathroom, made sure it was empty and started practising his best Elvis moves in front of the mirror, curling up his top lip and swaying his hips. *Yes, he still had it!*

Back at the bar the guys were laughing, Gary said, "I hope to fuck he does the hip thing, that is fucking hilarious."

Garnet chipped in, "I was going to leave but no way now, I'm not going to miss this."

John was back at the bar and Brian walked over.

"Any of you guys want to come up and sing? You seem to be in great form today."

Sammy put John's hand up, "He will, Brian."

The rest of the guys cheered along with others at the bar within earshot.

"The usual John?" asked Brian "*All Shook Up*?"

"Yeah sure Brian, but don't put me up first."

Brian walked back to the piano and looked at the couple of names that had been dropped off during the break.

"Okay, let's have Paul up to the stage, Paul is going to sing '*Sweet Caroline*' and I want you all to join in with the chorus."

The bar cheered loudly for Paul, but mainly for the song, which was always a great one to sing along to.

"Good times never seemed so good!"

"SO GOOD, SO GOOD, SO GOOD!" roared the crowd right back!

The bar was rocking, and you could hardly hear the singer, just the revellers busting a gut singing along.

John thought he might have to ask Brian to turn his microphone up so that the crowd could hear him. He didn't want to be drowned out by his audience.

"Thank you, thank you Paul!" shouted Brian over the loud cheering.

"Now we have another one of our regulars, John, who will sing '*All Shook Up*'. Up you come John."

The crowd cheered, for many who had witnessed John singing before knew that this was going to be hilarious. The gang at the bar looked at each other, winking and smiling. Saturday afternoon just got better.

"Hey Brian, crank the mic up, will ya. I want them all to hear me."

"No worries John," said Brian as he pretended to twiddle with the volume knob.

With a swivel of the hips, John said in the corniest Elvis impersonation ever, "How's everyone doing out there, are you ready to be all shook up?"

The audience cheered, they could not believe that even though he had sung this song a dozen or so times, he still did not know that he was crap, tone deaf, and displayed the "moves" of a geriatric elephant.

John started the song and was immediately lost in his own world. He swivelled, gyrated, moved his upper lip so high that it almost covered his nose. He got on his knees then jumped back up, the audience were in hysterics, but John was not looking. In his mind, he was on stage at the "Grand Ole Opry", he was the main act and the crowd was going wild.

He even thought at one point that he should have worn a button-down shirt rather than a t-shirt. He could have unbuttoned it mid-song and driven the women wild. *Next time John, next time*.

At the end of the song he dropped to his knees. Sweating profusely, he shouted out to his adoring audience.

"Thank you. Thank you very much!"

The bar went wild, it was the funniest thing many had seen in a while and this would make the Facebook rounds tomorrow. Brian turned to the Dog Pound, they were laughing uncontrollably. Brian shook his head and smiled at them. They had set John up again.

"Wow! You were brilliant John," said Sammy.

"Best ever!" piped in Claude.

John had a big smile on his face. He had nailed it once again.

As John went to the washroom to dry off, Nancy walked by and said, "If he sings on Saturdays then I'm booking them off, I've already got a killer fucking headache."

Sammy whispered to the guys, "Maybe we should pay John to sing on Saturdays if it keeps her away."

They all laughed at this, but from quite a few feet away Nancy called back.

"I heard that!"

This caused the guys to laugh even louder, as normally when you ordered a beer she was as deaf as a post.

Ben's Story

"See ya tomorrow bright and early, Ben, we've got a big day."

"Yep, see ya in the morning, Ian." The lack of enthusiasm in my voice is nothing I can ever mask, even to my boss. Another day, another dollar. We're all like that, us construction guys. When we wake up in the morning, our jobs aren't exactly something we look forward to. After years of labour our hands are callused, our backs are wrecked and our lives revolve around 10-12 hours of bullshit day after day, week after week and year after year. But, at the end of it all we do it anyway. We do it because it's all we're good at. We do it because it's all we've ever known. We do it because we have families and it pays the bills. Well, most of us have families. I really have no idea what exactly I'm working for anymore, just to stay busy I suppose.

"Hey Ben!" I hear Ian shout just as I'm about to pull off site, "I just got word from dispatch, we're coming back to this job on Wednesday. They need us at Queen and Woodbine tomorrow at seven thirty, alright?"

"Queen and Woodbine, sounds good boss."

As I roll up my truck window and leave work in the rearview for another day it slowly sets in as I scan my mental map.

Queen and Woodbine…Queen and Woodbine, that's south, near the lake…near the beach.

It's now I realize that the thought of work tomorrow just got a lot more daunting.

"What perfect timing," I said out loud to myself.

The drive home from work is usually pretty boring and tedious, but not today. Before I know it, my hour-long commute is over and I'm pulling into the Black Horse without even thinking. I barely remembered the journey home, my mind was preoccupied the entire time. Clearly, my subconscious took over. I mean, I did make it back to Ashington alive…regrettably.

Well, I'm here now, might as well go in for a pint, I thought to myself. It's Monday which means Mel is probably working.

As I get out of the truck I see all of the familiar vehicles. The goings on of this place and the people in it were like clock work. I don't think I would consider myself a "regular" here per say, but it's nice to come and get out of the house a few nights a week. For some people, their home is their sanctuary, for me it's a prison where I'm trapped in my own thoughts.

I walk into the pub and see the usual suspects. We never really talk much and so I greet them with my usual nod and take my seat at the very end of the bar and away from the loud mouths.

"Ben! How's it going? It's nice to see you!" Mel said with an excited greeting. She was always happy no matter what. Me on the other hand, well I was a different story.

"Oh, not bad I guess," I say with a quick smirk.

"Well…that's alright then," Mel replied with pity in her voice. "Coors Light?"

"Please."

I've known Mel since the good old days at Markham High. Back when everything was simpler and the only thing any of us were concerned about was who was going to buy us booze for a Saturday night house party. We'd never been particularly close, but we ran around in the same crowd. To me, Mel hadn't changed a bit since those times, she was just as bubbly back then as she is today. Guys went nuts for her when we were teens, but she wasn't the type to date just anyone. She was classy for a high school girl, she never slept around and she could always see right through any guy who asked her on a date.

I'll never forget the day I came into the pub about two years back and saw her with, wow, a blast from the past, little Ricky Wainwright. Or shall I say, *Richard Wainwright* as he calls himself now. She was behind the bar when he swept through the door in a hurry. Before I could even notice who it was, he called for Mel and starting going on about some pink polo he couldn't find.

"I've been calling you Mel, why don't you ever answer your phone?"

"I'm working babe! My phone's in the car," she replied with wide eyes.

"Well isn't that a great place for it. It's the Breast Cancer tournament today and I can't find my pink polo, where did you put it?"

"It's your shirt Richard, I haven't touched it."

"What do you mean you haven't touched it? You do the laundry!"

"Well, I don't keep tabs on all of your garments, babe. Did you check all the drawers?"

"Do you think I'm some sort of fucking mor—," his face started to turn red when he stopped himself.

"You know what, never mind, looks like I'll have to go and buy myself a new one." He turned around and left just as quickly as he came in.

"Okay…bye…" Mel said under her breath with a hurt look on her face.

I guess I couldn't hide the look on my face, she knew what I had just witnessed.

"Was…was that Ricky Wainwright?"

"Ummm, yep sure was."

"I haven't seen him in forever. I had no clue he even lived around here. Is he…are you guys dating?"

"Yeah, we've been together a little while now. He's having a bad day apparently," she said as she looked down with two raised eyebrows.

"He was just a little dweeb back in the day, who woulda thought," I said with a laugh without even thinking.

"Thanks, Ben," Mel replied with a smirk.

"Uh..haha, I'm sorry. I mean, good for you. Ricky always seemed like a nice guy."

From what I understand now he's some sort of aspiring golf pro. He sure looks the part. He lost his braces and filled out quite a bit since High School. He actually turned into a decent looking guy. It was actually "being" a decent person in general I wasn't so sure about. I'd never seen him redeem himself for the way he treated Mel those years back. He was rarely seen at the pub and when he was, he was usually there to badger Mel about something or another.

Even though Mel was always her upbeat self at work, there was a certain spark in her that I'd seen fade over the years. That was something we had in common, I guess.

"So, Ben, how's life?" Mel says with a sweet inquisitive smile.

"It's life," I reply. I always felt like such a downer compared to her, but I couldn't help it and she knew that. I hated the thought of dragging down her mood, but she always managed to stay positive despite my constant pathetic demeanor.

"Everything's going good with work and stuff?" she says making small talk.

"Oh ya, it's alright," I say looking down at my beer.

"You sure about that, you seem down?"

"You mean more down that usual?" I reply with a laugh.

"That's not what I meant," Mel said with a playful eye-roll. "Seriously, what's on your mind?"

I hated spilling my feelings, but with Mel it was different. I mean she knew why I was the way I was,

there was really no reason for me to hide anything.
"I've been dispatched near Woodbine Beach tomorrow morning," I said while I start ripping bits of my coaster apart, nervous habit. "You take that and the fact its October 13th today… a perfect storm."
Mel let out a long sigh with the look of sadness in her eyes. "Ben, I'm so sorry."
"What can you do? I mean it's work. They say you're not supposed to let your personal life interfere with your job, right? So that's what I'm going to try and do."
"Don't go. I'm sure if you just explain to your boss--"
"No," I interrupted, "I'm not going to do that." I took one last swig of my beer before throwing down a ten. "I'm sorry Mel, I've got to hit the road, I'll see you later."
"Okay, Ben. You know if you ever need—"
"I know, Mel. Thanks," I said with a quick smile before I headed for the door.

This time of year is always rough on me and had been for quite some time. While everyone else rejoiced over the thought of the Halloween and the beautiful colours of fall, I absolutely dreaded it. Those cool October days and the smell of the changing season brought me back to some of the best times of my life, however, that couldn't help but be overshadowed by the worst.
We loved this season, my family and I. Lydia was an avid animal lover and taught our little Annabelle the beauty of autumn. How the world got less busy, the days got shorter and the forests would be bursting a kaleidoscope of colour as the trees and animals prepared for their long winters nap. Living in the city, we tried our best to get Anna out into some form of nature from time to time. Woodbine beach was only a bus ride away from our apartment. We'd take our girl there to watch the ducks and pesky seagulls.

It was a popular dog walking spot too and Annabelle attracted curious pups like no other. She was just like her Mom in that way.

Our walks on that beach were some of my most favourite times of us together, until some drunk took that away from me.

There was a point in time where I actually didn't mind my job. It put a roof over my wife and daughter's head and even let me put some extra money into savings for my girl's college fund. That's where I was that Saturday, work. We had plans to go to Woodbine beach, but that morning I was called by my desperate boss who needed a crew, stat, for an emergency job. I said I'd do it, which in hindsight turned out to be the worst decision of my life.

My wife understood but little Anna on the other hand wasn't too impressed. I can still picture her that morning with her tiny hands on her hips and adorable four-year-old scowl, "No Daddy! No work today!"

It took some sweet talking but eventually she let me off the hook. I promised her we'd go and see *Horton Hears A Who!* at the theatre that night. I kissed my two loves on the forehead before heading out the door. Little did I know that that would be the first day of the rest of my miserable life.

I got the phone call around noon. It was a number I didn't recognize, so I ignored it. Moments later my cell rang again.

"Hello?"

"Mr. Whitley, we're calling from emerge at St. Michael's hospital. We have two patients here who we believe to be your wife and daughter."

My heart sank, I felt like I was on the verge of passing out instantly.

"What's wrong? What happened? Are they okay?"

"There's been an accident. Are you able to come here?"

"Yes, yes I'll be there as soon as I can," I said dropping my work tools and racing for my truck.

"Get here safely, sir."

By the time I arrived I was drenched in sweat and I could tell I was probably white as a ghost.

When I got to the front desk, I knew it wasn't good.

"Where are they?" I said with a cracked voice and tears streaming down my face.

"One moment, Mr. Whitley, let me grab the doctor," the front desk nurse said to me with sad eyes.

A man with a white lab coat approached me and pulled me to a private area of the hallway, he swallowed hard as he gave me the news.

"Sir, I'm so sorry to be giving you this news. We did everything we could, but we couldn't save your wife."

"And my daughter?" I say before totally absorbing what he had just said.

"She's still in the OR, I've got a full team in there right now and we're not giving up," he said as he put his hand on my shoulder. "If you have any other family members to call in for support, I'd consider doing that now."

It hit me like a wave. "He doesn't think she's going to make it," I thought to myself. But I knew better, or, at least thought I did. Anna was the strongest little girl I knew, she was going to pull through. A saying popped into my head, "God only gives us what we can handle." Well, I couldn't handle losing her and so that wouldn't happen. It couldn't. What a fool I was.

After a half an hour of pacing and wracking my brains in the waiting room the man in the lab jacket reemerged. The look on his face told me everything I needed to know. My baby was gone.

The days that followed were a dark blur. The police told me it was a hit and run, a fucking hit and run. What kind of monster hits a woman and her child and doesn't even have the decency to stop? A monster driving a Lexus, driving way too fucking fast past

Woodbine beach, that's who.

That's just about all I know about that person. The one human being on this planet that completely destroyed my life and all I know about them is the car they drive. Or, at least the car they drove two years ago. A piece of their headlight cover is still sitting in some evidence room at the Toronto Police Station. The cops told me they'd do everything they could to find the driver but without any witnesses, no traffic cameras, and not much else to go off, the trail has gone cold.

I often wonder what they're doing. How they can live with themselves knowing what they've done. The two beautiful lives they took away and the one they've left shattered. I still have hope they'll be found one day. Until then all I can hope is that karma truly does exist, and that it eats them alive.

PING

I reach for my phone assuming it's from Ian.

"Let me guess," I say out loud to myself. "Earlier start tomorrow."

When I glance at the screen, I'm surprised to see it's a text from my buddy Mark.

"Hey man, hope you're alright.
Me and the wife are having a little get together this weekend.
Wanted to see if you could make it."

I wasn't dumb. I knew exactly what that was code for, what that was always code for. They had a woman they wanted me to meet. I loved all my buddies, I'd known most of them since we were kids and we'd been with each other through a lot. Whether it was bailing each other out of the drunk tank as teens, or break ups in college, we never left each other's side. What I had been going through the past couple years was different though. It wasn't some stupid fuck up that we could laugh about years down the road, and it wasn't a heartbreak that a few beers could heal. None of them knew what to do when the accident happened, and I don't blame them. How could anybody know? Mark helped me with funeral arrangements and his wife cooked me up a few months' worth of meals, though I barely touched them. Everyone else in our circle gave me their "If you ever need anything" spiel or checked up on me from time to time. I appreciated every little bit of it, I really did, it was just too hard for me to show it.

I know I pushed my friends away then, and I know I've been doing it now, but I couldn't help it. They always seemed to have some sort of ulterior motives when they asked to get together. It's been twice now that "beer and wings" has turned into surprise blind dates with women their wives are friends with. Was two years too long to me in mourning? I didn't think so. Was two years too early to be going on dates? I did think so. I had absolutely no desire to move on from the way my life was before. Even though it was so different, some parts still felt the same and it was comforting to me.

I did have to move away from the city though, away from the constant reminders. I packed everything up, all their clothes and belongings, and moved as far away as practical. I set up Anna's room the exact same way she had left it that day, her "stuffies" piled together on her bed. She always said they needed to be like that so they could cuddle and keep each other company while she was gone. Our bathroom had been redecorated by Lydia just weeks before they died. She was going for a beach-y theme, and the seashell trinket dish she placed on our vanity was still holding the gold hoop earrings I had bought her for her birthday. I did my best to re-create this room too, as near as I could anyway. Sometimes when I walked into the house things would feel somewhat normal for a split second.

I knew there was no exact timeline in dealing with things like this, and so I never pushed myself to clean out my daughter's room, or get rid of my wife's things. As much as my friends wanted to push me to move on with my life, I knew I wasn't ready for it, and I never *wanted* to be ready for it.

Why move on to another life when I'd already had the perfect one? Well, maybe not perfect, but as close to perfect as it could be. How could I ever find another Lydia? Or ever again have a child like Anna? I couldn't. And so, in my eyes, what was the point of even trying?

It's not that I didn't want to be happy. I did miss being happy. I just couldn't.

My alarm is still another half an hour from going off and yet I'm already on my second cup of coffee. I couldn't sleep last night. The idea of having to drive near the beach is having such a hold over me. Realistically, that place holds many more good memories than it does bad. That beach was one of our favourite places. We'd taken Anna there from the time she was just a baby.

I think the part that bothered me the most is that I wasn't there when it happened. I knew the general area where they were hit, but not exactly. I had always imagined what the scene must have looked like, but I never knew exactly. I knew the only thing that would get me through this day was that I didn't have to drive by the scene. Not if I didn't want to.

I'd planned out my route and I had ample opportunity to avoid even looking at Woodbine Beach, yet I found myself totally ignoring it. I don't know what it was, but something inside me was driving me to that spot. I needed to see it. Whether it would bring me back to the happiest or most horrific time in my life I didn't know, but I was going to find out. As I made a left onto Lakeshore Boulevard I held my breath. A red light had me stopped at Coxwell

Avenue, giving me a perfect view of where it had happened. When I looked toward the street I saw a little purple stuffed bear tied to a streetlamp. It'd been there for a while but it was still in pretty good shape.

Who put that there?

Maybe it was the asshole, a small trinket of guilt for what he did. Maybe a witness who saw what happened. Or, maybe just someone with a big heart who recognized the souls lost that day.

My heart began to warm as I peeked over to the lake and saw one of the most beautiful sunrises an autumn morning could ever produce.

I needed this.

On my way home that afternoon, the Black Horse was calling me. I pulled into the parking lot and spied a few regulars out for a smoke. I gave them a quick smile and a nod before heading for the door.

Mel was behind the bar, looking as smiley as ever until she saw me.

"Hey, Ben," she said in a sorrowful tone, "How was work today?"

"You know what? Not half bad."

"Yeah? You're doing okay?"

"Way better than I thought I would, to be honest."

There was a light in her eyes, an almost surprised look on her face.

"I drove there today," I said looking down at the pint she just handed me. "And I don't know why but it kind of gave me a sense of peace if you can believe it." I gave her a quick smile too. "Can you believe that? It's the second anniversary of my wife and daughter's death, and I actually feel at peace."

I looked up at Mel, and she seemed shocked. "Why are you looking at me like that?" I asked.

"Oh, sorry," she said breaking her stare. "It's, it's just that I've never heard you talk about it so openly before."

"Yeah, I guess not, eh?" I said with a sort of surprised tone myself.

Mel began nervously wiping down the bar. I could tell she had something further to say, though.

"Honestly, Ben. Forgive me if I'm out of bounds," She took a deep breath before continuing, "Lydia was a friend of mine back in high school, you know that. She was one of the most vivacious people I ever knew, and so were you. She would never have wanted to see you living this way. She'd want you to be happy."

I stared blankly at her, absorbing all she'd just said.

"I'm sorry, Ben, I hope that didn't upset you. It's just something that I've wanted to say to you for a long time, I just didn't know how."

"No, don't be sorry," I replied. "You're right."

As I left the pub, I couldn't stop thinking about what Mel had said. I'd spent so much time consumed in my grief it had seemed almost selfish at this point. Lydia and Anna wouldn't even recognize me if they saw me today. They knew me as a person full of love, full of happiness and smiles. All I had been full of these last couple years was self-pity. I wasn't living the way they would want me to live. That wasn't to say I should just drop everything that happened and move on, but I needed to get a grip on my life, for myself and for them.

As the sun slowly started to make its way down to the horizon, I decided there was one more stop I had to make before I headed home.

"Two years, Lyd," I said with tears in my eyes, talking aloud to a gravestone in the Markham cemetery where they were buried. "I can't believe it's been two years. Some days it feels like yesterday and others it feels like a lifetime."

As the yellow roses I placed by my girls' grave fluttered in the cool breeze, I look over to the sunset. I felt a wonderful wave of peace coming over me again.

"Nice work you girls did today with the pretty skies," I said. "I needed that."

My voice began to break as I choked back tears.

"I owe you girls an apology. I haven't done right by you in the least."

I pulled a tissue from my pocket before I made them both an important promise.

"Things are going to change. I know they need to, and I know you'd both want them to," I said as I wiped two tears flowing down my cheeks.

I could feel every single tear of the past two years well up in my eyes and release like a volcano. I knew my life would never be the way it used to be, not in a million years and there's nothing that could ever change that. But I knew I needed to give life another chance. The world had been cruel to me, been cruel to my sweet wife and daughter, but I was still here. Instead of wasting my life away feeling sorry for myself I had to make them proud.

"I'm going to start living again. I never imagined I'd have to do that without you two, but here we are."

I sat by their grave in silence for a few moments, taking in the evening breeze and feeling their love all around me.

When the last tear finally left my eye, a feeling of serenity came over me like everything was going to be okay. It was then I could feel that good things were on the horizon.

With the second anniversary now behind me, things started happening in baby steps. I still had my bad days, but I wasn't going to let them define me anymore.

I started seeing everyday as a new opportunity rather than something I had to suffer through. I finally started texting my friends back who were happy to hear from me. I'd even started meeting them for wing nights at the Black Horse now and again. The first time Mel saw me in there with a buddy I thought she was about to faint. When I asked her what the shock was about, she gave me a wink and replied with, "Oh nothing, it's just nice to see a smile on your face."

That was something I'd been hearing from a few people actually and it was refreshing.

I got rid of my permanent five o'clock shadow and got a professional hair cut for the first time in forever.

I'd even started thinking about what to do with Anna's bedroom. Changing anything in there was a step I wasn't quite ready to take, but making plans for it was a good step, I thought.

While getting on with my life was something I knew I had to do, I was never going to forget about my girls or what happened to them.

The determination I had to make them proud by living again would never override the determination I had to find the drunk bastard who killed them. That is something I would never give up on.

Merry Christmas Tony Romano: Tony's Story

As Tony looked at himself in the "Gents" washroom mirror, a wry smile lit up his face. He could not believe it, maybe things were finally starting to turn around for him. A few days earlier, standing in the same spot, Garnet had entered the washroom behind him. Tony and Garnet had never really talked much before, maybe the occasional hello or nod and that was it. Tony did not care for Garnet or any of the others who called themselves the Dog Pound. Instead of using the urinal, Garnet had just been staring at Tony to the point that it was becoming embarrassing. Tony turned around and said, "Can I help you Garnet?" To which Garnet had replied, "Keep this to yourself, I am looking to sell my property and you are the only realtor I know. Can we meet somewhere private to chat about this?"

An astonished Tony stammered back.

"Of course, Garnet, I can do it all for you. I'm a bit busy at the moment, but your property won't take long to sell. Developers are all over this area looking for land."

Garnet solemnly added, "Not a word to anyone, I don't want anyone knowing my business."

Tony nodded, handed Garnet a business card and said, "Call me to arrange a meeting. I have an opening Thursday morning."

Well it was now Thursday afternoon and it had been quite a good meeting at the Newmarket Tim Horton's. 200 acres of property right next to a major highway and close to many amenities. This would be his biggest sale ever, by a longshot!

He had struck gold and the only stipulations were no "For Sale" signs or local newspaper advertising. Garnet really did not want the Black Horse crowd knowing anything about it. This would be easy for

Tony. First of all, he had no proper real estate signs and no extra money to spend on expensive ads anyway. He would just inform the developers directly and then sell to the highest bidder. The commission for this sale would be sweet and more than he had ever made in a single year before. He could pay back his outstanding gambling debts to Gerry the Bookie, who had recently threatened him with death if he did not pay up soon. Whether Gerry would actually kill him was something else, but he did have connections to quite a rough group and Tony did not want to meet any of them. Ever. He would call Gerry up and let him know that the money would be paid in full, with interest, very soon. If Gerry was on board then maybe he could start parking his car in front of the pub again, rather than out of sight behind it.

The other good thing happening was Rhonda. Apparently, she was now single and obviously wealthy. Her husband must have had to pay her quite a bit after he left her, as they had been business partners and he was loaded. He had started flirting with her and she seemed receptive to his moves. It was costing him a small fortune buying her glass after glass of wine, but now it would all be worth it. Hell, the money he had been stealing from his mother's hidden stash to pay for his daily pub visits could be replaced too, and no one would be the wiser.

All in all, it had been a very tough year for Tony. It had started well enough, when he'd won $1500.00 on a Super Bowl square at his local bar in Toronto. Obviously, the bar's football squares were blind luck, but to Tony, it was an omen. He knew football well, so maybe a flutter here and there and twenty or thirty bucks each week on Pro-line wouldn't hurt. He had not sold a condo for over six months, but he knew things would turn around and for now he could afford it. After all, he had made a killing last year when the housing market had exploded.

As he looked at his reflection in the mirror his

smile dropped a bit, reminded of the day a friendly bartender named Mike had introduced him to Gerry the bookie. Twenty bucks soon became two hundred, two hundred became two thousand. It was bet after bet, good money after bad. Money on horse racing, football, baseball, UFC fights, you name it. If it was a sport, he gambled on it. In the beginning he promised himself he would quit, but then he would win a small bundle and before you know it he was hooked. He was now into Gerry for $180,000 and the betting had eaten away all his savings. He had been forced to give up his high-end rental condo when he could no longer afford the rent. He stopped drinking at his usual watering hole in the city and instead drowned his sorrows daily in the Black Horse, up in the middle of nowhere. He moved in with his elderly mother and was sure Gerry would never find him here in the small town of Ashington.

The stupid locals still believed he was a big "wheeler-dealer", and thought he only visited his mother to help her out.

It was all different now. His troubles would soon be over. Christmas had come a few weeks early for him, pay back Gerry and get that off his back, and then maybe he could start a serious courtship with Rhonda. Hell, maybe he would even move in with her, last he had heard was that she lived in one of the biggest homes in the golf course's gated community. His luck was really changing, he could feel it and even taste it now. Maybe a last flutter on the next Super Bowl and that would be the end of his gambling days forever. Yes, times they were a changing.

A smile lit up his face once more. He straightened his tie and exited the washroom, quietly humming Jingle Bells.

"Well hello, Mr. Romano, finally we meet face to face."

Two of the biggest guys Tony had ever seen were now standing in front of him in the narrow hallway that led to the washrooms. For a moment Tony thought he might just piss himself right then and there.

"Gerry has been looking for you for quite some time now, and we're here to ensure that you finally get the message and pay the fuck up."

Tony stunned, finally stammered back.

"I was about to call Gerry, I swear. I'll be paying him back very soon, I promise. I have a huge commission coming!"

"Gerry said you might come up with that one again," said the guy who looked like a stunt double for the Hulk. "Hear that Charlie, we wasted a trip. He was about to call Gerry."

Charlie, who was only slightly smaller, answered, "That's what they all say. You're coming with us asshole."

Charlie grabbed Tony tightly by the arm and proceeded to march him down the hallway, while the Hulk went first to make sure that no one was watching. They would beat the crap out of Tony around back where they had spotted his car a few minutes ago. It had taken them a few months to locate this scumbag, but a 'tip' from someone in the area had led them to Ashington, and the Black Horse.

The pub was fairly busy, but the hallway led to a side door that most patrons had their backs to. Out the side, round the back, and then this pretty boy would get his just desserts along with the message that you did not fuck around with Gerry the bookie. Tony was shaking like a leaf and he burst into tears as they left the pub. He knew that nothing he said would get him out of this.

Dear God, get me out of this and I will never, ever bet or steal again.

He started sobbing loudly.

"Save your tears for later, shithead," said the Hulk. "You might need them when you see the repair bill for your fucking car."

This made Tony sob all the more, his car was the

only nice thing he had remaining in life, the only valuable thing too.

As they turned the corner to the back alley of the pub Sammy stepped out of the kitchen's back door.

"Get back inside," said Charlie menacingly,

"Nothing for you to see here, dipshit," Hulk added, "Listen to the man. Fuck off, and you ain't seen nothing."

Sammy just stood and stared at Hulk. There was something about him that unsettled Hulk slightly, but only slightly.

Sammy spoke softly, "I don't care what you do with this asshole, but I need a quiet word. It will only take a second and it may prove to be very valuable to you."

Hulk was intrigued, this guy had no fear, and if it was bullshit Charlie and him would just have another dickhead to beat up.

"Hold on a second Charlie. Alright num-nuts, what is it?"

Sammy walked up to Hulk and whispered in ear. Hulk immediately spun around and scanned the area.
Sammy again said a few quiet words to which the Hulk blanched visibly.

"Charlie, let him go and let's get the fuck out of here."

Charlie screamed back, "Are you fucking crazy! We have pretty boy here on a plate, Gerry will go nuts!" Hulk walked over to Charlie and grabbed his throat, emphasizing each word.

"We are getting out of here now!"

Charlie realized that this was very serious as they both walked briskly around the corner and back across the parking lot to their car. Sammy could see Hulk talking to Charlie animatedly. They both looked around the parking lot and jumped into their car. Charlie, behind the wheel, sped off with a screech of tires.

Tony had stopped sobbing but still could not find

his voice. Sammy had saved his life, or at least saved him from a serious beating. His beloved car was intact too. Tony turned to Sammy, but he was already gone.

Tony went back into the bar, and there was Sammy sitting quietly with the Dog Pound. He was chatting away with the rest of his cronies as if nothing had happened.

Tony ordered a double Grey Goose with one ice cube and, with shaking hands, quickly downed it.

What the fuck had just happened? What did Sammy say? Tony looked over at Sammy, who never even glanced his way.

"Rosie, another double Grey Goose, please."

Rosie nodded and thought that this was strange, as Tony had never drunk Grey Goose at the pub before.

"There you go Tony, take it easy though. Hey, you're shaking, everything okay?"

"I'm okay Rosie, it's been one of them days."

Just then Tony saw Sammy head to the washroom. He put his drink back down and went after him. He needed to thank him for what he'd done, and he also needed to know just what the fuck he had said.

He waited for a moment, taking a deep breath before opening the door. He entered the washroom just as Sammy was drying his hands.

"Hey Sammy, thanks so much, man. I owe you my life. I can't thank you enough."

Sammy turned and looked at him, "Don't mention it. Now please move out of the way so I can get out of here."

Tony had to ask, "What did you say Sammy, it must have been something serious for those goons to leave."

"Another day Tony, another day."

Sammy brushed past Tony, who was about to ask him again, but after seeing the look on his face, thought better of it.

Alone again in the washroom, Tony looked at himself

in the mirror and whispered to himself, "Merry Christmas, Tony Romano."

Meanwhile, back in the snug…

The background music in the pub was playing a little louder than usual but Tommy and Jack did not mind as it was on the 60's channel.

Tommy and Jack tried to out-guess each other on the artist and title and both were fairly even so no one was getting angry at the other.

"I Want to Hold Your Hand" by the Beatles came on and Jack smiled and said, "Now here is the greatest band in the world, you can't argue with that Tommy boy."

"Bullshit, Jack," Tommy replied sharply. "The Stones were much better than this manufactured boy band."

"What the fuck does that mean?" Jack retorted. "Lennon and McCartney were the two best song writers in the world."

"No way! In later years they wrote some classics but in the sixties my granny could have written their crap. *'She loves you Yeah! Yeah! Yeah!'* how hard was that to put together, eh! Now Jagger and Richards wrote songs against the system, they were a huge part of the sixties revolution plus they wore what they wanted and grew their hair long, not like the four mop heads who got their hair cut using the same bowl."

Jack was stunned, he had known Tommy for so many years, and they had argued about almost everything and anything, but how the fuck could someone not like the Beatles? This was sacrilege.

"The Stones were just a wall of noise, I could never understand a word that Hot Lips was singing. *'I Can't Get No Satisfaction'*, no wonder, dressed like that. He looked like a real pansy with his skin tight lycra pants."

"We all live in a Yellow Submarine, a yellow

submarine, a yellow submarine," sang Tommy mockingly "Sounds like something from Sesame fucking Street."

Jack was fuming now, "At least they were clean back in the day, not like the Rolling Stoned."

"Clean? For fucks sake, Jack, they couldn't hardly travel anywhere because their luggage was so full of drugs. And let's face it, you would have had to be under the influence of something serious to date that Yoko OH NO!"

Tommy was enjoying this, he was actually getting the better of Jack. *Who on earth argued against the Beatles?* Certainly, Tommy would not usually do so, as he loved the Beatles, but this opportunity was too great to pass up.

"The Stones were the bad boys of rock, they were a terrible influence on kids back then with their shouting and devil worship," blurted Jack who was not liking the way this argument was going.

Tommy was about to let Jack know that he was only taking the piss, but just then Evelyn came out of the kitchen to help Rosie deliver food to the table next to where they were sitting.

"Would you?" he said to Jack with raised eyebrows.

"Bloody right!" he replied.

The two went back to their pints grinning cheekily at each other, while *"Yellow Submarine"* started to play in the background.

The Road Trip: Buffalo or Bust

It was 8:30 in the morning, barely 30 minutes into the trip, and already the first victim had fallen. The sound of puking, hopefully into a bag, was coming from someone at the rear of the school bus. The throng of people seated near him, were either collectively mocking or cheering him on wildly.

"Soft cock!"

"Get it outta ya!"

"Who brought this fucking wanker?"

"Have another beer!"

The bus had just made its way onto the westbound Highway 407, and the 30 odd revelers, most dressed in their Buffalo Bills regalia, were already fully into 'party' mode. Some, obviously, had been drinking all night, and well into the morning, but the mood was fun, the energy was high and the expectations for a great day remained strong, despite the loss of Uncle Dave and his organizational skills. The only knock on the trip so far was the use of a school bus, with no toilet, rather than the traditional coach express that Dave had always procured. It was going to be an ugly ride home.

It was Ben's first trip with the Black Horse crew, and though he felt a little intimidated, he was happy to have come along. It was a big step for him. He was also happy to be spending some social time with Mel, who had convinced him to tag along. Cajoled, harassed and pretty much outright ordered him, was perhaps a more apt description of why he was there, but he was glad for it. He really needed something like this now. And to be able to spend some time with her was a wonderful added bonus. He leaned over to Mel sitting beside him and asked quietly.

"Who booked this bus anyway?"

She nodded towards John at the front, talking

animatedly to the driver.

"John".

John had been Uncle Dave's "unofficial" second in command for all these years, and probably the biggest Bills fanatic in the group. He had insisted on taking over the arrangements after Dave's passing, almost as a rite of passage. But sacrificing comfort to save a few dollars on transportation was definitely not a wise choice. His organizational skills were found to be a little wanting as well, their annual special order t-shirts emblazoned with the "Black Horse Bills" logo hadn't arrived in time for their trip either. To his credit though, all the beer and beer paraphernalia; key rings, bottle openers, hats and cups, were there, and were doled out with great solemnity. Four large coolers full of beer were spaced out on empty seats for self-service, snacks and paper towels were handed out, and John was just now making his first pass down the aisle with a large garbage bag to collect the empties and other detritus produced so far.

"Come on guys, let's keep the bus clean! No muss, no fuss!"

Ben just smiled as he passed by, dropping his Tim Horton's cup into the bag.

"Does he have a clue what he's doing?"

Mel punched him playfully on the arm. "Don't worry, I saw the envelope of tickets, that's the most important thing," she said laughing. "And there's plenty of food for the tailgating too. I saw him load it earlier with the barbecue."

"All right then," Ben replied with a genuine laugh of his own. "It's my first time! Care for a beer?"

Mel nodded and smiled brightly. "That's the spirit! Make sure to grab one for yourself."

"You got it, coming right up!"

They were sitting up front in the third row, and as Ben got up to walk back to the nearest cooler, he took a quick look around at the group on the bus. He was surprised to see so many faces that he didn't recognize. A lot of them must have been friends or family of Black Horse regulars that didn't often frequent the pub themselves. On the plus side, there were many familiar faces too, including a surprising one. He had just spotted Mary sitting a few rows back. What was she doing here? He never figured her for a football fan, or for one to socialize in a large group like this. But then again, he hadn't been one for this type of activity either, hadn't been for a long while anyway.

She was sitting with Gary, and for a moment he wondered if there was anything going on with the two of them. They were often found sitting quietly together at the corner of the bar, reading and talking and laughing amongst themselves. He was glad to see Gary though, he liked him. Gary had always been open and friendly towards him. He respected his privacy when he popped into the Black Horse on his way home. Most of the other regulars would keep intruding on his thoughts, trying to get him to join them at their section of the bar, the infamous Dog Pound, and sometimes he would relent, just to appear friendly. Gary would just smile and say hello, maybe some quick chit chat, but it was genuine. He was a good, honest guy. He understood personal space.

Gary has a girlfriend, doesn't he? And a little boy, too.

He was struck suddenly with overwhelming sadness, thinking of his daughter, knowing she was gone, that they were gone. The floor seemed to sway under his feet. He had to reach out and steady himself from his grief. Ben closed his eyes and took a deep breath, felt the new calmness coming back. This wasn't the time or place for those feelings. He had a lifetime of moments ahead of him for thoughts of Lydia and Annabelle, but not here and not now. He was finally starting to heal and needed something like this trip to get out and get away from those thoughts. Besides,

Mel would probably kill him if he got all dark and morose on this trip.

"Hey Mary, how are you? Gary, glad to see you too."

He reached out and shook both their hands.

"I didn't know you were a football fan, I'm a bit surprised to see you here."

"I just thought I'd see what all the fuss was about," Mary replied, but Ben quickly interrupted her.

"I was talking to Gary," he said with a giggle.

Their initial confusion quickly turned to shared laughter as they got his feeble attempt at humour.

"Yeah man, Mary promised to teach me everything about the game and show us all the finer points of 'tailgating' culture," Gary added playfully.

It was good to see Mary laughing too, she must be feeling a little uneasy in this setting, but it sure didn't show. She looked as comfortable as can be beside Gary.

"Listen, when we go into the stadium, why don't the two of you sit with Mel and me. It would be awesome to be next to you guys instead of whoever it was that was heaving up his breakfast."

He looked from Gary to Mary and back, seeing smiles and acceptance. "If that's okay with you guys."

They both answered almost simultaneously, "Yes!"

"Great, that's settled then. I'm so glad to see you both. This is going be a lot of fun. I'm just going to grab a couple of beers, are you guys okay for drinks?"

Gary answered first, "I'll take one, thanks. None for Mary."

Mary smiled sheepishly as she pulled a can of wine cooler out of her bag and gave it a little shake.

"I'm sticking to wine. Or what passes for wine under these circumstances."

It was good to see that she was really enjoying herself. He wished he could be so relaxed. Ben liked her too and was happy that she was making an effort to fit in, just like he was. Another "Black Horse Bill" first-timer.

"Alright, be right back."

He grabbed three beers from the cooler, listening to the shouts and laughter sounding from all over the bus. This trip was a great idea, getting out and about again. He passed one to Gary, and with another shared smile between the three of them, made his way back to Mel. Yes, it looked like this would be a fantastic day after all.

He handed Mel her drink and sat back down.

"Did you have a nice chat with Mary and Gary?"

Ben was surprised, Mel had been watching him. It made him smile even more.

"Yes, I was surprised to see her, that's all. I asked if they would like to sit with us at the game. I hope you don't mind?"

"That's perfect, what a great idea! They're both such cool people. It'll be so fun to hang with them."

She got a little twinkle in her eyes now. "But maybe you'd have more fun sitting with John."

John was currently arguing with someone at the back of the bus about the lack of toilet facilities.

"We'll pull over at a rest area before we hit the border! What's wrong with you guys? We just fucking left the pub! Hold it in will ya!"

"No, I think they're the better option."

They both laughed again. He'd been expecting to see Sammy, but he wasn't here. Ben found that weird, seeing as how Sammy was such a big Bills fan.

"Hey Mel, how come Sammy's not here? I figured this sort of thing would be right up his alley."

"He never goes on these trips."

Swivelling her head to see if anyone was listening, she continued, "I don't think he's allowed to cross the border. I don't know if he even has a passport. To be honest, Ben, I don't even know his real name."

"What? He's been going to the Black Horse for years. Are you kidding me? Doesn't he own a garage or something?"

"I don't know if he owns it, but he runs it, I think. Nobody knows anything for sure when it comes to Sammy. I saw his driver's license once, it sure as hell didn't say 'Sammy'."

"That's so wild." Ben was amazed. "Has anyone asked him about it?"

"Let's just say Sammy doesn't like answering questions about himself. And he has a very intimidating way about making sure you know that."

Ben was genuinely shocked. Granted, he didn't know Sammy very well. He'd only spoken to him occasionally in the Black Horse, but this was big news to him. Talk about being out of the loop.

"Is he dangerous? I mean, is it okay that he's in the pub?"

"Don't worry, Ben, he's a good guy, just a bit mysterious. Well, a lot mysterious! But he's nice, he's friendly. And he's stepped in and helped me out a few times too, like when some drunk won't take 'no' for an answer. He never hurts them though, he's not violent. He just makes them think he's going to hurt them! I'd have to say he's more sad, I think, than anything else. He's scary, but that's just the cross he has to bear."

After a moment she added with a laugh, "I wouldn't want to piss him off though and test that theory!"

"Maybe it's because he has a criminal record and can't cross into the U.S. That would make sense, I guess," Ben was thinking out loud now. "Where is he from by the way. Originally, I mean. I can't place his accent."

"I don't know. He could be middle eastern I guess, or Turkish. Maybe even Russian. No one knows!" Mel shrugged her shoulders and added, laughing, "He loves tequila but I'm pretty sure he's not Mexican!"

"It's weird, you're so right. I can't even figure out how old he is. I'd guess mid-forties, but he looks so fit and yet so battle-scarred that I could be off by fifteen years either way!"

Mel contemplated for a moment before turning to Ben and whispering in his ear so as not to be overheard.

"Rosie might know. They're very close, you know. They talk all the time."

He felt her breath on his neck, surprised at how good it felt. He wanted her to go on whispering, but she had already moved away.

"You're kidding me. Rosie?"

"Yes! He's an absolute sweetheart with her. Maybe I can discreetly ask her a few questions about him. She must know something."

Ben nodded in return.

"Enough about Sammy, how are you and Richard doing?"

Gary accepted the beer from Ben with a nod of thanks. He seemed to be a completely different person lately, what a dramatic change from his usual moody self. It was nice to see him pop out of that shell. Mel must be working her magic again. He knew they were friends from way back in high school, and if anyone could help raise a person's spirits, it was her.

"That was nice of Ben to ask. He seems much happier these days, doesn't he?"

Mary pursed her lips before answering. She wasn't sure just how much the other regulars actually knew about Ben. He was always so quiet, and never talked about himself when he was at the Black Horse, but Mel had told her little bits and pieces of his story and it broke her heart. Mel had made her promise not to tell anyone else. If Ben wanted people to know, he'd let them know when he was ready. It wasn't her place to blab, even to Gary.

"Yes. He looks much better too, he was actually smiling! I hope this new Ben manages to stick around. Speaking of 'new', what else have you gotten me into here today, besides drinking wine at 8:30 in the morning?"

Gary's eyes lit up, he was excited to talk about their day ahead.

"Well, the strategy is to act as normal as possible until we cross the border, which should be in about an hour. Then, it's party time! Drinking games, bus karaoke, everyone has to tell at least one joke. At least that's how it was when Uncle Dave was running the show. He'd have us in stitches by the time we pulled into the stadium lot, everyone lubed up just the right amount to tailgate like experts."

He looked to the back of the bus where John was cleaning up more garbage.

"I doubt that will happen with John at the helm, but there's going to be some delicious food grilled when we get there, don't you worry. And the stadium is electric once the game starts. 80,000 people yelling and screaming, it's awesome to witness. Nothing even close to this ever happens in Canada. We're not allowed to have fun, too many rules."

Mary was nodding along with his further descriptions of what to expect, the game itself, the speed and quality of the athletes, the popularity of the sport, the rabid local fans, and the perpetual disappointment that their beloved Bills were to all their diehard supporters. The more she heard, the more she liked it.

In Nigeria, she had gone to many Premier League Football games during her time at university in Lagos. She still wasn't used to calling it "soccer". The "Mountain of Fire & Miracles Football Club" was her local team, and they'd all make their way out to cheer on their purple and gold heroes, the "Olukoya Boys" at the Agege Stadium. They'd eat, drink and enjoy the action on the pitch, singing along to the club's songs all afternoon. But their stadium barely held 5000 spectators. She couldn't wait to see what 80,000 avid football supporters looked and sounded like up close. It must be deafening!

Mary had been nervous about accepting Gary's invitation at first, but the more she'd thought about it, and the closer the game day became, she got more and more excited. This was a real adventure; her first trip to America, her first live football game, and her first outing with some of the people she knew from the Black Horse. It felt so wonderful to belong, and she was going to try and enjoy every minute of it. Having Mel and Gary by her side would make things so much easier.

The one flea in the ointment she had to deal with, however, was another internal dilemma she had involving secret information. It was strange, she'd had several serious boyfriends in her past, in fact, Mary had almost gotten married to one of them, before discovering that he had been cheating on her for almost a year. To her, infidelity and dishonesty were unforgiveable sins, and she would never put up with a man who wasn't devoted to her.

She liked Gary, she liked him very much. It surprised Mary to realize that she had never felt as comfortable being with a man as she was with Gary. He was intelligent, he worked hard, and he had a solid moral compass that she admired greatly. It didn't hurt that he was quite handsome as well. She definitely felt her heart flutter when he was near and she was pretty sure that Gary had feelings for her too. He never crossed the line with her, though. He maintained a wonderful propriety at all time. She was grateful for that. It was a wonderful quality. He had a girlfriend and he had a young son at home. It broke her heart to know that little Ryan was almost certainly not his biological son. His odious girlfriend, Stephanie had been cheating with the equally, if not more, odious Claude. She'd had her suspicions about him from the way Claude looked and acted whenever Stephanie was in the vicinity, there was a palpable sense of discomfort and guilt about him in those situations. What she couldn't figure out

Dozens and dozens of RV's and other buses were lined up in neat rows, most were comfortable coaches, and the smells of barbecued meat and smoke wafted over the entire area. Music was blaring, some tailgaters even had large screen TV's set up to watch all the pre-game shows and highlight reels.

Mary was astonished, she'd never seen anything quite like it before. It was like a giant street festival! Everywhere she looked, she saw people having fun, most wearing the blue, white and red of the Bills. Jackets, jerseys, hats, even a few brave souls wearing t-shirts only. It was wonderful, so boisterous, crazy and celebratory. Her concentration was broken by Gary as he pulled a package out from behind his back. He looked so boyish and shy all of a sudden, and very happy.

"I never got you a graduation gift for passing your dental exams. Congratulations Dr. Okuoimose. I'm so proud of you!"

With that he handed her the carefully wrapped package. She had tears in her eyes and couldn't help but hug her dear friend.

"Thank you, Gary, you didn't have to do that. It's so sweet of you."

Gary nodded and smiled in return. "Go ahead, try it on!"

She tore off the wrapping paper to reveal the beautiful blue of a Buffalo Bills jersey within. A good one, with stitching and patches and everything, not like some of the cheaper ones she'd seen on the bus and all around her. It must have been very expensive.

"Oh Gary, it's beautiful. I can't believe it! You really shouldn't have. You should take it back. It's too much."

She thought she might have offended him, but his smile got even bigger.

"I can't take it back. Look."

He gently pulled the folded jersey from her hands

and held it up for her to see. The number '1' was sewn on front with the small Bills logo on one side of the upper chest. He then turned the jersey around to reveal a larger '1' on the back, just below the beautifully stitched letters that spelled out her name, "OKUOIMOSE".

She let out a sob as she once again thanked Gary, hugging him once more. What a precious, thoughtful gift. He knew how much she wanted to fit in today and he had found the perfect gift for her.

"Put it on Mary! I can't wait to see how it looks on you."

She thought it would be far too big, but it fit snugly over her jacket. She pulled it down and spun around in front of him. She felt like a Queen.

"Well, what do you think?"

"You look amazing Mary. Absolutely amazing."

It didn't really matter what he said, the look on his face told her everything she needed to know. She couldn't remember having been so happy for such a long, long time. Her tears of joy were clearly a testament to that.

"Houston, we have a problem!"

John was digging around furiously in the storage compartment looking for something, coming up empty handed.

"Shitballs!"

The crowd of pub regulars and guests hanging out by the BBQs had been watching John confidently place pounds of meat onto the two grills, one for burgers and sausages, the other for chicken. Now it appeared that panic was setting in.

"I forgot to bring the BBQ tools."

Initially, it was just loud groans that escaped from the hungry group. Then the insults flew.

"You useless twat! How could you forget those!"

"Dave wouldn't have fucked up like this!"

"What are we supposed to do now? Use our fingers to

flip burgers?"

"I know, I know. Don't worry, I'll go borrow some."

John appeared to be truly aghast as he made his way from bus to bus begging to borrow a big spatula or some large forks. Eventually he returned with a filthy set of tongs. He'd even forgotten to bring plastic cutlery for the chicken. Well, people could just tear apart the breasts and use hamburger buns to make sandwiches. It wasn't a complete lost cause.

"Hang on a sec, guys, I have an idea."

Gary stepped up with a large screwdriver he'd found in the bus's toolbox. Grabbing an empty beer can he placed the end of the tool into the can's opening and then set them down on the ground between two pieces of cardboard scavenged from empty beer cases. He then proceeded to stomp on the can several times until it was perfectly flat. With dramatic flair, he pulled the screwdriver-beer can combo out to reveal a makeshift spatula.

"Voila!" he said to the cheers of his friends, taking a bow after handing it over to John. "John, get back to work!"

Relief clearly expressed on his face, John replied with hearty gusto.

"Yes sir!"

Soon after, the happy Black Horse crew were scarfing down their pre-game meals, talking and laughing and having a great time. More than a few complimented Mary on her personalized jersey, making sure that she was enjoying the full experience of the day. She was taught how to throw a spiral, how to punt the ball and quizzed on her knowledge of the rules. She passed all three tests with flying colours, reveling in the camaraderie of the trip. She was pleasantly surprised at how warmly welcomed she was. Perhaps she'd not given all these people enough credit. Maybe she could let her guard down a little, and open up more.

In fact, the only difficulty she encountered all

day was the effort required to resist sliding her hand into Gary's as they made their way to the stadium entrance. She would have liked that more than anything.

Rosie looked at Sammy watching the game on the pub's big screen TV. The pub was quieter than usual for a Sunday afternoon as almost all of the folk who came in to watch football were down in Buffalo watching the game live. A few couples having lunch, and Garnet keeping Sammy company at the bar.

"Do you see them? I think they're sitting near the twenty yard line, upper level."

Sammy had indeed been scanning the crowd for any sign of his friends but to no avail.

"They must be on the opposite side, I don't see them," he said as he turned back to Rosie. "This new screen is fucking fantastic by the way! So much definition!"

Rosie smiled, she was happy. Business had been good lately, so good that upgrading the big TV with the latest and greatest had finally been possible, and her regulars deserved it too. She was pleased that Sammy had not only noticed, but was impressed.

"Garnet, can I get you another?"

Garnet nodded and accepted with a quiet, "Yes please."

Sammy got her attention and pointed at his chest. This one was on him.

As she poured, Sammy shuffled over one seat to be right beside the old farmer.

"Everything okay there, Garnet? Haven't seen you around so much these days."

Rosie shared his concern. Garnet was looking thinner and more dishevelled than normal. He was quieter too. She hoped it was just some temporary money problems, and nothing worse. She wasn't ready for another funeral.

Garnet turned to Sammy with a confused look on his

face.
"What do you mean? I didn't know you guys were keeping tabs on me."
"We just miss you, that's all. The place isn't the same without you."
Garnet's face softened as he realized Sammy's concern was genuine.
"I've just been doing some work around the property, cleaning it up a bit. I want to get it all finished before winter sets in for good."
There had been a couple of light snow falls so far, but nothing had stuck for more than a few days. The weather was warmer than usual, and the frost hadn't set in yet, but time was running out for outdoor work. If he was going to sell his farm, he figured he'd best get it looking presentable for prospective buyers if he wanted to get top dollar. After visiting the property, that weasel Tony had suggested a general cleanup would be helpful. He was full of suggestions, that Tony was. He was full of something, that's for sure. As long as he kept his mouth shut about the sale and did his job, he'd be very well compensated. There was something about him though that bothered Garnet. He couldn't quite put his finger on it, but he didn't trust him. He needed him though, so he'd just have to keep an eye on him. And no funny business either, he wanted a straight and simple sale. No complicated deals.
"Let me know if you need any help. I'm pretty good with a tractor."
"Thanks Sammy, I might just take you up on that." He meant it too. His back was aching and there was still so much left to clean up and clear off.
"I'll tell you who really needs help, those fucking Bills! They're horrible."
Sammy laughed and put his arm around Garnet, careful not to crush him.
"You said it, pal. That they are!"
They both looked up at the TV, the screen

highlighting the half-time score: New England 35 Buffalo 3. At least the weather was good.

Mel and Mary were returning to their seats after going on a half-time washroom break. What an expedition that had been! There definitely weren't enough ladies toilets for the size of this crowd.

"Another wine, Mary?"

Mary was having the time of her life, she'd really been getting into the game. Her voice was hoarse from all the yelling and cheering she'd been doing.

"Why not?"

She'd probably have to slow down after this one though, she was getting more than a little tipsy. She'd likely sleep the entire way home.

"Let's get some more beer for the guys too."

"That's my girl!" Mel replied, "We are on a mission!"

They lined up at the nearest concession stand. Thank god this line was moving faster than the one for the washrooms.

"I'm having such a great time, so glad I came."

Mary was more talkative than ever, a result of the wine, the excitement of the game and the friendships she was cementing with people in their group. She felt absolutely giddy, definitely only one more wine!

Just then Mel nudged her and pointed down the concourse.

"Hey, look, there goes John."

It was John, and he was with a different group of fans. Locals by the look of it, and he was the centre of their attention. They were all laughing and slapping him on the back, like he was the king of their court.

"I wonder where they're going?"

"I don't know, but they look like they're leaving. Maybe John has finally found someone who hasn't heard all of his corny jokes before."

"Haha, now that would be a miracle!" After a quiet moment, Mary added, "What a crazy day."

The group was getting frustrated. *Where the hell was John?* No one had seen him since Mel and Mary at half-time, and he wasn't answering his phone. It was just going straight to message, probably dead.

"What the fuck are we supposed to do now?"

The bus had already been paid for, but had to be back on schedule, and many of those on the trip had to get back home in time to get a good night's sleep before work on Monday morning. It was just like John to screw things up for the rest of them.

"Should we call the police?" asked someone from the back of the bus.

"Maybe he's been kidnapped!"

Mel had described the situation of their last sighting of John. It hadn't looked like a kidnapping. She'd pity the gang who'd ever hold him as a hostage though. Nothing could prepare them for that headache!

People turned to Gary for guidance. He was the most experienced of the group when it came to these trips, and he'd just stepped back onto the bus along with their driver.

"Look guys, this is what's happening. We're going to get going in a few minutes, and it looks like we'll be leaving John behind. He's an adult and he knows how to take care of himself. He obviously chose to go off somewhere else, and he knows the rules. He'll be okay. We'll keep trying to get hold of him though. Hopefully he responds, but in the meantime, if he's not here in five minutes we're out of here without him."

The news put a bit of a damper on the crew, but choosing to just sit there and wait for who knows how long, was not an option. They had to go.

Almost half of the group were passed out in their seats already, the rest staring out the windows or talking quietly amongst themselves. A few true diehards were still drinking, John had done a good job of stocking the coolers, and the occasional crack and "whoosh" of a can opening could still be heard.

Eventually the bus rumbled to life and began the long trek home. Gary took his seat beside Mary. She was looking a little worse for wear.

"Are you okay Mary? It's been quite a day."

"I'm good", she slurred. "Just tired."

Gary took off his coat and balled it up.

"Here, put this against the window and use this as a pillow. Try and get some sleep."

She gratefully accepted, and after a bit of trial and error positioning, she started to nod off.

"Thanks Gary, you're wunnerfulll."

He smiled and put his arm around her. If anyone was wonderful, it was her.

you don't have to say a word
it is, always
that bright shimmer in your eyes
the way that tiny musical notes
appear at the corners of your mouth
when you smile
these are the things that speak to me
and what a song
such a wonderful song
they sing

gary harrison

A few rows up, Mel was speaking quietly with Ben. Somehow, the conversation had veered back towards Richard. Why was Ben so insistent on talking about him?

"Listen Mel, I don't want to upset you, you're one of my closest friends, but I have to be honest."

She was listening, arms crossed in front of her, no longer smiling.

"I know you don't like him, Ben. It's a common feeling. But it's not really any of your business."

"It's just that I don't like the way he treats you, the way he puts you down. You don't deserve that. I know you love him, I'm just concerned, that's all."

Mel stared out the window, not replying at first. She didn't like the way Richard condescended to her either, but he was always so stressed about work and his future that she let it pass. It was getting worse though, more frequent, and she was getting tired of his aloofness too. He was snappy with her, then silent, then all lovey-dovey. There was no consistency. She worried that he was cheating on her. He didn't seem to want to let her move in, and she was no longer sure that she wanted to anymore either.

Mel was struggling with her thoughts. What did she see in him? In him now, that is. She wasn't getting any younger, and if she was going to get married and start a family, it looked less and less likely that it would be with Richard. What was she going to do? What was she supposed to do?

"I don't know, Ben," she said to the window, "I just don't know what to do anymore."

Turning to face him again, she grabbed his hand.

"I don't like how he has changed, how he has changed me. I only know what I don't see in him anymore, a future. A future with me. I just feel so lonely, even when we are together. I need to move on."

Once she had vocalized it, heard the words, she knew she was right.

Why had it taken her so long to come to her senses?

Ben was silent, offering nothing but a kind face as he put his arm around her and pulled her close. This was not a time for words. Mel rested her head on his chest and closed her eyes. She felt so tired all of a sudden, so worn out. Though exhausted by inner turmoil, she still found sleep elusive, and spent the next hour listening to the calming sound of Ben's heart beating.

As the bus approached the US/Canada border, the sleepers were nudged awake, passports were retrieved, and silence reigned supreme. As long as nobody said or did anything stupid, they would be back in Ashington in two hours. Those still visibly drunk were warned to be on their best behaviour, and the "piss jug" was hidden from view.

There had been no more news about John, their lost leader and organizer. The few remaining drinkers tipped one out in his honour and drank up as they pulled into the inspection area. It turned out to be an uneventful crossing, and the crew were pleased that they'd be home before 9:00. As the last remnants of daylight faded, the bus picked up speed and made its way east, back to the friendly confines of the Black Horse.

Mary was awake now, still reeling a bit from all the wine she had consumed, but alert and conflicted. She needed to tell him. Tell him everything, no matter the consequences. He deserved to know the truth.

Gary looked over and smiled his lovely smile. She handed him his coat, took a deep breath and spoke the words that she had been dreading to speak.

"Gary, I have to tell you something. I'm so sorry, but you're not going to like what I have to say."

He looked at her with a calmness that surprised her.

"It's okay, don't worry. Whatever it is, I know it's been bothering you for quite a while. Just tell me. It's okay, I can take it, whatever it is."

She was on the verge of saying, *"It was nothing, never mind, I'm just being silly,"* but steeled herself instead and went on.

"It's about Stephanie. And Ryan."

Tears flowed from her eyes as she related all she

knew, all that she had found out over the past few weeks. Other than putting his hand on her shoulder to comfort her, he said and did nothing. He was still trying to comfort her! This poor, sweet man was trying to make her feel better, even as his own world crumbled around him.

After what seemed an eternity, his face changing with the conflicting emotions that coursed through him, he spoke softly as one solitary tear rolled down his cheek.

"He's my son, Mary, my baby boy. He's mine! I don't care about biology, Ryan is my son. Period. And no one is taking him away from me."

He took her hand in his, she was still shaking.

"I know how hard this must have been for you. It's not your fault, Mary, you've done nothing wrong. You're right, I believe you. I needed to know. I feel so bad though, that you had to be the one to tell me, it's not fair to you."

Gary hung his head and took several deep breaths.

"That fucking cunt, I'm going to kick the living shit out of him!"

"Don't Gary, don't do it. He'll call the police, he doesn't share your values, your sense of honour. You'll only get in trouble. You'll maybe even lose Ryan."

He was almost shaking with rage, but he knew she spoke the truth. That fucking asshole would have him charged for sure, play the "victim" all the way. And he might lose custody of Ryan. Stephanie was another story. He'd fight for all his rights with her. He knew his boss would give him all the time off he needed for court battles. Hell, he'd probably help find a good lawyer too. He would keep Ryan in his life, no matter what. And he'd never give up his role in the boy's life, ever.

"Don't worry, Mary, I was just venting," he said with exasperation. He could see the concern in her eyes, knew that this was so difficult for her, that she had actually believed he might cut off their friendship for it. "I'm glad you told me."

Mary felt as if the weight of the entire world fell off her shoulders. *He didn't hate her! He understood!*

Gary went quiet for a few minutes but didn't let go of her of her hand. Lost in thought, lost in his emotions. With a shudder, he came back and gave her hand a squeeze.

"I love you Mary, I've loved you since the day we met. I just want you to know that."

The Dog Pound were almost all present and accounted for, except for John. It was Monday afternoon and their "MIA" was starting to become an even bigger source of concern.

"What the fuck happened to John?" asked Claude.

Sammy was laughing nervously, trying to lighten the mood.

"That fucker is probably running for Mayor!"

"Just what Buffalo needs, another dumpster fire."

Gary wasn't laughing. He was staring daggers at Claude, clenching and unclenching his fists. Claude was trying his best to avoid Gary, never even glancing his way.

Rosie came by and put some appetizers in front of them. Something was off. There was too much tension in the air. Something was wrong. Maybe some free food would settle them down. Sammy looked at her and shook his head, he was just as in the dark as she was.

"What the hell, Gary. Why so down? Two tequilas please Rosie, no fruit!"

Gary thanked Sammy. Only two. Somehow Sammy knew that Claude was the source of all the tension, and wanted to let Claude know about it. Garnet and Tony were off talking in the corner, Ben was sipping a coke. Claude was keeping his mouth shut too. It was a strange atmosphere, like the calm before the storm.

Just then, as if destined, the front door of the pub opened and John rushed in, still wearing his clothes from the day before, his treasured Bills jersey stained with various colours of wing sauce.

"Holy shit guys, you'll never believe what happened!"

Like a whirling dervish, John stumbled his way to the seat that Sammy held open for him. Gary and Ben each ordered a shot for their long-lost companion and crowded around.

"Explain, motherfucker! What the hell happened? Where did you go?"

John settled himself into his seat, swallowed both shots, one after the other, ordered a beer and took a deep gulp. He had his audience just where he wanted them.

"Do you know where Buffalo chicken wings originated from?"

Over the next hour John recounted his tale, acting out most of the important moments with flailing arms.

Bonding with the locals sitting in front of him at the game, John had impressed them with his Buffalo Bills knowledge and love for the team. They in turn had regaled him with tales of their trips to Toronto, and their love of the cheap Canadian dollar. When John mentioned that he'd always wanted to visit the Anchor Bar, where "Buffalo chicken wings" were first created, his new friends bundled him up and dragged him out of the stadium to visit the legendary place.

Once ensconced on the heated patio and plied with two-dollar beers, John had proceeded to not only tell every joke he knew, but learned a few new ones too. Somewhere along the way he'd lost his phone, but his new friends had sworn upon a bible that they'd get him back to the stadium in time for the bus. It must have been an abridged version, because when he asked when they'd get him back, he was met with cries of "drink, drink, drink!"

So, he did, and he made Canada proud!

"I slept on someone's couch, got up and took a cab to the bus station. From there I went to Niagara

Falls and walked across the border. Then I hopped on the Go Train, then a Go Bus, then finally a cab. I'm not one hundred percent certain, but I'm pretty sure I robbed the whole lot of those guys!"

With that, John opened his wallet to show a mass of American money, mostly twenties and tens, but there were a few fifties and even a couple of hundreds in there as well.

"I have almost a thousand bucks!"

To the collected laughs and cheers of those present he exclaimed with pride, "Rosie, a round of drinks on me!"

Gary was speechless, Ben was clapping, and Sammy was mock bowing in front of him.

"You, my friend, are a fucking legend!"

A Black Horse Happy New Year!

It was New Year's Day and Rosie was alone in the Black Horse pub, starting the big clean up from last night's celebrations. Hopefully, Mel and Nancy would be arriving shortly to give her some help. This was far too big a job for one person to handle, especially one slightly hungover person, no matter how energetic and happy she happened to be feeling inside. Dylan would definitely not be offering his assistance today, not in the condition he'd been in when she'd last laid eyes on him. She'd be lucky if he managed to make it in for his bar shift tonight!

The pub would not be opening until 2:00 pm today. This gave her almost three hours to get everything squared away and shipshape before her regulars eventually made their way back to the scene of their many New Year's Eve shenanigans.

What a crazy night it had been. For her most of all! What a wonderful, crazy night.

"FIVE, FOUR, THREE, TWO, ONE… ***HAPPY NEW YEAR***!"

With the cacophony of noisemakers, combined with the cheers and delighted screams of celebration coming from each and every reveller ringing in her ears, Rosie turned to her left and decided to just go for it. It was a tradition after all, what did she have to lose?

Grabbing Sammy in her arms, or as much of him as she could grasp, she shouted into his ear, "Happy New Year Sammy!" and proceeded to give him a nice, big kiss on the lips. She felt even giddier when Sammy had hugged her back, prolonging their kiss for a few seconds longer than typical in these situations. His initial look of surprise had quickly turned to one of pure delight.

"Happy New Year, Rosie."
And then he had simply smiled at her with a charmingly shy expression that she'd never seen cross his face in all the years she'd known him. This was the boy inside the man, Sammy finally letting his guard down.
"That was very nice," he added.
So, she kissed him again.

Earlier that night…

With the Dog Pound fully present and accounted for, and knocking back their drinks with ruthless efficiency, Gary and John turned the discussion back to Mel and the end of her relationship with Richard Wainright.
"It's about time she finally dumped that douchebag," John stated yet again. "Good for her!"
"He never deserved her," added Gary. "Not the way he treated her."
Mel was working the floor, selling shots and serving the dinners that were included with the Black Horse's New Year's Eve party package, which included free champagne at midnight. The guys were all looking at her now. She seemed to be holding up pretty well by the looks of things. They'd all heard about the incident that had taken place just a few hours ago and were concerned.
Earlier in the day, Mel had had another big public bust-up with Richard, this time in the pub. She was pissed that he had not invited her to attend the big New Year's Eve Charity Gala at the country club with him that night as promised. He'd only told her she wouldn't be going the day before, after she'd already purchased a brand new dress and shoes for the party. Mel couldn't believe that after all she had done for him, all her support for him over the years - she wouldn't be going to "the biggest party of the year" in Ashington. It was the straw that finally broke the

camel’s back.
She had accused him of cheating on her, of being embarrassed to be with her because she worked at the local pub, and wasn’t good enough for all the hoity-toity people at the club. Just throwing everything against the wall to see what would stick. All her rage and frustrations burst out in a stream of emotion.
“Fuck you, asshole! We are done. We’re finished! I never want to see you again!”
After storming out of his house, she had called Rosie to let her know she’d be able to work New Year’s Eve after all, and to vent about her breakup with Richard. Rosie had listened to everything she said, offering both sympathy and righteous indignation, assuring Mel that it was the right thing to do, she’d be better off without that “piece of shit” in her life.
As the Black Horse staff was setting up and preparing the room for their New Year’s Eve party, Richard had showed up, barging into the pub and demanding that Mel return all the jewelry that he had bought her throughout the course of their relationship.
“Are you for real? It’s mine, I’ll do with it want I want, even if that means throwing it away!”
“Give it back. Or else!” Richard had fumed.
“Or else what?” Rosie interrupted. “What are you going to do?”
Richard looked from Rosie to Mel and then back to Rosie again, sneering.
“Stay out of this Rosie, it’s none of your fucking business!”
“Get out of here Richard, you’re not welcome here. You are not welcome in my pub. Ever!”
Mel had started to sob quietly, embarrassed for what was happening, angry with herself for not realizing just how toxic her relationship with Richard had become.

"Just leave, Richard. Just get the hell out."

"Not until you give me what I want. I'm taking you home to get my jewelry. Then you can come back to this shithole and hang out with the rest of your asshole friends!"

With the expectation of a wild night ahead, most of the regulars had gone home to get some rest. As a result, the Black Horse was almost empty. Almost.

As Richard made to grab Mel and physically drag her out the door, Sammy rushed over from the bar, flying past a shocked Rosie and pushing Richard against the wall. Before he could even react, Sammy delivered a short but fierce punch just below Richard's rib cage. As all the air flowed out of him in one long groan, Sammy held Richard up against the wall with one strong hand, the other squeezing his jaw and pushing his head back even further.

"Listen carefully and listen good. If you ever set foot in here again, I'm going to hurt you real bad. I will fucking cripple you. You'll never walk properly or swing a fucking golf club for the rest of your life."

As Richard started to struggle, Sammy squeezed harder, staring into Richard's frightened eyes, hissing, "And if you ever lay a finger on either of these women, I promise I will fucking kill you. Do you understand?"

Richard's eyes flashed anger, despite his position of helplessness.

"I don't think he's getting the message, Mel."

With another lightning quick movement, Sammy struck the heel of his hand into Richard's Adam's apple, dropping him to the floor in a spasm of choking cries and gasps for breath.

"Sammy, no!" shouted both Rosie and Mel in unison, attempting to pull him back from the prone man on the floor.

"I think he gets the message now."

The two women bent to help the struggling Richard

to his feet.

"Just go Richard, get out of here," Mel said flatly. "We're done, you should be happy about that."

"And don't even think about going to the cops about this, Richie. That would be a very stupid idea. It would really upset me," said Sammy as Rosie opened the door for Wainright. "That would not be a wise thing to do."

After the door closed behind him, Rosie turned to Sammy.

"You shouldn't have done that. You could have killed him."

Sammy looked down for a moment, sighing, then gently placed a hand on each of their shoulders.

"I'm sorry you had to see that, but I know what I'm doing. Trust me, he's not hurt, there won't even be a mark anywhere on him. I just scared him, made it difficult to breathe for a few seconds, that's all. He'll be alright, don't you worry."

"You still shouldn't have done it," Rosie said, more gently this time, then punching him playfully in the arm with a smile. "What are we going to do with you, you big oaf. It's not like I can ban you!"

Mel had finally regained her composure and gave Sammy a big hug that ended with a soft kiss on his cheek.

"Thank you, Sammy."

As he reddened, she stood back, holding her fists up in front of her and laughed.

"Can you teach me how to do that?"

"Sammy fucked him up good, that's what I heard," said John.

"I'm not sure that's true," Gary replied.

He had spoken to Mel when he'd arrived. She'd looked a bit frazzled, so he had asked her if everything was alright.

"I'm better than alright, Gary. I feel great, I

feel…free."

Mel had given him the bullet point explanation of what had occurred earlier. He couldn't hide his shock with the news.

"Please don't make a big deal about it. I'm sure it'll get out but let's not worry about it tonight, okay."

"Don't worry Mel, it's all good."

Gary understood, probably better than anyone else. He'd just put an end to his relationship with Stephanie, their "together" relationship anyway. He'd be dealing with the fallout of Stephanie's betrayal for a long time, but he wanted to keep it civil for Ryan's sake. He had his doubts that she would be able to keep herself under control, but he didn't have much choice. They both loved their son. They'd have to find a way to make it as painless and as seamless as possible for little Ryan. To both share in raising him and to still spend some time together as a family, even if they'd be living apart.

He was fortunate to have found another place so quickly. John had spoken to the management at his building, and when a unit would become available in a month's time, Gary would be able to move in. In the meantime, he was sleeping on his co-worker Cameron's couch. He'd left his car for Stephanie to use, except when he would take Ryan out. She'd actually appreciated his generosity, which was a positive sign as they moved forward. She would be moving back to her mother's place soon, he couldn't afford to pay two rents, but it was a separate apartment within the home, and she'd have all the additional care and support from her mom she needed.

His life, on the other hand, was currently in so much turmoil he didn't quite know what to do. He was conflicted about everything. He was struggling to control his anger towards Claude, coming close on several occasions to physical violence, but he remembered Mary's advice and resisted the impulse. It hurt, but not as much as getting arrested and losing Ryan would hurt. Claude knew that he was pissed off at him, but he hadn't let on the reason why. He doubted that Claude even cared, but not being able to get some form of revenge really stung.

"He's not worth it," Mary had said.

Maybe that was true, it sounded like sensible advice, but it didn't feel right, it felt as wrong as wrong could be.

None of the other guys knew specifically what was up, or why Gary was so pissed at Claude, they just figured it was Claude being Claude and did their best to keep themselves between the pair. Gary didn't want anybody to know about it, about the real reason for his conflict with Claude. There was no question of where their loyalty lay though. They'd made that clear to Gary with the recent increase in their offhand remarks and gibes at Claude's expense.

He was conflicted about Mary too. *Why had he confessed his love for her on the way back from Buffalo? Why had he been so freaking stupid?*

Whether it was the beer buzz, the incredible closeness between them that he'd felt that day, or simply the weight of what she had told him on the bus, he just couldn't help himself. "*In vino veritas,*" he supposed, but Mary had appeared a little shocked by his confession and the last thing he needed was to lose her friendship on top of all he was dealing with.

She had called him a few days after the trip to see how he was holding up. They'd both skirted around what he had said to her, focusing on Gary's immediate problems, until Mary eventually touched on it.

"I care about you too Gary, I care deeply, but with all you are dealing with right now I don't think the time is right to be jumping into anything so suddenly. You need to focus on yourself right now."

He had understood what she was saying, it was exactly the type of advice he would probably offer her in the same situation. He, his emotions, everything, were all over the place, and only a fool would want to place herself in that environment. And Mary was no fool. She was the most sensible person he had ever met. He figured he'd blown it for sure, which saddened him even more.

"You're right Mary, I'm so sorry. I should have just kept my big mouth shut. Let's pretend the whole thing never happened, okay?"

As if that was ever going to be even remotely possible.

"Don't start getting all self-pitiful on me now, Gary, it doesn't suit you, it's not who you are. I'm just looking out for you. I hope you understand that. You need me to be honest with you right now, we've always been honest with one another, that's why we're so close. I value our friendship more than anything, you have to know that. I don't know how I would have made it through this past year without you. Maybe we have a future together, maybe not. I don't know, but I really hope we do because I love spending time with you. All I'm saying is that we shouldn't rush into anything until you take some time and are sure about exactly what it is you want."

"I understand Mary, I really do. You mean the world to me too. I don't want you to feel all weirded out and uncomfortable by all this though, or to worry about me. I'll be fine, no matter what."

"It's for the best dear Gary. I'll see you soon, okay?"

"Okay, thanks for calling. See you soon."

Gary's feelings were hurt a little, but he had to admit she was right. Now was not the time to feel sorry for himself. He needed to focus on sorting everything out with Stephanie and Ryan and getting his life back on track. She was just being a good friend and that's what he needed most right now. If only it didn't make him love her even more.

When Gary had seen her at the Black Horse a couple

of days later, their initial awkwardness was quickly washed away by the genuine affection and comfort they felt for each other. They talked and laughed and enjoyed their shared time together, just as they did before, not mentioning Claude or Stephanie once. Gary felt relieved, even as he confirmed his love was not an illusion. He could wait. Mary was worth it.

"I meant what I said," she had whispered to him before leaving, placing her hand upon his for a moment before adding, "If, and when, the time is right, we'll know."

"Yo no soy esa que tú te imaginas
Una señorita tranquila y sencilla
Que un día abandonas y siempre perdona
Esa niña si, no
Esa no soy yo…"

"Wow, Rosie! Where did you find this band?" asked Ben. "They're amazing!"

A trio of musicians; keyboard, drums and guitar, were accompanying a beautiful, dark-haired, Latina woman, who was entertaining the Black Horse crowd with a series of classic standards, singing in several languages depending on the song. Her sultry voice and exotic presence held the room rapt, with thunderous applause and whoops erupting after each new song.

"Evelyn and I saw them play downtown when we were doing some 'research' about six months ago. I figured they'd be perfect for tonight, so I booked them on the spot!"

"Are they ever, I've never seen or heard anything quite like this before! You're a genius!"

Rosie smiled at Ben's enthusiasm, and from what she was seeing, the rest of the pub was feeling the same way. It had been a bit of a gamble to bring in this type of entertainment, but for New Year's Eve she wanted something special for all her loyal regulars and guests. Her heart swelled with pride in knowing that everyone was enjoying the band as much as she had, and was again. Garnet was actually tapping his feet on his stool, without a single mention of the evils of immigration! He'd even requested a song, "*Can't Take My Eyes Off Of You*", dutifully performed by the stunning chanteuse. John was mesmerized, partially by the wonderful music, "not classic rock, but not bad", he claimed, more so by the singer herself.

"I bet she has the sexiest feet. Do you think she'd let me see her toes?"

"Not in a million years, pal!" Sammy replied laughing. "Try to behave yourself tonight, will you."

Maidali, the singer and leader of the group, was originally from the Dominican Republic, and performed an amazing range of music, from "*I Want You Back*" to "*The Sound of Silence*", and everything in between, including a stunning version of "*The Tennessee Waltz*". Having just finished "*Yo No Soy Esa*", the band thanked their audience and took a break before their final post-midnight set. The Black Horse celebrants, especially the Dog Pound crew, were excitedly getting ready for the arrival of the big countdown. She'd never seen the place so energetic. Rosie had been worried about Mel, keeping an eye on her for signs of trouble, but she seemed to be having a great time too.

Rosie waved the band over to the bar to see if they needed anything to drink. As they approached, Maidali was intercepted by Claude. She couldn't quite hear what he was saying, but he kept leaning in closer and closer, eventually placing his hand on her shoulder. Maidali's expression soon changed from a curious smile to a frown. Just as Rosie was about to rush over and intervene, Claude began whispering in her ear.

"Oh no," said Rosie.

All of a sudden, the elegant singer reared back and with an audible "smack", punched Claude square in the face! Those within ear and eye shot looked on in stunned amusement as Claude stumbled backwards against John, blood gushing from his nose and staining his crisp white dress shirt. After a moment, a round of applause burst forth from the crowd surrounding the wounded Claude, including Rosie herself. That made two jerks receiving swift and deserved justice within the last six hours. What an unforgettably crazy day this was turning out to be!

"What a punch! Did you see that?" Dylan shouted, laughing hysterically. "That was awesome!"

"She should have kicked him in the nuts," added John. "Put those gorgeous feet to good use!"

Now smiling contentedly, Maidali sidled up to Rosie.

"Some people have no manners. Soon they learn though," she said with her wonderfully accented English.

"You're a very good teacher, my dear," Rosie replied as they both giggled.

They watched happily together as the crowd parted to allow Claude passage to the washroom to clean himself up, repeating all the way, "She broke by dose, she broke by dose."

Tony and Rhonda were sitting comfortably in the snug they had reserved for New Year's Eve, holding hands and sipping the last of their wine. It was just past 2:00 am, the crowd was quickly thinning out, and as he reflected on the night, he couldn't imagine it having gone any better. Seeing that beautiful woman smack Claude had been the icing on the cake. That poor bastard ended up leaving before midnight to howls of laughter and the classic, "Na-na-na-na, Na-na-na-na, hey, hey…goodbye!" from the crowd at the bar. He could only imagine what that idiot had said to piss her off like that.

Tony still hadn't decided when to tell Rhonda his big news, the best news he'd had in ages. A consortium had made a very generous offer to purchase Garnet's land for multiuse development. If he told her, she'd want him to start spending money right away, lots of it, and he was still technically broke. He'd have to play this one just right to keep her on the hook. She knew nothing about his gambling debts either. He'd have to figure out how to massage that news into the ongoing situation as well. It could be a deal breaker, so he'd have to tread very lightly, or better yet, bury it completely.

He'd done a little research on the developers, and with access to their planning proposition he'd discovered that a huge mosque was going to be a big part of the development. The region had been trying to find a suitable location for the mosque, a difficult task with the opposition from constituents and private landowners, and not enough suitable public lands available. Knowing this, he'd been able to play hardball and get well over the going rate for Garnet's 200 acres. On top of that was the extra 2% commission he'd snuck into his agreement with the naïve old farmer. He stood to make a killing, over half a million dollars! He'd been sitting on this offer for a week or so, but having spoken to Garnet quickly the day before, and after advising him to accept the offer, without mentioning anything about a mosque, it looked like it was pretty much a done deal. The old farmer seemed greatly relieved, thanking him for his help. He would become a very wealthy man indeed. It would still be a few months before the closing date, when he'd finally see his commission, but it seemed that the weight of the world was finally sliding off his shoulders.

What a whirlwind the last month had been for him, what an absolute roller coaster ride! Tony was so confident that his luck had changed that he had called Gerry the Bookie to let him know roughly when to expect his debt to be fully paid off. He still didn't know what Sammy had said to scare those goons off, but he figured they'd be back sooner or later, and Sammy might not be there when they did.

Gerry had begrudgingly accepted his terms, with a definite warning about his life being worthless if he didn't come through this time. There was still menace in his voice, but Gerry appeared to be pleased about the big commission, and finally getting his money, plus interest, back soon.

He glanced over at Sammy, sitting at the bar talking to Rosie. Just what the hell had he said to Gerry's men? Whatever it had been, he definitely owed him one. A strange guy that Sammy, he never mentioned the incident or held it over him at all. It was as if it never happened.

As Rhonda put her head on his shoulder, murmuring, "Let's get out of here, babe," he kissed the top of her head.

"Yeah, let's scoot. The Uber will be here any minute."

Having seen the last of the staff and revellers out the door, Rosie locked up the Black Horse doors and let Sammy walk her to her waiting cab. After one final kiss, she closed the door and watched him wave as the taxi pulled out of the parking lot.

"Happy New Year, Rosie," she said to herself. "What a Happy, Happy New Year."

Meanwhile, back in the snug...

Meanwhile, back in the snug, Tommy and Jack were quietly sipping their second pints of the afternoon, just recently dropped off with a scowl by the irascible Nancy.

"Why'd you have to go and piss her off like that again?" Jack asked.

"I don't know what you mean," Tommy replied as wide-eyed and innocently as possible. "All I said was that I've had faster service from a drunken, three-legged sloth. It's not my fault she's fucking slow."

Jack just shook his head, trying not to laugh out loud and draw further attention to the pair of them. Nancy was fully capable of unleashing her unique brand of misery on their lives when properly motivated. They'd weathered several of those "storms" before and it definitely wasn't fun.

"By the way Jack, how are your daughter and grandkids getting along on their visit?"

Tommy was smartly trying to steer the conversation back to safer waters.

Jack's daughter, Shelley, and her husband, along with their four year old twins, Bobby and Christopher, were in town for two weeks on their annual visit. They'd moved out west a few years ago, just north of Vancouver, and he really missed having them around. He loved seeing Shelly and Brian again, and playing the doting Grandpa to the two boys. They all loved spending their time with him too.

"The house is bursting at the seams, Tommy! Emma is cooking for an army and running herself ragged, but we wouldn't have it any other way. And I'm catching back up on Sesame Street each morning with the lads. Shelley loved that program too when she was their age. You know, Big Bird, Oscar the Grouch, Ernie and Bert, the whole gang."

"Ernie and Bert are gay you know," Tommy said matter of factly.

"What the hell are you on about you bloody fool? Gay? They're frigging puppets for Christ's sake. How could they possibly be gay?"

"Just saying, Jack. Two men, sharing a room like that. No girlfriends. Have you seen the way they look at each other?"

"You are absolutely insane! How do you even know that they're adults to begin with? Puppets aren't real. They don't have romantic relationships with anyone. They don't even have sexual orientations. I'm pretty fucking sure they don't have penises either, you deviant old bastard. They're just puppets."

"I'm not saying there's anything wrong with it, Jack, settle down. But you're wrong, don't kid yourself. Isn't Kermit the Frog boinking Miss Piggy? Doesn't Oscar the Grouch have a girlfriend too, Grundgetta! They wallow in filth together. Shamelessly! Ernie and Bert are gay as the day is long. How can you not see it?"

"Tommy, you've completely lost it."

"Let me finish! Bert watches Ernie have baths. Ernie sits on Bert's lap all the time. They're always exchanging little gifts. They love each other! In the morning when Bert tries to read the paper; and by the way, what kid reads the morning paper, Ernie always annoys him by trying to talk to him. Just like an old married couple, Jack! You know it's true! And I for one am very happy for them. You should be too. Don't be so damned intolerant!"

With that said, after a few stunned seconds of silence, Tommy burst out laughing, tears in his eyes. "Oh Jack, you should see the look on your face. You are like the proverbial deer in the headlights!"

Jack could not help but stare at his friend with a confused look on his face. How he always managed to let Tommy wind him up like this he'd never know. He had to admit defeat yet again and joined in with a

howl of laughter and a shake of his head.
"How the hell do you know so much about Sesame Street you crazy old bastard? That's the scariest part of this whole thing! You are totally demented, and I mean that in only the ugliest possible way!"
Tommy nodded in response, "Ha, you want to see demented?" He then gestured towards Nancy, who was serving drinks to another table across the room. "Use your imagination then. Gay or straight, would you?"
Jack's reply was almost immediate and delivered with as much solemnity as could possibly be mustered under the current conditions.
"Not even with Kermit's big, green, amphibious dick!"
The sound of their raucous laughter was soon shattered by a shrill, Banshee-like cry, "I heard that!" coming from across the room.
Tommy and Jack looked at each other in semi-mock horror. They knew they were in trouble and that the rest of their day was not going to be as pleasant as they'd hoped.
Jack leaned forward and whispered to his friend, "Today's Black Horse visit is brought to you by the letter 'F', as in today we are absolutely fucking fucked!"
A few moments later, Nancy sidled by, glaring daggers as she collected their un-finished pint glasses from the table.
"Wrong! It's brought to you by the letter 'A', for assholes! Now who's laughing, you dirty old dogs?"
As Jack and Tommy looked up with the admonished looks of young schoolboys caught passing notes, Nancy turned and made her way to the bar to replace their drinks, barely concealing her own big smile the entire way.

Sammy's Investigation

Sammy was having a tough time dealing with what he had just heard. He was upset, of course, but didn't want to let Rosie know exactly why. The news that Mel had confided to Rosie, that she had now confided to him, was so sad and tragic enough all on its own, there was no need for him to add further with his unconfirmed suspicions.

Ben's family, his wife and young daughter, had been killed in a hit and run accident two years ago in downtown Toronto. His heart broke for the senseless, overwhelming pain that his new friend must have gone through, and obviously was still was.

"Oh Rosie, that is such a terrible tragedy. The poor guy, no wonder he's always been so quiet and downhearted."

The two of them were talking quietly in the Black Horse. It was just after 11:00 on a Tuesday morning, so they pretty much had the place to themselves for the moment. Sammy had made an off-hand remark about the noticeable change that had come over Ben in the past few weeks, his increased sociability and more positive outlook. Rosie sat down beside him, and as was her way with these types of chats, leaned in so as not to be overheard by any prying "ears".

"I think Mel is finally working her magic, Sammy. I'm so glad to see him start to move on. He's still so young."

With that said, she explained to Sammy that Mel and Ben and Ben's wife, Lydia, had all been friends together in high school, that's why Mel was the only one who ever really talked to Ben in the pub. She fought back tears as she explained what had happened to shatter Ben's life.

"It's so sad what happened to Lydia and their wee Annabelle, so terribly sad. That poor young man, what he had to deal with. I couldn't imagine what he must have gone through."

Sammy listened intently as Rosie related the details of the accident. The two of them out for an early morning walk to the beach, taking advantage of the nice fall weather to watch the birds feeding. Ben, already at his job site, was unaware that a speeding car had apparently blown through a stop sign, sending them flying. The driver, probably drunk, not having the decency to stop and help, or even call 9-1-1. The lack of witnesses or intersection cameras put the investigation into a deep hole from which they were never able to escape from. The only piece of evidence found at the scene was a fragment from a headlight assembly bracket and some pieces of shattered glass lodged in their hair. Experts determined that the headlight bracket was from a late-model Lexus, black in colour, but they couldn't pin it down to anything more than that.

As Rosie continued to relate the known facts of the tragedy, Sammy's mind was racing, his senses screaming out to him in unison.

"What was the date of the accident, Rosie? Do you know?"

"October 13th. That's what Mel said."

Sammy watched the news regularly, but a random hit and run accident in Toronto would not have made much of an impression on him. Unfortunately, it was not that uncommon an incident for the big city. He hadn't even known Ben back then and only now was he learning about this tragedy. But the rest of the details felt familiar to him.

A little over two years ago. Mid-October. Black Lexus. Shattered windshield and broken headlight. Could it be?
Claude.

Sammy finished the last of his beer, but as Rosie

went to re-fill his glass, he waved her off.
"I have to take care of something back at the shop, Rosie. I'll see you later."
"Okay Sammy, I'll still be here."
Rosie smiled and watched him leave her pub. It must be something important for him to leave so soon. He did seem a little distracted though. Hopefully it was nothing serious.
"Better get back to stocking that fridge," she said to herself.
Sammy sat in his office, more a glorified storage room than anything, with a series of files on his makeshift desk. It may look like chaos, but his filing system worked for him, and that's all that mattered. He could find anything he needed at the drop of a hat. Sammy always kept meticulous records of his work. He was staring at the open folder in front of him, and the parts orders it contained. They matched. So did the date.
The memories came flooding back with startling clarity. He was right, he knew it, and now he thought he might be able to prove it.

On October 13th, two and a half years ago, Claude had called him early in the morning in an absolute panic. He'd struck a deer on the highway and shattered his windshield. Could he fix it, fix it right away? He didn't want to go through insurance. When he arrived at the shop, Sammy had Claude bring the car into his main bay.
"Must have been a big fucking deer!" exclaimed Sammy.
The windshield was indeed badly damaged, and some blood stains still remained visible. That deer must have exploded on impact. There was some front-end and hood damage as well, nothing too serious though. His "body guy" would make it good as new, once the parts arrived of course.
Claude had been acting strange, very nervous,

muttering to himself. He looked dishevelled, he was sweating, was really shaken up. He also slightly reeked of alcohol. It must have been a good night for him.

"Relax, man, it'll be okay. We'll have you up and running in a day or so."

"I need it done fast, Sammy. Please, I need my car back soon."

Sammy threw a number out, a large number given the rush. Cash. Claude didn't even hesitate, nodding his acceptance immediately. He was good for it, Sammy knew. That's why it felt a bit strange. He could easily afford a rental for a few days or even a week. Why the rush?

"Come by tomorrow evening. We'll have it done." Two days was just enough time for a job like this.

"Thank you, Sammy. I'll drop off the cash later today. You're a life saver."

When Sammy had popped into the Black Horse later that day, Claude was there. From the state of him, he must have been there all day. He'd never seen him so drunk before. Hitting that deer must have affected him more than he figured. Yes, it was a scary thing to have happen, but he'd thought Claude was made of much sterner stuff.

Upon seeing him, Mel had immediately approached Sammy and asked him for help in getting Claude into a cab and sending him home. He'd been cut off and wasn't taking the news very well, arguing belligerently with the entire staff. It was only Sammy's entrance that had calmed him down.

"Claude, come on. I'll run you home myself."

Claude resisted at first, but Sammy picked him up by the shirt and marched him out into the late afternoon sunshine.

"Get a hold of yourself, Claude!" he hissed. "You're embarrassing yourself. It was only a fucking deer."

At this, Claude had stopped and swallowed hard,

staring straight ahead. A single tear rolled down his cheek, but he shook it off.

"Yeah, just a deer. Thanks Sammy, thanks. Let's go."

"You're fine Claude, it's going to be okay. Your car will be fixed tomorrow. Be a fucking man."

"Please don't tell anyone about this Sammy, about the deer. Please. I'm so embarrassed."

"Don't worry Claude, no one needs to know."

Sammy had driven Claude straight home before returning to the Black Horse. "What a fucking pussy," he thought, but as a man of his word he'd said nothing to the other guys about Claude's accident.

Claude returned and picked up his car the next day, as scheduled, displaying again his gratitude. Sammy and his crew had worked fast, and the results were nearly perfect. You would never know that the car had even been scratched.

Claude had also gone on a two-week bender, getting dropped off in a cab, then getting shit-faced in the Black Horse all afternoon, keeping to himself for the most part. He'd stopped shaving and his usual natty clothes became wrinkled, as he mechanically downed drink after drink in a desperate effort to get obliterated.

Eventually, it reached the point that Rosie had to step in. She banned him for a month and told him that if he didn't "smarten up and smarten up soon!" the ban would be extended permanently.

The tough love must have worked, as about a month later he popped into the pub one evening, back to his normal confident and obnoxious self.

Sammy had observed the whole transformation happen and was happy that Claude had finally recovered from his frightful experience. He'd also noticed that Claude had purchased a new car. Another black Lexus. *Why would he have the old one fixed so quickly if he was just going to get a new one?* And it wasn't even that old, he'd bought it new only three years ago.

When he questioned Claude about it, he said the lease was coming up anyway, why not get a new one now, rather than later. Come to think of it, Sammy hadn't seen the old car since Claude had picked it up from his shop that day. Strange. The whole thing had felt a little odd, but who was he to decide what Claude did with his vehicle. To each his own. At least the Dog Pound was back to normal, or as "normal" as this group of misfits could ever be.

Sitting at his desk, Sammy considered what his next move should be. After much careful consideration, he made his decision. Pulling the middle drawer of his desk completely out, he recovered a piece of paper that had been folded and taped to the back of the drawer. It contained nothing but a single row of numbers. Using a simple "shift" cypher, he converted the numbers to another set, a phone number. Taking a deep breath, he pulled a burner phone from out of a different drawer, plugged it in and dialed.

"I want to speak to Superintendent Ronan Gibbs. Tell him it's Kresimir Jurisic. He can reach me at this number."

Sammy was sitting on a bench in Sunnybrook Park, a large, snow covered field in front of him, as he waited for RCMP Superintendent Gibbs. It had been many years since the two had last met, and it had been Inspector Gibbs back then. Sammy too had been an Inspector, with the Croatian National Police force. With a large multi-national team cobbled together through Interpol, he had worked for years to bring down a notoriously brutal human trafficking ring. Working undercover, Sammy had infiltrated the group who preyed on young women, even children, from Eastern Europe and forced them into prostitution and slavery all over the world. The evidence that Sammy had managed to put together was enough to take down some of the groups top leaders and put a massive dent in their operations. Or, it would have been. The criminal organization had been more sophisticated than any of them imagined, with tendrils and informants in many of the police forces of the different countries themselves. When they swept in to make their surprise arrests, they were in fact walking into a trap. Their operation had been betrayed, and Sammy was very fortunate to have escaped with his life. Three other officers were not so lucky, it had been a bloodbath. A big price had been placed on Sammy's head, and these people would stop at nothing to get their revenge. Sammy, his wife, and young son were moved and put into the witness protection program, but Sammy knew it was only a matter of time before they would be discovered and executed. Europe was not a big enough, or safe enough, place for them.

RCMP Inspector Gibbs was tasked with creating new identities for Sammy and his family, providing for a new life and future in Canada, where they would finally be safe. His wife, however, refused to go. Their marriage was irreparably broken, as she could never forgive Sammy for putting them all in danger, for not placing them above his job. He didn't blame her, he understood. They were victims too, and it was all his fault. She, and his boy Frano, went into a protective program somewhere else and he had no idea where. It was better that way, there would be no further contact between them. They were simply more collateral damage, more innocents suffering for the crimes of the animals who trafficked in human misery. Not a day went by, however, without Sammy thinking about them, wondering how they were, where they were. He took solace at least in knowing they were safe.

He saw Gibbs making his way across the field, waiting patiently with hands in his pockets, as the Superintendent slogged through the snow.

"Couldn't find a more convenient location? Maybe one with hot coffee and some heat."

The two men shook hands.
"Superintendent! You must be getting on very well now."
Sammy was genuinely happy for his former colleague. Patting him on his protruding belly, he added, "Maybe too well."
Gibbs laughed at the slight. "Working behind a desk all these years does take its toll. You still look fighting fit though."
Pleasantries aside, the two men got down to business.
"What did you want to talk about Sammy? Is everything alright up there in Ashington?"
"It's all good, no problems there. I need your help on something unrelated. You still have good contacts in the Toronto Police?"
Sammy detailed the history of Ben's family and the unsolved hit and run accident, and his suspicions about Claude's involvement. He pulled an envelope from his jacket pocket, purchase orders and the repair invoice for the work done on Claude's car.
"Get these to whoever needs to see them Ronan. It might be enough to re-open the investigation, bring this asshole to justice."
"If he's guilty. Maybe he really did hit a deer."
Sammy glared at his former colleague.
"He did it. I can feel it. Just do as I ask, please."
The Superintendent took the envelope from Sammy and placed it into his own pocket.
"I'll see what I can do, I know just the man for this. He's a tenacious fucking bulldog. Just like you."
"Thank you, Ronan. This guy, Ben. He deserves closure."
Gibbs put a hand on Sammy's shoulder.
"While I have you here, let me ask you something. The credit cards we provide for you, why don't you ever use them? We've renewed them many times, but

they've never made a single purchase."

"I make my own way. I don't need them."

"You've earned them Sammy. You deserve to be compensated for all that you did, what you went through. What you lost. It's the least Interpol can do. Same with the passports. You've never gone anywhere, taken a holiday." He waved at the frozen field all around them. "Look at this shit, why don't you head down to Mexico or something and lie on the beach for a change. Enjoy yourself."

"They're still looking Ronan, they'll never stop."

"Your new identity is safe, Sammy, they won't ever connect you to it. It's been almost fifteen years now."

All Sammy could remember was the ambush in the "safe house", the bullets flying, the blood, the bodies dropping all around him, the betrayal. He'd been told he was safe before. He'd believed it then. He'd never believe it again. He didn't want to leave a record of his new name anywhere. No scan at the border, no traceable purchases, nothing. He craved anonymity. It kept him alive.

"Just get this information to the right person. If they need to get in touch with me, have them call the shop."

He reached out and shook Superintendent Gibbs' hand.

"And let me live my life, my way. I appreciate what you've said, Ronan, I do. I'm good as is. Things are working out okay. No need to tempt fate."

With a nod, Gibbs slowly made his way back across the large, snowy field. Sammy turned and made his way down through the forested hillside to his parked car, with the ease of an expert mountaineer. He liked his shortcuts. And his escape routes.

Rhonda & Tony - A Match Made In Heaven

The romance between Tony and Rhonda was the talk of the town – just the way they liked it. Little did they know the chatter they were the subject of wasn't exactly as expected.

"Do you see those two twits over there?" Garnet could sometimes be heard yammering at the bar as he stared toward the snug. "Two arses in love," he'd continue with a hoarse laugh.

While the bar's grump couldn't help but focus on the couple's sleazy demeanor, everyone else at the Black Horse could see right through that and knew who each of them really were.

Claude had vented to The Dog Pound about Rhonda on more than one occasion.

"Ugh, I can't stand that bitch," he proclaimed loudly one day.

"Why? 'Cause she won't screw yah," John teased him back.

"I wouldn't touch her with a ten-foot pole!" Claude replied, something everyone knew was a lie, since Claude would sleep with just about anything that could walk.

"She's just a pretentious bitch. I've heard she's living in her mother's basement down on Sparrow. Can you believe that? She acts like she's the queen of this god damn town, yet she doesn't even have her own house!"

"That can't be true! I thought she was loaded, she's a Wallace!" Garnet said back in shock.

"Jesus, where the hell have you been, old boy? Her husband ditched her for some hot piece of ass and took off down south," Claude replied smugly.

Garnet looked over to Sammy for some validity, as he always seemed to have a secret low-down of people in this town.

"It's true, pal. I heard that too," Sammy said looking down.

Garnet went on, "And now she's fucking around with that tool? Ha, what is she thinking?"

"Isn't it obvious? She thinks he's rich," Gary piped up. "She may be nice to look at but she ain't the sharpest tool in the shed."

He'd gotten this intel from his pal Mary. She'd been unintentionally eavesdropping on the two for weeks now when they sat in the snug. She couldn't help but chuckle about it with Gary when they would chat.

"Think about it guys, we all know Tony's full of shit. But if you didn't know any better you might not."

"Well if that's the case, you're right, Gary. She's definitely not the brightest crayon in the box," John chimed in with an eyeroll.

The relationship between Tony and Rhonda started off slow, for all of a month or so. But after that, they were full speed ahead. Rhonda tried to be sneaky with Tony, she still wanted him to think she was well off and not just a desperate gold-digging divorcee. This made it all the more easy for Tony to be just as sneaky with Rhonda. He filled their conversations with his bullshit stories of closing multi-million dollar deals downtown and she ate it all up.
Rhonda couldn't have Tony knowing she lived in her mother's basement and so they spent most of their date nights together at hotels in the city.
Tony would manage to scrape up enough money to get them set up somewhere decent, he would explain spending time together downtown made more sense since he was there all the time for work. He was too embarrassed for Rhonda to ever see the mediocre bungalow he owned outside Ashington, which hadn't been properly cleaned in, well…ever.

Rhonda had something she wanted to bring up Tony

but wasn't quite sure how to do it. But, after a couple Merlots at their hotel one night, she was able to lure him into bubble bath and hope that her seduction skills hadn't worn off.

"So, hon, these last few months have been fabulous. Don't you think?" Rhonda hinted as she slipped into the bubbles clasping her glass of red.

"Sure has, my love. I've enjoyed every minute," Tony responded with crimson stained lips.

"So have I. I'm really looking forward to a future with you Mr. Romano," Rhonda paused for a moment before spitting out, "Possibly as Mrs. Romano?" Tony's eyes grew wide as he nervously reached for the bottle of wine to top up his glass.

"Mrs. Romano, huh."

"Yes, don't you think that would be wonderful? You, me and the rest of our lives together?"

"Of course."

Rhonda wasn't exactly getting the response she wanted from him. She had to turn her nudge more into push for the clueless twit.

"So, then what are we waiting for? I love you and you love me. Let's get married."

Tony was now gulping his wine rather than sipping it, his mind was going a mile a minute.

Marriage? After only a few months? This chick is off her rocker.

The voices in Tony's head were somewhat logical. However, they usually only had one thing in mind.

But… she's rich. I'd be set for life.

Just as the voices were starting to calm down, Tony remembered one very important thing.

Fuck, she thinks I'm rich too. How the hell am I supposed to continue that tall tale?

"Um, well. The thing is honey. I've got a lot of my finances tied up at the moment. Until I close one of these big Toronto condo deals, I don't think I could give you the wedding you deserve. At least not right away."

"And exactly how long is that going to take," Rhonda responded with a bratty eye-roll.

"A couple of months at most, Sweetie," Tony reassured her as he took her hand.

"I'm going to hold you to that! Don't keep me waiting too long though," she replied with a wink.

"Now all I need is a ring! You best make sure it's sparkly, my love," Rhonda said with fluttering eyes and an outstretched left hand.

Tony spent the entire next day scavenging around pawn shops. With $150 in his pocket and his eye on the finest jewelry any of them could offer he was getting two different responses from shop owners, uncontrollable laughter, or the odd, "Get the fuck out!"

He eventually found something half decent which he knew would probably be total trash in Rhonda's mind, but he had to work with what he had.

One Sunday he decided he was going to bring her up to the Muskokas, which she had hinted to him many times was one of her favourite spots in the entire world.

With a bottle of red wine in tow, the two love birds took a small walk to a lookout over Three Mile Lake.

Tony was nervous, not because of what her answer would be – he already knew that. But because of what she would think of the ring, and the little fib he had to try and back it up with.

"Will you marry me?" Tony blurted out, down on one knee with sweat beading from his forehead as he opened the box.

He almost wanted to close his eyes in order to miss her reaction, but he had to grin and bear it – and it wasn't pretty.

"Rhonda, my love. This ring belonged to my Great, Great, Great Grandmother. It's been in my family for generations and has seen the purest, and truest, love anyone could ever know. My Great, Great, Great Grandfather, *it was three Greats… right?* bought it for the love of his life after he returned from the War of 1812. It's been gussied up a few times over the last century or so and I couldn't think of someone who I would rather give it to than you."

"So…what you're saying is, it's vintage?" Rhonda responded with one eyebrow raised.

"Well, sure. You could call it that. But, more importantly it holds great significance in my life. It's an incredibly valuable heirloom, Sweetheart. It belonged to my —"

"I know you told me," she said cutting him off. "I — I love it! I don't know a single other woman who has an over 200 year old engagement ring! It's incredible!! Yes, yes, and yes again!"

"Phew, that was a close one," Tony thought to himself on the car ride home.

I'm either an excellent liar or she's as naive as they come.

"Do you mind if we make a quick pit stop, hon?" Rhonda said hesitantly.

Something had been badgering at her since the moment they entered Muskoka.

"It's just…Donald and I used to have a property up here. We put a lot of money into that place and I'm kind of curious to see what the new owners have done with it."

"Sure thing, my love. Whatever you want."

The two took a turn off the highway and headed down Oastler Park Drive. Tony couldn't believe his eyes once he laid them on the waterfront mansion which once was his new fiancé's.

"Holy smokes!" He exclaimed. "Maybe I need to get into real estate up here, look at this thing!"

"Ah, yes. This was one of our smaller investments, but it was one of my favourites," Rhonda coolly replied.

When she noticed the owners weren't around, she led Tony down to the dock and told him stories about the parties she'd thrown here with her former girlfriends, while her ex was travelling the world working.

"I guess you've probably heard by now that he was a filthy cheat… in more ways than one."

Tony was a bit surprised by this statement but nodded his head in agreement.

"This property was actually one of his main money laundering hubs," she said with a laugh. "He'd hide wads and wads of cash all over this property and keep surveillance on it 24/7. That was one of the main reasons I'd stay up here in the summers, to keep an eye on his stash."

"How much money are we talking here?" Tony said curiously.

"Oh, probably in the millions," Rhonda responded looking out to the water.

"You uh, you think he might have left any?" Tony asked jokingly with a nervous laugh.

"Over his dead body would he have ever left even a penny up here, that neurotic ass."

It was in that moment Rhonda had an epiphany. You could almost see the lightbulb shining above her head as she looked at her fiancé.

"You know what? He was in a big rush the day he fled. He knew the cops were onto him. Could you imagine? That dumbass might have forgotten one of his stashes here?" She threw her head back laughing before shooting Tony a devilish grin.

"Are you up for a little digging, my love?"

Ten two-foot holes and a bucket of sweat later, Tony was regretting even putting the dumb idea into Rhonda's head. He'd been digging for what felt like forever while she bossed him around from spot to spot.

I mean really, what were the odds that they'd find

anything of value on this damn property?

"HONEY, HONEY, GET OVER HERE!"

Tony rushed over to Rhonda who had been lurking around the guest house.

"YOU'RE NOT GOING TO BELIEVE THIS!" She continued to shout.

As Tony rounded the corner to the back of the building, he saw the most beautiful sight he'd ever laid eyes on.

There was his fiancé, with the biggest smile he'd ever seen on her face, holding a wad of cash.

"I forgot about this spot!" She exclaimed as she continued to pull stacks of bills out of a secret false wall in the building.

Her excitement was evident, there had to be at least a quarter of a million dollars in there.

While that might sound like a lot to most everyone in Ashington, it was nothing for her. She looked at the cash as more of an investment, you might say. In her head, she still needed that title of "Mrs. Romano" before she could finally be financially set in the life that was always meant to be hers.

"This could help pay for our wedding, darling! We could get married next month!"

Tony ran to his woman, picked her up off the ground and spun her around as he embraced her with a kiss - only because he couldn't do it to the money itself, of course.

Meanwhile, back in the snug...

It was just another day for Tommy and Jack who sat in their snug sipping on pints and watching the news on one of the overhead TV screens.

"You see this shit, Jack?" Some poor young lady was beaten up again by one of those stupid fucking cell phone drivers."

"Cell phone drivers? What in the hell are you talking about, Tommy?"

"You know, one of those damn cab drivers you order with your cell phone. They're all fucked, every other day you see this shit about them assaulting women on the news. I just don't see why anyone would use them," Tommy replied

"Hey Dylan!" Jack yelled to the bar, "Come over here for a minute."

Dylan sauntered over with regret, he always knew when he was about to be dragged into one of the two old boys' arguments.

"Don't you do them cell phone driving services?" Jack asked him.

"Cell phone driving services?" Dylan replied with a confused look.

"Damn it!" Tommy said in frustration as he couldn't keep up with any of these new age terms. "Whatever it's called when you order taxis off your cell phone!"

"Oh…like ride-hailing apps. Yep I do that on my nights off from here."

"They're fucking ridiculous," Tommy exclaimed.

"Don't you see what's happening on the news, all these people getting attacked by their drivers?"

"Yeah, it's unfortunate," Dylan replied.

"Unfortunate? That's all it is? Unfortunate? And you're supporting these cows! You should be ashamed!" Tommy said with a shaking finger.

"Dude, chill out!" Dylan said with a snarled lip as

he walked back to the bar.

"Jesus, Tom. Don't abuse the poor kid for shit other people have done. You're just pissed off you're so old that you can't keep up with all of the new technology these days!"

"Oh *I* can't? Fuck off, Jack you old prick, you thought it was called 'cell phone drivers' just like I did."

"Well, all I'm saying is all this new stuff isn't such a bad thing. A woman could get attacked by a regular cab driver, there's no difference!"

"Back in the 2000's everyone was telling their kids not to meet people over the internet or get in cars with strangers. Today people are literally *ordering* people they don't know fuck all about on the internet and getting into cars with them!"

"Well anyone can be a bad person, Tom. Just because someone does the cell phone drivin' for a living doesn't mean they're a damn rapist. Look at Dylan for instance, he's a good kid."

"He's a nit wit, Jack," Tommy replied as he sipped his beer.

"Well sure, we all know that. But that just goes back to my point that you can't keep up with the damn kids these days."

"Damn it Jack, you're pissing me off. You're old as dirt too and you know it! Don't be talking to me about 'keeping up with the kids' when you don't even know what Facegram or Instabook is."

"Sure I do! Those are the things on cellphones that bloody zombify my grandkids. Trying to get a word out of either of them is like pulling teeth when they've got those damn phones in their hands."

"Well, I think I can agree with you on that one, buddy. Look at Dylan over there, on his phone while my damn glass is bone dry," Tommy said in a loud voice trying to get the distracted bartender's attention. "YOU HEAR ME, BOY! MY GLASS IS PRITNEAR BONE DRY!"

Dylan looked up from his screen, startled at first until he realized it was Tommy yelling to which he responded with an eye roll.

"I may be deaf, boy but I ain't blind! Keep rolling your eyes, maybe you'll find a brain back there."

"Christ, Tommy, one of these days that boy's gonna thump ya if you keep talkin' to him like that," Jack said to his pal.

"I'd like to see him try, Jack! You've seen me in a bar fight or two, you know the power behind these babies," Tommy replied, holding his wrinkled arthritis-ridden balled up fists to the sky.

"Well, sure, maybe 50 years ago, pal. Keep dreaming," Jack said with a swig of his beer.

"You truly don't think I could knock that little nit wit off his feet?"

"No Tom, I truly do not."

"Well, I'd prove it to yeah but I don't want to be banned for life."

Jack nearly spit his beer all over the table laughing so hard.

"Shut the fuck up you old bastard."

"I'm being serious, Jack! You don't want to mess with me," Tommy said again, shuffling his fists back and forth looking like a drunk octopus.

"Here's you beer, you old Grump," Dylan said as he set the pint down on the table and turned to walk away.

"Hold it, hold it, boy," Jack said as he turned to Tommy. "Tom, I'll pay for your beer for the next week if you can beat Dylan in an arm wrestling match.

"Pfffft, I don't want to embarrass the boy in front of the entire pub, Jack, come on."

"No I need to see this. If you can beat the boy I'll never doubt 'those babies' again." Jack said as he grabbed Tommy's fists.

"Dylan, are you up for a challenge?" Tommy said to him with a wink and smirk.

"A challenge? And, what do I get if I win?" Dylan

replied smartly.

"If you win, I will personally see to it that Tommy leaves you the hell alone from now on," Jack promised.

"Huh," Dylan paused. "Ok, deal."

"Ha! If you insist. Sit on down, boy. Let's see those pipes in action!" Tommy said as he bit his tongue between his front teeth to prepare his concentration.

The two got into position as Jack cleared the table of pint glasses.

The scene began to catch the attention of some bystander's.

"Ah, an audience. Prepare for an embarrassment, boy. And, you can thank Jack!" Tommy said, wiggling his butt in his seat in anticipation.

The two locked hands and positioned their elbows on the table, adjusting their grips and staring each other down.

"Alright, tough guys. On the count of three, you're going to begin. One, Two, aaaaaaaaand, THREE!"

Their fists tightened as Tommy's concentration face quickly turned into a look of constipation. His blue and purple veins began protruding through his paper-thin skin.

Dylan was smiling as his arm slowly started to take Tommy's down to the table.

The match lasted all of 3 seconds before Jack started clapping and yelling "OOOOOOOOOHHHH!"

"I…I wasn't ready, you fuckers!" Tommy said in protest. "Best two out of three, that was bullshit!"

Dylan got up from the table, "I gotta go, man. People at the bar are waiting."

"You..you better come back, boy. I'll get cha, I swear it!"

Dylan walked away totally uninterested.

"Jack, tell him we need a re-match!"

Jack turned to Tommy, his face beet red from holding back laughter.

"Tommy, you're my best bud, and there's no way I'm letting you embarrass yourself like that in this pub again. Just face it, you're an old bastard, just like me, and we just can't keep up with the kids anymore!"

"Fuck it Jack, you're right," Tommy said as he snatched his pint from the ledge beside him. As he took a sip, he zeroed in on a blonde-headed beauty across the bar, her long hair flowing down her back.

"Would you look at that, Jack. We may be old bastards but I think we've still got enough pep in our step to woo a woman like that," he said as he nodded towards her, ensuring Jack got a good look too.

"Huh, don't think I've ever seen her around here before. How in the world did she get into those jeans?"

"Not a clue buddy, but I'd sure like to get her out of them!"

The two laughed into their pints before asking the obvious question.

"So, Jacky boy, whattya think? Would ya?"

"Ha! Would I ever!" He replied, as expected.

"Oh, look, look! She's walking over, be cool!"

It took all but a few steps toward the snug as the old men's eyes began to refocus on the blonde bombshell they'd been eyeing up.

"For fuck sakes Tommy, she's got a goatee!"

"You're right Jack, and them damn jeans reveal WAY too much in the front."

It became clear to them both, as the beauty that walked by them suddenly turned into a beast.

"It was a fuckin' man Tommy, you asshole! How many times have I told you to bring your damn glasses with you," Jack groaned.

"You fell for it too you old prick! Since when does a man have any business wearing jeans like that or growing their hair that long?"

"It's these damn young'uns I tell ya!"

"You're right, maybe being an old bastard ain't all

that bad after all," Tommy said as he raised his glass.

"Cheers to that, buddy!"

The Wedding

Gerry the Bookie

Dylan looked over towards the front door of the Black Horse after placing a couple of drinks in front of Sammy and John, who were happily sitting and chatting away in their regular seats. The wedding guests, including all the pub regulars, were starting to arrive for Tony & Rhonda's reception, half of the tables were already full, with a full sixteen at the bar expected soon. The actual wedding ceremony had been a very private affair, but it looked like it was going to be a full house for the "after party". Although it was going to be an open bar for the whole night, Dylan was looking forward to receiving a big tip from the happy couple on top of what Rosie had already included in her event pricing menu, and what the regulars would generously add themselves. As long as everything went smoothly, he would make a bundle tonight and end up drinking for free!

Tony and Rhonda were suitably ensconced at their little table of honour, drinks in hand and looking happier than he'd ever seen them. Rhonda was looking especially hot, her sculpted legs finely on display in her tight-fitting dress, looking ten years younger than he knew her to be.

Dylan's appreciative ogling of Rhonda was interrupted by a sudden exclamation from Sammy.

"Shit! This is not good!"

As Sammy turned from looking at the bar's mirror to the front door, Dylan followed his gaze to see a pair of giant thugs enter the pub. The same pair of giant thugs that had scared the shit out of him last fall, when they'd popped in looking for someone. They were staring at Tony. No, this was definitely not good at all.

As Sammy stood, another large man followed them into the Black Horse. He was older, fatter, wore a very expensive looking suit, and was holding two small, gift-wrapped boxes in his hands.

"What the fuck is going on?" Dylan muttered.

"I don't know for sure," Sammy replied, "but I'm going to find out."

As Sammy made his way towards the front of the pub, the two goons blocked his path.

"It's okay Sammy, they're my guests," called Tony, who had risen from his seat.

If Sammy was shocked, he didn't show it. He simply nodded at Tony and made his way back to his seat, although he sat facing the door just in case.

As the rest of the guests continued to arrive, and those already present continued to talk amongst themselves, Tony shook hands with the older man, but not his goons. With a wrapped package of his own under his arm, he led the trio of strangers to the bar, slightly nervous but still looking happy.

"Dylan, can you get these guys a drink? Whatever they want."

"We won't be staying, Tony, thanks anyway. I just wanted to drop of these gifts for you and your lovely bride. Matching Rolexes, special editions."

As the man handed over the two boxes, Tony accepted them and replied, "Thanks Gerry, you didn't have to do that! I have something special for you too."

"You better!" growled the larger hulk of a goon.

"Hey, no need for that," cautioned Gerry, "we're invited guests. I'm sure Tony understands why we're here. Right, Tony?"

Dylan could sense Sammy tensing up, the veins on the side of his neck were beginning to bulge and his death stare had returned. "Please don't do anything stupid," he thought to himself. "Don't fuck things up for all my tips tonight."

Tony handed over the package he'd been holding. "I have a little gift for you too, Gerry, just a little something to say thanks for all your patience and understanding."

Gerry hefted the package carefully then passed the gift to the bigger goon.

"I knew I could count on you Tony, you're not a dumb guy. It'd be a shame if we'd had to end our relationship on a bad note." Tony's eyes followed Gerry's gaze as he glanced towards Rhonda, who was showing off her wedding ring to an admiring Rosie. "That's when people get hurt, when they don't respect their obligations. Sometimes there's collateral damage that can't be helped too. I'm just glad we were able to work things out."

Tony gulped, but recovered quickly, "You're right, Gerry. This type of misunderstanding won't happen again, I promise."

Gerry slapped him on the back and placed his bejewelled hand heavily on the Groom's shoulder.

"I'm happy to hear it, Tony, I always liked you. I hope we'll hear from you again soon, too. I miss doing business with you. Just give Mike a call and we'll open your account again."

Tony looked relieved, smiling and nodding in response.

"Okay boys, let's get going," Gerry stated. "Congratulations once again to you and your lovely bride," he added as they made their way to the door.

Once the door had closed behind them, Dylan exclaimed, "Will somebody please tell me what the fuck is going on? Who the hell are those guys?"

"Aren't those your former business partners, Tony?" Sammy deflected, covering for Tony as best he could while staring directly at him.

"Uh, yeah Sammy, I did some deals with them a while ago. It took some time to work out the details but it's all good now."

"You're sure?"

Tony looked and sounded thoughtful as he answered, "Yeah, I'm sure. Everything's good, thanks for your concern, Sammy. You know I truly appreciate it." He shook Sammy's hand warmly and continued, "And you know I truly appreciate all you did to help. How can I ever thank you?"

"Just don't do any more deals with those guys, okay? Stay away from them and stick to what you know. You're a married man now, you have a wife to consider, a future. No need to take such risks anymore, right?"

"Right, Sammy. I won't, don't worry. I've learned my lesson."

Sammy doubted that what Tony was saying was true, he could tell from his body language and the timbre in his voice that he was trying to convince himself more than anything else, but what more could he do?

"Okay!" Slapping his hand on the bar, he cried out,

"Dylan, a round of tequilas for the boys, no fruit, and one for the Groom!"

"I'll drink that shit on one condition," Tony replied, laughing and pulling Sammy away from John.

"What's that?"

"You gotta tell me what you said to those guys that night, when you saved my life. What did you say?"

Sammy smiled and pulled Tony close, hugging him with one bear-like arm, speaking quietly so as not to be overheard. "I told them I was a CSIS operative and they were fucking up a long-running investigation involving you laundering money for a known terrorist group. There were surveillance units all around and if they didn't leave immediately, they'd be rounded up, held as accessories, and turned over to the Americans. Maybe even taken to one of their secret rendition camps and tortured."

Tony listened intently, with a stunned look upon his face, as Sammy continued.

"I told them I only wanted the big fish, the terrorists, and that you were going away for sure, but if they interfered and blew the rest of the operation, they'd pay for it."

"Holy shit Sammy, that's crazy!"

Sammy stared hard at Tony, erasing the smile from his face.

"The world is full of crazy shit, Tony. What you see, what you think you see, is just the tip of the iceberg. Remember that."

"Who the hell are you Sammy? Really? Who are you?"

Handing him a shot glass of tequila, Sammy barked, "Drink up Mr. Romano! Drink up everybody! To Tony!"

They all downed their shots, Tony included, and wished the Groom well. As Tony wandered back to his table, and to his bride, he glanced back and gave Sammy a "thumbs-up" while shaking his head. Sammy responded the same way.

Don't do it, kid, stay away from those guys. Nothing but trouble there.

"Good luck, Tony. You're going to need it," Sammy said aloud to himself. Turning around and re-joining his friends at the bar, he said loudly, "Right, whose round is it now?"

Rosie & Sammy

Tony and Rhonda's wedding reception was well under way and becoming a raucous affair. The private ceremony held earlier that afternoon at the Ashington Town Hall had been a mere formality, the real celebration for all the invited guests, and pub regulars, was held afterwards at the Black Horse, and the place was absolutely heaving. This hallowed room had never experienced such a unique occasion, and no expense had been spared to make it a special one as well.

Rhonda, looking absolutely gorgeous in her cheekily

short designer gown, soaked up both the adoring and jealous attention she was receiving with equal pleasure. Tony, sporting a bespoke tuxedo, could not stop smiling, hugging and kissing his bride at every opportunity as they moved from table to table accepting all the congratulations and handshakes from the festive gathering.

Rosie and her staff were weaving their way through the throng of celebrants with plates of the delicious specials that Evelyn had prepared for the happy couple and their well-wishers. Steak and lobster had followed the delicious soup and salad course, plates of appetizers had already been devoured, and a magnificent crème brûlée and cherry chocolate torte combination was still waiting in the wings. Everyone involved was proud of what they had managed to produce and accomplish for this special day, none more so than Rosie. She was feeling over the moon, happier than she could ever remember.

Sammy had played a big role in Rosie's renaissance, their relationship had grown closer and stronger with each and every day that passed. This was a somewhat unexpected but greatly valued experience for the both of them, bringing them the comfort and happiness that had been missing in their lives for a long, long time.

They had both been nervous and a little embarrassed when they'd seen each other again on New Year's Day. Neither of them could have imagined that they'd be making out like teenagers the night before, ignited by that simple kiss at midnight, but it had happened, and they'd been forced to deal with the immediate fall out.

Sammy had arrived at the pub ahead of opening to help Rosie with the clean-up, barely able to make eye contact with her. She, too, struggled with her words, not knowing what to say to him. Finally, after a few minutes that seemed like hours, Sammy had raised his head and spoken softly to her.

"I'm not sorry. I'm glad it happened."

Having unburdened himself with those simple words, he'd opened his arms to her. Rosie rushed in to embrace him and echo his sentiments, sealing the start of their new and improved "friendship" with another passionate kiss. They understood each other well and felt no need to rush into anything beyond what they already obviously felt and shared. They'd just decided to take it day by day and see where it took them.

As Rosie delivered the last dinner plates from her tray, she glanced across the room at Sammy, chatting away with John, Ben and Garnet in the Dog Pound's section. Sensing her lingering stare, he turned and gave her a quick smile accompanied by a roguish wink. It made Rosie feel so good to have this man in her life, the type of quiet strength and affection that he provided was something she'd never been blessed with before. It made everything else in her life so much easier to manage. Maybe one day she and Sammy would be hosting their own wedding reception here.

Rosie's tender thoughts were interrupted by Mel's appearance at her side.

"Snap out of it, lovebird, we need more wine. Stat!" she said, laughing. "I don't know where they're putting it all, they're drinking like fish!"

"On it," Rosie replied with a mock salute. "Let's get this party really started!"

Sammy was enjoying himself immensely. He was genuinely happy for Tony and Rhonda, but especially for Tony. Maybe this would finally straighten him out and get him back on track. He knew that this was a marriage of convenience for both of them, but when two like-minded individuals get together for the same ill-conceived reason, you never knew what could happen. And they seemed to be legitimately happy with the situation, so who was he to judge. Rhonda was the type of woman who would give Tony a swift kick in the ass when needed. Probably when it wasn't needed too!

She'd put a stop to his reckless gambling one way or another. It did seem that Tony was flush with cash all of a sudden, and it couldn't have been from betting either. His behaviour had undergone a full 180 in the past few weeks, even to the point that he now parked his car out front, not hidden away in the back lot. There was a bounce to his step that Sammy hadn't seen in, well, ever, and putting two and two together, he figured that Tony had managed to make some big money selling real estate. The only thing he couldn't figure out was why he wasn't bragging about it. It wasn't like Tony to keep quiet about his success. Oh well, that wasn't really any of his business, he was too busy being happy with his own life right now.

John had been talking non-stop for about ten minutes now about Rhonda's shoes and how beautiful her feet were, how he'd pay to drink out of her sweaty shoe. Sammy needed a break from his running commentary on phalanges, metatarsals and the erotic joys of "toe-sucking", so he decided to head outside for a breath of fresh air.

"Excuse me boys, save my seat will ya."

The first thing Sammy noticed when he stepped out of the pub was an unmarked police car with two plainclothes officers inside. The second thing he noticed was a marked cruiser circling the parking lot. Something was about to go down, and he had a pretty good idea what it was. Fuck. Why today? Why today of all days?

"Claude Gingras, you are under arrest for two counts of vehicular manslaughter. Place your hands behind your back."

Two uniformed police constables closed in on Claude, and as he resisted their instructions, resorted to using physical force in order to subdue him. Grabbing his flailing arms and placing him in a partial choke hold, they were finally able to get him to the ground for cuffing as he fought frantically to get loose.

The wedding guests were shocked by the scene unfolding right in front of their eyes. They were silent at first, a few audible sobs pierced the shouts and grunts coming from the battle in front of them, but that quickly changed to loud questioning of what was happening. The officers were forced to clear some space around Claude, knocking over a few chairs in the process as he continued to fight against their efforts.

"What the hell are you talking about?" Claude raged, his eyes bulging and spittle flying as he refused to go quietly. "This is all a big mistake! Get off me! Leave me alone!"

As one of the plainclothes detectives supervised the uncooperative, but handcuffed, Claude being lifted by the pair of constables, Sammy grabbed Ben and walked him to the hallway leading to the washrooms at the back of the room.

"What's going on, Sammy? What's Claude done?"

"Claude's being arrested, Ben. He's being arrested for the accident that took Lydia and Annabelle."

Ben couldn't comprehend at first what Sammy had told him. His thoughts were all over the place, confused, he was numb with shock. As he slowly began to realize the implications of what Sammy had said, he was overcome by pure, blind rage.

"YOU FUCKER! I'LL FUCKING KILL YOU! YOU…"

Unable to complete his sentence, Ben's screams had brought the entire pub, cops included, to a standstill. Red-faced and sobbing, he tried to force his way past Sammy to get at Claude.

"I'LL KILL YOU, YOU BASTARD! YOU… MURDERER!"

Struggling mightily in Sammy's firm grasp, Ben pleaded with him to let go, to let him get at Claude, but Sammy was too strong, absorbing all the rage and pain that Ben was releasing, while trying his best to soothe him.

"No Ben, no. He's going to get what's coming to him. I know what you want to do but it's just not worth it. It won't solve anything, Ben. I'm so sorry."

With the sounds of crying and shocked gasps coming from the dining area, Ben finally began to calm down, almost collapsing into Sammy's arms. Tears flowed down his face as he began to collect himself, sniffling a reply.

"You can let go now. Thanks, Sammy. I'm okay. I'm okay."

They watched together as Claude, head hanging low with a stunned, and now emotionless face, was led out of the Black Horse by the two constables. The regulars and other guests made way for them, watching with angry expressions and derision.

"Fucking baby killer," Gary said with a clenched jaw as he approached. One of the cops held out his arm to prevent Gary from getting any closer. "You're fucked, asshole. You are so fucked," he added, as Mary gently pulled him back.

The tall plainclothes detective made his way back to where Sammy and Ben remained standing, an expression of empathy on his face.

"Mr. Whitley, I'm sorry that you had to witness this. I'm Detective Jennings. We've just arrested this man for the accident that took the lives of your wife and daughter. I need to speak with you for a few minutes. I know this is a big shock, do you understand what I've just said?"

"Yes. That's the bastard that killed them. You finally caught him. Finally."

"We recently came across some new evidence that allowed us to re-open the investigation and move forward with identifying the perpetrator. Would you please come out with me to my car so we can sit down and talk about a few things, let me explain what's going to happen next."

"Okay. Let's go," Ben replied softly, "Let's get it over with."

Once Ben was out the door, the entire pub erupted in a series of conversations and questions.

"What the hell just happened?"

"He killed Ben's family?"

"What are we supposed to do now?"

It was Rhonda, surprisingly, that eventually took control of the situation and brought a sense of order to the chaos in the room.

Tinkling her wine glass with a spoon to attract everyone's attention, she waited until the chaos abated and she had everyone's focus on her.

"Listen up everyone, please! Can you all just take your seats." The firmness in her voice was balanced with compassion. That alone was enough to compel compliance. Once everyone was seated, she continued.

"I know we've all just had a big shock," looking at Tony, she grabbed his hand, smiling, and went on. "We're just as shocked as all of you are. This is very upsetting news, but there's nothing we can do about it now. This tragedy, this horrible, horrible tragedy happened, and now it appears that it's finally being brought to some sort of conclusion. I understand if you all might not feel like celebrating right now, I know that my heart goes out to poor Ben and what he's dealing with, I can't imagine what he's feeling, but it's out of our hands. We're both so happy to have shared this day with you. We understand if you want to call it a night, but we'd love to have you all stay and try to enjoy yourselves a little bit longer. It's still early and maybe we can try and end the night on a happier note. What do you say?"

At first no one spoke up, nobody wanted to be the first to reply, waiting for someone else to make the first move.

"She's right." It was Mel that finally broke the

spell. "Rhonda's right. There's nothing we can do about it now. It's so unfair, Rhonda, Tony, that this had to have happened on your special day. Come on, everyone. Please raise your glasses and let's toast the happy couple!"

Glasses started to move slowly, but soon everyone's were eventually raised, smiles slowly returned to faces, and a few laughs were even heard.

"To Tony and Rhonda, who found love in the Black Horse pub and strength in each other. May your life together be a long and joyous one."

"Cheers!" everyone cried, clinking glasses.

"And a prosperous one too!" John shouted to wild laughter. "Ching-Ching!" he added, rubbing his fingers together in a gesture of imaginary money.

"Cheers!" came the cry again, this time mixed with laughter.

"Alright, everyone, let's get back to work," Rosie added. "Who needs more wine?"

Despite heavy hearts, and the significance of the events surrounding Claude's arrest, the guests soon returned to celebrating, knowing that this was not the time and place for dealing with that tragic situation. It would best be left for another day.

The front door suddenly opened, and Ben walked back into the pub. Mel immediately ran to him, hugging him tightly.

"Are you okay?"

"I'll be fine Mel, really. It's going to be alright. Justice will finally be done. It's been so long, but they finally got him."

"Just let me know if you need anything, anything at all."

Ben squeezed her hand in return, "Thanks Mel, you don't know how grateful I am to have you in my life."

Rhonda and Tony wandered over to Ben as Mel went back to work. "We're so sorry, Ben," Tony said solemnly. "I can't imagine what you're going through."

"I'm sorry too, guys, that your day had to be spoiled by all this drama. I'm truly happy for you both. What do you say we try and forget about my issues for the rest of the night and concentrate on having a good time, okay?"

"Okay," Rhonda said, kissing Ben on the cheek. "We're so glad you're here."

The noise in the pub was soon back to its earlier level, as Ben made his way over to take his seat beside Garnet and Sammy.

"Thanks, Sammy, for everything. Sounds like you might have had something to do with the big break in the case."

Sammy put his big hand on Ben's shoulder and leaned in.

"Listen to me Ben," he said quietly, nodding his head towards Garnet, who was listening too. "Garnet's learned this also. You can't live in the past. Never forget, never stop thinking about them, but don't get consumed by the grief. You have to move on, or you'll die inside. It doesn't mean that you don't love them anymore, or love them any less, but you have to love yourself too."

"Sammy's right, son," Garnet added. "Listen to him. You're a good 'un, you have a bright future ahead of you. Don't waste it. Like I did."

Ben smiled at them both, responding to their concerns with silent acquiescence.

"Jesus Christ, I'm taking advice from Garnet now. What the hell's in this drink?"

Sammy's hand slapped the table, rattling the glasses.

"Ha! Another round for my friends please, Rosie!

Garnet

8.5 million dollars! 8.5 million, that was what Garnet had deposited into his bank account two days ago. Tony had actually come through! He had made Garnet nervous earlier, as he'd turned down two previous offers for the old man's farm. Eventually this buyer gave in and agreed to the inflated asking price. Garnet was, all of a sudden, a very wealthy man, getting on in years, but now he would live out the rest of his life without wanting for anything. His daughter and son in law had welcomed the news that he had sold the farm, and his desire to go and live with them, especially once he'd informed them just how much money he now had. Their small farm in P.E.I. was going to get brand new equipment, and the house would undergo a complete renovation, including adding a small in-law apartment for Garnet. "Happy Days" were here indeed.

Tony did not say much about the buyer, and to be honest, Garnet had not really wanted to know. All Tony had said was that it was a big developer who wanted to build a gated community complete with Condos and detached homes. Garnet was glad to be leaving. Ashington was now going to get yet another influx of new people and he bet that most of them would be freeloading immigrants.

Garnet hadn't told anyone at the pub yet about his departure, he didn't want the regulars to know anything about his business. That is, until today. He sat on his stool in the Dog Pound and contemplated the best way to say goodbye. He had figured this wedding would be the perfect opportunity to reveal his news as everyone he knew would be there, especially since Tony the wop was paying for everyone's drinks. His flight left tomorrow, so these would likely be his final hours at his beloved Black

Horse. He figured he should definitely go to the wedding as Tony had been a man of his word and had got him the best deal possible.

Maybe he should have purchased a wedding gift, but fuck that, his commission was probably the best gift Tony would ever receive. The party was in full swing and everyone was happy and laughing except for poor Nancy who was absolutely rushed off her feet. Rosie was half-working and half-partying; in fact, she looked like she'd had more than a few glasses of wine.

Mel was sitting and chatting to Ben, who now seemed a different person than the quiet, sullen man he had been before.

Garnet would really miss this place, and he wondered if he would be able to find another little pub out East that he could call his own. The hell with it, he would build one if he had to! At this thought Garnet let out a loud laugh which caught Sammy by surprise.

"Jeez Garnet, that's the first time I've ever heard you laugh like that. You usually only have a sly grin on your face."

Garnet felt embarrassed and replied, "Just thinking of that joke John told us yesterday."

Sammy shook his head in disbelief as John's joke yesterday had probably been one of his worst ever. Looking at Garnet, Sammy suspected that he was hiding something.

A few minutes later, Tony walked over to the gang, just as Garnet was about to tell them all about his big news.

"Hey guys, thanks for coming to the wedding," shouted Tony over the sound of Brian hammering away at "*Taking Care of Business*". "Did you all say goodbye to Garnet?" he yelled with his arms around Garnet and Sammy's shoulders. "This crusty old son-of-a-bitch is moving out East, I got him a real sweet deal on his farm."

Garnet tried to interrupt but Tony was on a roll,
"He's leaving tomorrow I think, but of course you'd all know that already, as you sit with him nearly every freaking day."
Sammy looked at Garnet, "Is this true Grump? You're leaving the pack without even a word?"
"What the Fuck Garnet, you weren't going to say goodbye!" John piped in.
Garnet blushed and wanted to say that he was about to tell them, when Tony came out with a zinger that even shocked Garnet.
"The old farm is going to become home to one of the biggest Mosques in Ontario! The planning's already been approved. It's going to be a huge facility, including a learning centre, with parking for almost 2,000 people. They're putting town homes in as well, it's going to be like 'Little Kabul' over there."

Garnet suddenly turned as red as a beetroot. He had never really inquired who the buyer was, but now it all made sense as he recalled that group of Asians in the pub one day looking at maps and such. Gary had hinted that they were looking to build a temple or something in the area.
"So that's why you never told us," said John.
"I..I..I didn't know," blurted out Garnet. "I didn't want to tell anyone until the deal was done and the money was in the bank. I only got the money a couple of days ago."
"Oops!" said Tony, walking away laughing to greet other guests. He figured it was best to leave Garnet on his own to say his farewells to all his misfit friends. He had managed to stir that particular pot very well though!
After a bit of friendly banter to and fro in the Dog Pound, word got around that Garnet "the Grump" was leaving Ashington for good. Astonishment turned into a sort of sadness that one of the regulars would no longer be a part of the Black Horse's crowd.

People now lined up to hug and say farewell to Garnet, just as they had done to congratulate the Bride and Groom.

Garnet's face had returned to normal, and he'd even had to wipe away a tear in his eye when he realized that in a way, this was his home, and maybe he should stay. He'd made his decision though, he concluded, it was the right one, and he should quit being such a goddamn pansy. He could fly back for a week or so next summer for a visit.

"A bloody Mosque," he thought, still stunned. His father would be turning in his grave.

Just then, another stranger appeared in front of him, one of Tony's special guests. Garnet had no idea who he was as he did not personally know any Asian people. The man vigorously shook Garnet's hand with glee as he shouted out, "Mr. Garnet, thank you so much for selling us your land, you have made our group so very happy. We have been trying to purchase land in this area for years now, but always faced too much negativity, or got outbid by other developers. We were exasperated until Mr. Tony came to us with such a great deal." Smiling broadly, he continued, "In your honour, we are going to call the roadway up to the Mosque '*Garnet Wilson Way*', so that everyone will know who was responsible for blessing us with this land and this Mosque! Have a wonderful life out East, Mr. Garnet, you will always be remembered here now for what you have done."

Unable to speak, Garnet fainted dead away.

Mary

Mary couldn't stop laughing, this startling news was just too funny, Garnet's land was going to be turned into a mosque with an Islamic Learning Centre. The old coot must be losing his mind, wondering how the hell this "abomination" had transpired.

Oh Tony, you sneaky little devil, thanks for making my day.

She almost felt sorry for the old farmer. At least he would be living with family again, and maybe that would soften up his bigotry a little bit. And he was now a very wealthy man, that too would go a long way to easing his pain. She had a feeling though, that Garnet was not the type of person whose heart would change one iota just because of money. He was just too set in his ways, too unwilling to see the benefits and legitimacy of "otherness". Miracles could happen she supposed, but she wouldn't be holding her breath.

She hadn't gone over with Gary and the others to congratulate him and say goodbye, she no longer felt the need to pretend and mask her feelings. She was always cordial with Garnet, but that was as far as she was willing to go. She was glad he was leaving. It would make the Black Horse a much more comfortable place for her. It looked like Claude would be out of the mix too! What a crazy day this had been. Her heart broke for Ben but at least, at last, he would be able to get some sense of closure. It must have been so hard for Ben and Lydia's family to go on, knowing that the guilty person was running around free. The look on Claude's face when he was dragged out by the police said it all. He was guilty and he was going to pay for it now, finally.

Mary had been impressed by how Rhonda, and Mel, had handled the situation, how they had brought the people gathered back to a sense of normalcy after Claude's arrest. Sammy too had done well in containing and comforting Ben's rage and all the other emotions that he was going through. It almost seemed that Sammy had anticipated the reason for the arrest and pre-emptively pulled Ben away.

How did he know. He'd pulled Ben away pretty quickly, how did he know it involved Ben's family?

She'd been so preoccupied in keeping Gary from getting at Claude that she hadn't paid much attention to it at the time, but she was certain now that Sammy knew something. That man certainly was an enigma. He sure was making Rosie a happy woman though, she'd been walking on air ever since New Year's, and even though they were trying to keep it all low key, everyone knew that there was definitely something going on between them. Sammy hadn't changed much outwardly, but she did notice the odd smile and a glint in his eyes whenever she was near. Rosie was apparently good for him too, and Mary felt very happy for them both.

Mary had to admit that she was feeling blessed and happy herself. Her boss, Dr. Sharif, had welcomed the news of her Certification with the Royal College of Dental Surgeons of Ontario, and almost immediately placed her in charge of the Ashington office, with a nice pay raise. She had also placed Mary on a pathway that would allow her, over a period of years, to earn up to a 40% ownership share in the business. She was so grateful and proud to finally be achieving her dreams, the dreams she'd had since the age of twelve. She was starting to feel like a welcome and valuable part of the community as well, something that she'd been longing for too. To top it all off, her relationship with Gary was growing steadily and they were closer than ever.

He had, as Mary expected, been a man of his word. Gary had given her, given them both, the space required to sort through their strong feelings for one another, and his awful responsibilities in sorting out the chaos that his breakup with Stephanie had wrought. Not once had Gary ever made her feel uncomfortable. Quite the opposite, he had made sure she understood that their friendship was extremely important to him above all else, and they continued to share their time together at Library Corner, with growing closeness. They communicated through texts and occasional phone calls as well, and Mary was proud of the way Gary had moved on while maintaining an amicable relationship with Stephanie and a wonderful one with his son.

Having his own apartment seemed to assuage many of the frustrations he'd had with his prior living situation and despite all the drama, Gary seemed to be in a much happier place. He saw Ryan whenever he wanted to and the formal arrangements that had been made with Stephanie were being respected by both parties. Mary had been elated that Gary was moving on with such maturity and confidence, and hopeful that they could start to slowly pursue a romantic relationship now that the time felt right.

It was Mary that made the first move, inviting Gary out on a dinner date downtown. They'd both dressed up for the occasion, Gary looking sharp in a fitted grey suit, and Mary in her best little black dress that she felt really flattered her figure. Seeing Gary's eyes nearly popping out of his head when he picked her up assured her even more that it had been the right choice. Before dinner, they spent a couple of hours visiting the exhibits at the Art Gallery of Ontario, sharing their thoughts and showing each other their favourite works of art. At one point, Gary had gently grabbed hold of her hand as they walked through the galleries. Despite the difference in their heights and leg length, neither one of them had to adjust their stride as they walked hand in hand. Their paces were perfectly matched, so natural in fact that Gary had joked that it was as if they were in a three-legged race. To Mary, it was a simple sign, the Universe speaking to them, that they belonged together.

Dinner had been just as wonderful, with delicious food, interesting conversation and an unmistakable feeling of intimacy growing between the two of them.

Mary had very seriously considered inviting Gary into her apartment after he dropped her off back at home but decided it was maybe just a bit too soon for that next step. Their long goodnight kiss tempted her though, but Gary, ever the gentleman and sensing her hesitation, thanked her for the fantastic date, and said he'd plan the next one.

Mary's tender thoughts were loudly interrupted by shouts coming from the Dog Pound.

"Garnet! Garnet! Are you okay?"

Mary rose and turned to see what all the commotion was about, spying the old farmer slumped on the floor. She immediately made her way over, ordering the concerned people surrounding him to move out of the way as she approached.

"What happened?" she asked.

Sammy replied immediately, "He was just standing there, then he got quiet and passed out. I caught him on the way down."

"Is he dead?" Gary asked with concern, suddenly behind her.

Mary could see Garnet's chest rising slowly and see that he was breathing comfortably. Good, not likely a heart attack.

"Sammy, lay him flat on his back. It looks like he's just fainted."

Sammy did as she instructed, elevating Garnet's legs once he was positioned. He knew what he was doing, another good sign. She leaned down and loosened Garnet's collar, speaking to him as she did so.

"Garnet! Can you hear me?"

Mary started shaking his shoulder as she repeated her question louder, yet still no response came from the old farmer.

Sammy nodded at her and said, "Slap him."

After a couple of solid slaps to the side of his face, definitely made a little harder than necessary, accompanied by cries of, "Garnet, wake up!" his eyes

fluttered open.
Unable to focus at first, Garnet saw a blurry figure hovering over him.
"Where am I," he thought to himself. "Why am I lying on the ground?"
He heard his name being repeated, clearer and sharper than before. As his vision improved, he was able to make out a pair of rather magnificent, dark-skinned breasts, barely contained by a low-cut dress. Also, the side of his face really seemed to sting for some reason. Looking up further, he recognized Mary, the African woman that Gary was now seeing, looking down at him with concern in her eyes.
"Garnet, you appear to have fainted," she informed him.
Then Sammy's voice rang out, "Welcome back, Grump!"
As Gary helped Mary to her feet, Garnet allowed Sammy to assist him into a chair.
"Get him some water," she said to Sammy. "He'll need a ride home too, maybe call a taxi."
"I'll ride along in the cab with him, make sure he gets in alright. I'm sure you can hold the fort until I get back," Sammy replied with a smile. "Good work, Doc!"
"Yes, great job sweetheart," Gary added, admiration in his eyes. "You are one cool cucumber."
As Rosie cleared the way for Sammy and Garnet, everyone else returned to what they had been doing before. It would take more than an arrest and a medical emergency to keep this crowd from celebrating. This was the Black Horse, after all!
"What a crazy wedding!" Gary exclaimed, taking the words from her mouth.
"Would you expect anything but crazy from this place?" she replied with a giggle. "Come on, it looks like the music's going to start up again and you promised me a dance."
"As you wish, my love. As you wish."

Ben & Mel

"You really do clean up quite nicely there, don't you Benjamin?" Mel with a wink, checking him out in his very best wedding attire.

"Benjamin!?" He said back with a giggle.

"I'm sorry, I guess we're not 'there' yet are we?" she responded back with air quotes.

"It's funny actually, that's what Annabelle used to call me when she'd try to call me out on my bull," Ben stated with a laugh as he looked down. "She heard my mother call me it once and she never let it go. Anytime I'd try to tell her a fib she'd respond with 'Yeah right…Benjamin!' I nearly fell on my ass the first time she said it, 'I'm Daddy to you, young lady! I'd say to her with a few jabs at her tummy. When she saw how hard it made her mom and I laugh it was game over, she'd say it almost daily."

Ben continued to stare at the ground, cracking a smile with misty eyes. "Ugh, man. I'm sorry Mel. Now isn't the time for that."

"You never have to apologize for keeping their memory alive Ben, especially to me. It's actually really nice to hear you talk about them," Mel said as she gently placed her hand on Ben's shoulder.

"That Annabelle of yours sounds like she was really something," she continued, trying to lighten the mood.

"Oh, was she ever, Mel. If you liked that story, I have about a thousand more that you'd love."

He knew this wasn't exactly the type of depressing conversations one should be having at a wedding. As he looked for an escape, he peeked over at the Black Horse's makeshift dance floor where it looked like the crowd was getting ready for another embarrassing dance session.

"What do you say we show up this riff raff on the

dance floor?"
"You? Dance?" Mel said with two raised eyebrows. "Now that I'd like to see."
As Ben whisked Mel away to the dance floor, Rosie couldn't help but get a little giddy from the sidelines.
"Would you just look at them, Sammy?" She said with a glisten in her eye, "They're perfect for each other. I hope Mel gives him a shot now that that loser-ex of hers is out of the picture."
"Oh, mark my words, Rosie, she'll give him a shot," Sammy responded with a know it all grin.
The two looked onto the dance floor as Ben and Mel goofed around dancing to classic wedding jams like *"Celebrate"* and *"Sweet Caroline"*.
Brian the Piano Man was getting quite the kick out of it, he made eye contact with Rosie, who shot him a nod, and he knew exactly what it meant.
"Alright, ladies and gentleman, we're going to slow it down here for a minute. So, grab that special someone and come out onto the dance floor."
As another classic, *"Can't Help Falling in Love"*, began to bellow from the speakers, Ben, with an awkward look on his face began to head back to his seat.
Before she could even stop herself (that damn wine), Mel grabbed him by the arm.
"Where do you think you're going, mister?"
He looked back at her with an apprehensive look on his face.
"Oh, come on, you can break it down to Neil Diamond but not a little Elvis Presley?"
"I haven't slow danced in a long time Mel. I'm warning you, you might lose a toe."
"If you didn't break one off during your *'BAH, BAH, BAH'S,'* I'm willing to take a risk with this one." She replied with a smirk as she took his hand and led him back to the floor.
The dance started off a little awkwardly. They

looked like two third graders being forced to dance by their teacher.

"Jesus, Mel, he doesn't have cooties!" Rosie said out loud to herself.

"Are you thinking what I'm thinking?" Sammy said to Rosie with a sly grin and side eye.

"And what exactly are you thinking?" She replied with a pensive squint.

"Follow me," he said as he grabbed Rosie's hand, leading her in a dance beside Ben and Mel.

"Whoa, I've got to say Sammy. I never pegged you as a dancer," Rosie exclaimed.

"Don't be ridiculous Rosie…I'm not. I'm just making an exception in this case," he said with a wink as he gave Mel a knock in the hip, plunging her deep into Ben's embrace.

"Ah, God! Sorry guys! Me and my two left feet," he said to the pair in the most sarcastic tone you'd ever heard.

"Oh! You little devil," Rosie said as she held back a cackle.

"Now that's how you get it done!" Sammy said as he winked at Ben.

Tony & Rhonda

"I'd like to thank everyone from the bottom of our hearts for coming out today to celebrate the Union of Tony and I," Rhonda slurred into the microphone as she looked out into the crowd of the Black Horse. "As you know," she giggled, "this isn't my typical style," she said out of the side of her mouth, alluding to the casualness of the event. "But, I'm so glad you all decided to join us."

As she raised her glass of red in the air, she

looked at her new husband. "Here's to you and I, Tony Bear. Thank you for making all my dreams come true. Now, where's the, *hiccup*, honeymoon going to be, sweetheart?" She said with a wink as she put down the mic.

Tony responded with a wide-eyed look, as he sucked back a rock glass of straight vodka and turned back to the bar.

As Brian, the Piano Man, began his next set, John loudly chimed to his friends in the Dog Pound, "Ha, Ha, Ha, I'd recognize that look anywhere! Pure regret, my friends, pure regret!" Getting Tony's attention, he continued, "Hey boys! Raise your glasses, this one's for you, Mr. Romano."

The entire complement of people at the bar raised their glasses as they gave a nod towards Tony. "Cheers to the rest of your life…with that one!" John added.

With the people at the bar roaring, Tony struggled not to spit his drink all over the place. He glared at John, but everyone was laughing entirely too hard to notice.

"Thanks, Pal!" Tony said with an eye roll as he walked away with the remainder of his drink.

"I love my wife and I love her money, I love my wife and I love her money, I love my wife and I love her money," Tony began chanting in his head as he wandered into the crowd in search of some less judgmental company.

"Heya, Tony!" Dylan said as he ran up to the groom with an order pad in his hand. "Your wifey over there just ordered a round of 'Patron' for everyone. She said you'd be taking care of it! I just wanted to double check before I charged the amount to your card."

"I, um, I'm sorry…and exactly HOW much is that going to be?"

"Well, let's see. They're around $10 a shot and I'd say there's what, maybe 35-40 people here right now?"

"So, you're telling me she just ordered $400 worth of tequila shots?"

"Don't forget the tax, dude."

"Thanks for the reminder, DUDE," Tony said as he took another swig of his vodka. "If that's what she wants, then give her what she wants I guess!"

I love my wife and I love her money, I love my wife and I love her money…

Tony wasn't proud of it, but it was precisely for times like this that he was thankful for sticking one of Rhonda's bundles of cash in his briefcase a week or so ago - just for emergencies, of course!

John

"*For, I can't help falling in love with you.*" John was loudly singing, and fixated on Rhonda, who was now sitting on a high bar stool exposing lots of thigh with her legs crossed. Many guys in the pub were catching sneaky glances at her legs but John's gaze was set a lot lower, he was staring at her feet. John loved women's feet and shoes, he didn't know when it had all started, but he guessed that wearing his big sisters high heel shoes as a kid was probably a sign that he was a sick puppy. He could imagine drinking a bottle of tequila out of those shoes then slowly sucking on a toe or two. This was really turning out to be a great night. Here he was, killing it on the mic, and Christ, people were even up dancing! He should have been a fucking singer he thought. It was in his blood. And he was living the care-free bachelor life for a few weeks too, with his wife and stepdaughter visiting family in the Philippines again.

The truth was most people were so drunk that, at

this moment, even John sounded half decent. Of course, Brian the Piano Man had turned down John's volume as an act of mercy for all involved.
John was high as a kite and loving the scene, free booze from the stuck up realtor, and many of the ladies in the room dressed to the nines wearing their best footwear to boot. He really should go to more weddings, this was paradise.

"Thank you, John, now Tony would like to say a few more words," said Brian as he cut John off a tad early, before he had even attempted to reach the last notes of the Elvis classic.

"Fuck Brian, I was saving the best for last, man. I was going to do '*All Shook Up*'."

"Later John, later, the night is still young," said Brian. This made John cheer up a bit, as he bowed to the distracted crowd, many of whom seemed to be more interested in Rhonda's legs than in applauding his performance.

A little chuffed, John waltzed over to the bar and hollered to Dylan for two shots of tequila, one for him and one for Elvis. It was an old saying that John thought was hilarious, and he laughed at his own wit as he downed the two drinks in rapid succession. Just then, looking down at the floor, something beautiful and sparkling caught his eye.

Could it really be? Could he?

John gestured to Dylan for two more shots, he had to order from Dylan because Rosie would cut him off in the state he was in. As for Nancy, she would probably just pour two shots of water, the miserable bitch.

John was drunk, but not too drunk to hatch a brilliant plan for what to do with what he had seen on the floor. This was going to be an epic night after all!

"Who dares, wins, Johnny boy," he said to himself.

A Few Hours Later...

John woke up groggy as hell. He did not recall much of anything about the night before. He did somewhat remember wowing everyone with his singing though, and making everyone laugh at his jokes, but he had absolutely no idea how he had gotten home. His thoughts, still muddled, John looked over to his nightstand where he usually kept a glass of water. Not certain at first what he was seeing, a huge smile soon lit up his face as a beautiful memory came flooding back. There, sitting proudly on the little table, was gold, pure gold. Size 7½ "carat" gold to be exact!

He remembered, now, how he had seen Rhonda's shoes sparkling under her chair as she let her feet breathe after all that dancing. John's heart was pounding loud and fast as he initiated his "master plan". He staggered over to the chair and pretended to drop something, then bent to pick it up. Next, he snuck his hand out and snatched a shoe, a shoe still wonderfully warm and damp from Rhonda's feet, and quickly secreted it under his shirt.

Now it was his, this precious possession, all his, and there it was, sitting barely two feet away from his face. He could still taste the sweetness of the champagne that he'd slurped out of it earlier.

"This is the greatest day ever!" he thought.

Just then he heard a groan behind him, and his smile swiftly morphed into a grimace. Timidly, he turned around to see a head popped out from under the covers.

Shuddering in recognition, he suddenly remembered who had driven him home.

"What the Hell are you looking at?" squawked Nancy.

The End

Meet the Authors

Bill Perrie

Bill is the author of eight guide books featuring the best pubs in Ontario and Canada, and a former radio host whose show featured pubs and beer. Known as *"Canada's Pub Guy"*, Bill is the part owner of a small town Ontario pub. Born in Dundee, Scotland, Bill now resides in Mount Albert, Ontario.

Ken Jorgenson

A published poet, Ken is a former feature writer for *The Pub Magazine*, a beer connoisseur, and an avid Sherlockian collector. When he's not reading or writing, he works as a Health & Safety Manager in Markham, Ontario. Ken's keen interest in beer and pubs developed during adolescence and is one that he continues to pursue faithfully to this day.

Alissa Heidman

Alissa is a small town girl from Udora, Ontario and a journalism graduate from the University of Toronto. She's written for *Canadian Living Magazine*, *Narcity Media* and *The Richest*, among other publications. She worked her way through school in pubs and continues to do so part-time, meeting some characters you just can't make up.